The Dad With a Flamethrower

By Don Shift

Special thanks to Frank Thornton

Stone Fruit and Orson Wells

Airport

Ross, you have really poor timing when it comes to vacationing, my inner voice chastised. Imagine the worst riots in US history occurring at the same time a massive polar vortex struck, causing a vicious freeze-then-flooding disaster a month before the most contentious election in American history. That's what was waiting for us after we landed back home in the great western state of Fremont. All the bad stars aligned just right to cause a perfect storm of environmental and human conditions for a near-collapse scenario.

Man, it was cold. Florida's 80° temps in early October were lovely but unfortunately the daytime high back here was only half that. You'd think being a hairy, slightly overweight middle aged white guy my genes would have been perfectly adapted for these far below-normal autumn temperatures. Nope. "This must be how Canadian tourists feel coming home," I said as my family and I shivered in the cold on the airport sidewalk.

We had just deplaned after two weeks in Florida hitting the beaches and taking our girls to spend a week with The Mouse. We knew a cold weather anomaly had hit the southern midsection of the country, but this was a shock. No one expected to deplane into essentially martial law and a disaster zone. Normally one of the busiest airports in the country, River City International was eerily dead. The last time the taxi stands were this deserted was after 9/11.

"It feels like *The Langoliers* movie," my wife Raelene said, referring to the Stephen King story where an airplane travels back in time to a yesterday devoid of all life. As in the story, the scene was unsettling, but not a supernatural kind of sinister. Real-life was probably more frightening.

Raelene and I had been married for seven years now. She was a traveling trauma nurse on an extended sabbatical and I was a software developer turned junior executive. We had a history of interesting vacation weather. Hurricane Emily made a guest appearance from afar not long after our wedding. Those rainy last two days of our honeymoon from the hurricane were charming compared to this.

"Daddy, I'm cold," Reya, who was seven, said.

"Sorry, honey. Rub your arms." It must have been in the high forties at sunset when it should have been 65°. Orlando was still having shorts weather so none of us had any jackets. I glanced at Remy, our two-year old, who wore her blanket like a cape.

"That's the second Uber to cancel," Raelene said. She looked up from her phone. "If we don't get a cab, I'm unpacking her bag and getting her long sleeve shirt out."

"Then let's walk down to the next terminal." A few cabs were parked over there. With the two kids in tow we barely made it to the sole minivan before a group of four businessmen did. "Where is everybody?" I asked the cab driver.

"Man, ain't you been watching the news? Nobody wants to fly in here thanks to the Big Freeze and all the riots. This is Hurricane Katrina bad. Probably worse," he mused.

We had been watching the news, particularly The Weather Channel, in the hotel because a tropical system was moving in on Florida. Since I was a techie, I was usually all over the Internet and on the bleeding-edge of the news, but not on vacation. My brother Grant let me know about riots in his medium-sized city of Red Rock in the rural north of the state—started by a police shooting of an out-of-towner—and we caught some coverage of what was being called "The Big Freeze" on CNN. What we were learning was that the media had been downplaying everything that was going on.

You may remember the storm-of-the-century cold snap Texas had not long ago. Fremont was experiencing something like that, but worse. This time the power grid did fail statewide. Powerplants were still trying to figure out their "black start" procedures while the national grid operators scrambled to send excess power in. We saw it all on the news, of course, but to us being so far away in Florida it was like it was happening in a different universe. My brother drove downstate and did some quick winterizing for us so we enjoyed ourselves knowing that everything would be fine by the time we got back.

However, like everything since COVID hit, this Big Freeze had second and third order effects no one anticipated. Since the entire region was affected, there was little help to send in from other states. Refineries shut down causing a gas shortage. Transportation delays led to stores, already emptied ahead of the freeze, meant that food wasn't coming in. Since the election was less than a month away, that combined with racial tensions and some unfortunate police shootings pushed things over the top. Riots developed and these were way more than the violent pre-election protests that had been happening since summer..

Riots go with looting the way that destroyed mobile homes go with tornadoes. While there was plenty of opportunistic looting for pecuniary or material gain, much of it was focused on getting necessities. In the early days, hungry looters ignored places like Best Buy and went to supermarkets.

One loaded cart running out the grocery store door served as a catalyst for many more to follow in a stampede. Closed restaurants were broken into for food. As the police's ability to cope waned, the scope of the thefts changed from substance to the pillage of the free stuff army.

Looting was so bad that the National Guard was *still* deployed in a police capacity across the country. There was an armored vehicle sitting on top of the airport parking garage for crying out loud. It wasn't just in River City, either. The entire Metro area of the state was dealing with the same thing and so were almost all the big cities across the county (minus the weather effects). The fractured politics of our nation had given us another riotous "summer of love" that threatened to spiral into a real civil war. Even my brother in the medium exurb of Red Rock City was embroiled in the unrest.

Red Rock, about two hours north, was pretty bad from what he told me. Refugees from the cold went up there from the cities and overwhelmed the locals. Looting and riots developed. Then Radical Community Reform, RadCom, activists (who had to change the official name because people started using it "negatively" and assuming that "com" referred to communism, which "seemed" bad to the official organizers) moved into inflame and exploit the situation. My brother called it a "literal communist revolution," which I thought was a bit extreme, but if terrorists were trying to blow up the regional powerplant—and they were—there could be a problem.

The reality here in River City was a lot different on the ground than the news depicted. I half anticipated the plane coming in high and fast to avoid gunfire and smoke from burning buildings when we landed. The streets looked quiet beneath us as we came in on final approach. Much of the snow was gone, too. The effects were subtle. The city was shrouded in an unsettling and deceptive tranquility, masking the severe distress beneath. The fallout so far seemed to be most of the airport concessions being shutdown and a lack of traffic.

"Where to?" the driver asked.

"West River City." It was on the west bank of the river that split the state and our metro area which was the oldest satellite city of the area. Our suburb was on a large island made by the main channel and a backwater ship canal.

"It's almost dark, so do you want me to avoid downtown and take the beltway? I gotta warn you the trip will be double the price if you do."

"What's the problem with through downtown? It's the shortest and fastest way."

He looked at me as if I had a horn growing out of my head. "Some folks don't want to go through downtown at night. With the curfew and all we'll be fine coming from the airport but its not the police they're worried about."

"Just get us home the fastest way, please. What are they worried about?"

"You'll see."

The fifteen mile trip from the airport to downtown that usually took half an hour during rush hour was done in less than half that. The cab driver was speeding along the empty freeways. I knew that there had been riots, protests, and gas shortages but the near solitude that we had on the highway was disorienting. The skyscrapers loomed up from above the sound walls. Except for their red anti-collision beacons, all the commercial buildings were dark. Even the residential towers showed a minimum of lights. *Were the blackouts that bad?*

Without warning, two cars going close to 150 MPH (the taxi was doing about 90 itself) shot by us on either side with a whirr and blast of air that shook the van. "Whoa!" the driver exclaimed. The cars were a half-mile away in ten seconds. "Yeah, that's a thing since the state troopers are too busy to chase speeders. Damn racetrack out here."

Beyond the retaining wall the glow of fires illuminated the city. Columns of smoke rose up in several places. Red and blue emergency lights flashed here and there. A police helicopter circled east of downtown shining their spotlights like the heat-ray of the Martian tripods in *War of the Worlds*.

Raelene and I shared a concerned look.

"Here," the driver said. "This is what I was telling you about." The headlights showed a massive patch of blackened pavement about a hundred yards long that stretched from the fast lane to the exit ramp. Scorching and soot went halfway up the freeway walls. "Protest shut the freeway down. Rioters came up the ramp here and scared everybody out of their cars. Then some arsonist came along and started chucking road flares in the windows. Fire department couldn't get here so like a hundred cars burned up. Freeway was closed for two days."

I felt like Marty McFly in *Back to the Future Part II* when he arrived in the paradox version of Hill Valley. Our town had, in the span of less than two weeks, turned into a city of perpetual night where mischief reigned. We had only been on the ground for an hour and I felt we had fallen into a world designed and stage managed by the director of a dystopian blockbuster.

"Uh oh," the driver said. A man was running down the shoulder of the freeway. In a moment we saw why. A semi-truck and trailer was stopped with two pickup trucks backed up to it. Six or seven people were rushing to unload boxes of what looked like vegetables into the pickups. Some carried guns and were standing guard. One person might even have been shot. Raelene gasped. The cab driver floored it. "Told you that y'all might wanna have taken the beltway."

"What are they doing that for?" Raelene asked. "Nobody got no food. Grocery stores are closed 'cuz that's happening if people just don't steal stuff the minute it hits the shelf."

Grocery stores being empty? The idea sounded preposterous to me. Shortages were part of the new normal, but empty was impossible.

"Do you have food?" Raelene inquired in follow up.

"Us? Yeah we got lots. We were smart and stocked up ahead of the store. No EBT cards in our family. Course we ate most of the freshies now and are eating out of cans 'n stuff, but it beats being hungry. Ate vegetables out of cans for most of my life. No ma'am, we're not French toast people."

"French toast people?"

"You know, the ones that run out right before a hurricane or whatever and buy all the milk, eggs, and bread, like they're going to make it into French toast and live on that alone. On TV all they show you are empty shelves—no milk, bread, and eggs. Never go down none of the other aisles. When the power started going out, we bought ourselves steaks. Bunch of 'em real cheap 'cuz they gotta be refrigerated, even if the heat is out and the store is cold enough. Paid cash and 'bout filled up a shopping cart."

All the talk of food was making me hungry. I hadn't eaten a meal since breakfast. There was a delay in taking off, so we bought the girls McDonalds in the terminal back in Orlando. Raelene and I ate snacks on the plane and hoped to get a bagel or something when we landed but we were lucky to get a coffee from Starbucks.

"What else did we miss?" I asked.

"Well, they got the curfew on. Can't go out dusk to dawn, but that's not stopping anybody from stealing or breaking in. The protests have stopped. The college kids who started it got scared when the rioting and looting started. Not like up there in Red Rock or in Portland. Get a whole bunch of hungry, cold, and scared people out in the street yelling and screaming then be surprised when they start stealing and burning stuff? Pinko idiots, as my dad woulda called them."

I did see something on the news about various activists leading initial protests against the horrible disaster response by the authorities and governor. A big march in the snow went from the state universities to the city hall or the capitol building. Thousands of people who lived in the cities and had nothing to do because they couldn't go to work joined in. Once police became overwhelmed is when the massive looting spree began. It was the riots of 2020 and Hurricane Katrina combined.

We made it past downtown and were circling along the river without any further incident. The city sat on the confluence of two rivers in a huge river valley that was spliced with irrigation channels, sloughs, and a ship bypass channel that went a hundred miles south until the river was wider and deeper for large draft ships. The main river, the Buenaventura, split the state in two and connected a chain of its major cities for over two hundred miles.

Just over the water by the I-21 bridge was West River City. It had been a sleepy town until the 1920s when the new US Highway System required a bridge across the river to connect the route that was now superseded by the Interstate. In the '60s through the '90s, the small town became a haven to the working class as the wealthier folks moved to the burgeoning suburbs across the river. It grew into until the suburbs were juxtaposed next to the ports and railyards.

As soon as we crossed the bridge, Raelene's and my phones began screeching with an emergency alert message. The driver laughed. "Flood watch. Never fails to go off right as you go over the river. Been doing that all day," he said.

Lots of amber lights were flashing on the bridge ramp and it was not for a toll plaza. "Weather damage?" I asked.

"No sir, bridges are fine, even with the water rising. Checkpoint."

Now I could see a pair of state trooper cars, multiple Humvees, and an armored personnel carrier. Curiously, the Humvees all had machine guns mounted in their turrets. I had never seen that before. The taxi entered a chute of orange cones. A soldier in a green traffic vest waved us to a stop in the middle of a pool of harsh spotlights. An officer approached us and four other soldiers with their M4s surrounded the vehicle.

The taxi driver had his hands firmly on the steering wheel. "Lower your window!" the soldier shouted. The driver pressed the button and put his hands back. Two MPs shined flashlights in all the windows and said something to the officer. "Driver, turn off the engine, leave the keys in the ignition, and step out of the vehicle and unlock all the doors."

"Yes, sergeant," the driver said. He did as ordered. I noticed that the driver was standing straight with his arms by his sides, fingers tucked into his fists.

"Ross, what's going on?" Raelene asked. She was worried. I was confused. The baby was asleep and Reya hardly looked up from the iPad.

"I don't know."

The MPs opened each door on the side of the van and shined their flashlights in. They said nothing but moved on to open the back hatch. "Sir, just a family with luggage. Two kids."

Their officer nodded. "Get their IDs." We went for our wallets without the MPs repeating the order to us. "Were you in?" the lieutenant asked the driver as he inspected the taxi permit.

"Yes sir, 5th Armored."

The lieutenant glanced at the driver's permit and handed it back. "At ease. Where are you going?"

"Dropping these folks off in West River City, sir. They wanted to go through downtown."

"Matches the address on their licenses, Ell-tee," an MP said.

The lieutenant indicated for them to give back our licenses. "Shut the doors for them, guys." He turned back to the driver. "Lots of looters trying to cross the bridge specifically in stolen cabs and commercial vehicles. Never can be too sure what they're driving. At this time of day with a van full of people and a backseat full of bags you fit the profile."

I stuck my head out the door before the MP could close it. "Excuse me, sir, but we've been out of town. Looting is still going on?"

He saw that the baby, slumped in her car seat, was wearing her Mickey ears. "Musta been nice seeing the Mouse instead of here. The stores are empty sir. If there's nothing to buy and nothing to shoplift, they're breaking into houses."

A chill hit me. I asked nothing more. Our house had been unoccupied for two weeks, save for my brother rushing down to hastily winterize it. A neighbor was supposed to watch for any surprise packages and keep a general eye on things, but we had no housesitter. For all we knew the place had been ransacked. We were waved on. I said nothing to my wife and anticipated the worst for the rest of the drive.

On the other side of the bridge we could see in the last glow of twilight that the river was nearly to the crest of the bank. Crews were working by portable lamps to shore up parts of the levee. Downtown West River City was dark. I noticed that the driver was rolling through the dark stop lights. You only did that if the neighborhood was really sketchy—a bad sign in this yuppie town. I wondered what other urban survival skills he learned in the last week that he wasn't sharing with us. Not a soul was on the street, so it had to be more habit than anything else.

The cab took the freeway connector bridge that went to the island. West River City might as well have been two cities. North of the shipping channel that bisected the city was the old town with the waterfront, the heavy industry, and residential areas that hadn't been fully gentrified yet. South of the channel was the suburbs, all built from the early 2000s when the housing market boomed. That's where we lived, protected from the floodwaters by levees.

Once we got home, I had to do a walkaround of the house to check for intrusion. I made up some mumbled excuse about the storm making the place unhabitable. The meter was still running so the driver didn't mind my family waiting in the warmth and safety of the cab. He knew what I was doing. Thankfully, nothing was amiss. I guess the Citizen Patrol vacation checks were useful after all.

Inside, we could still see our breath, but no puddles of water awaited us. Though the thermostat was set at 55°, a power outage tripped the unit's internal breaker, and the house was only a shade warmer than outside. None of the pipes in the house froze which told me the heater breaker tripped sometime after the worst of the cold. It might be tolerable by bedtime. All of us immediately scrambled into warmer clothing.

I made my actual damage check. The outdoor faucet bibs had been dripping slightly to prevent them from freezing up, but they did anyway. Icicles still hung from them. I turned the heat gun on them, and they were gushing water normally. *One problem averted.* The pool filter was off and drained; something my brother thought of that I wouldn't have. The pool itself hadn't iced over because it had to be really cold for the water to freeze. Our emergency water in the garage partially froze and had ice still in it. There was a lot of thermal mass that had to be reheated for it to go liquid again.

Some said the "Big Freeze" was due to the Butterfly Effect. A huge volcano erupted in Indonesia and the ash in the upper atmosphere scattered the sunlight, resulting in record low temperatures occurring over most of the world. Since the eruption in August, the temperatures had been cooler and the sunsets much more vibrant, but the meteorologists said we weren't facing a "year without a summer." Some were blaming the volcano and others said it was a result of anthropogenic climate change.

Whatever the case was, this autumn was an unusual one. The hunter's moon was blood red like something out of the Book of Revelation. Our normally dry fall, after the monsoon stopped and before the cold fronts swung down from Canada, was a wet. El Niño gave us two wet winters and summers before this. Then, be it the volcano, climate change, or the Great Pumpkin, the polar jet stream swung down into the far south of the US to bring winter in October.

Chyron graphics on all the news station warned of the coming "polar vortex" for several days in advance of its arrival. For those of us in balmy Fremont, fall was a time when we started playing make-believe that we lived at the North Pole. Parkas came out when the mercury dipped below 50° for the first time. Girls and women swapped their sandals for furry Ugg boots.

The months of October to February were a relief from the itchy heat that bracketed the monsoon's humid stickiness. Only those living in the far north of the state in the mountains ever experienced anything stronger than chilly weather. Snow made an appearance every twenty-odd years and shutdown the state if it was more than just a teasing of flakes. The last snow day had been in 1949.

Freezing temperatures happened here but usually not until December. Winter mornings in the twenties was normal and everyone got annoyed about having to jump start batteries and chip ice on the days in early February when we got into the teens. Overnight lows approaching zero were unheard of. Frost-proofing here in the Metro counties was minimal at best. It's easy to see why we were impacted so drastically.

After the cold, the snow, and the blizzard, the ice storm came. The temperature had not improved noticeably since then. The jet stream swung low for a prolonged stay and was still wearing out its welcome. While the blast of cold had tempered somewhat, the relative warmth brought with it rain. Freezing rain and sleet blanketed the state in nearly as much ice as we had snow. In fact, snow and ice was still on the ground. Our house had a miniature glacier beginning to form on the northern slope and I would have to get into the crawlspace to make sure there wasn't an ice dam forming.

My runny nose needed blowing when I came back inside. Raelene was on her phone and looked unhappy. "What's up?"

"None of the pizza places are answering. Even Dominos."

"No problem." I opened the freezer. What we had wasn't safe to eat after the power outages I noted with dissatisfaction. The few frozen meals we had sat in re-frozen soggy cardboard. Since Raelene was a fan of fresh food, we didn't have a pantry full of canned goods as my mom did when I was a boy. A can of chili, hominy, and Spam were the only savory things to eat. I doubt that even Raelene, as well as she could cook, would be able to do anything with the cans of tomato paste and fruit cocktail.

"Peanut butter and saltines will have to tide the kids over."

"I've still got some baby meals for Remy. You're gonna have to go out and find something to eat. Shopping can wait 'til morning."

I ran upstairs to get my keys and wallet. For a moment,

I thought of holstering up my handgun, but decided against it. Nothing was happening in the city tonight and I couldn't see needing it. The only times I carried a gun, other than when I first bought the Glock, was when we went camping. Even though a carry permit wasn't required in our state, I didn't feel the need to pack heat. We didn't go places or hang around in circles where it was likely to be necessary.

On attempting to start the car, it immediately indicated it was not happy with me. Raelene followed me into the garage to toss a bag of the suspect food in the trash outside, so I asked her "Why is the Tesla only at 23%?"

"You were the last one to drive it," she replied defensively. "Your brother must have unplugged it."

Or I must not have plugged it in like I thought, but I didn't say. Grant would have to take the fall. I plugged it in. The stylized T symbol went red, and I got the warnings "Unable to charge" and "Charging disabled." *Okay...Let's see what this is about.* A new message popped up on the screen. "'Due to state regulations charging is disabled during an electrical grid crisis.' Fan-freaking-tastic." Our smart meter was communicating with the Tesla now. We were down to one car until this mess is over. Where are the keys to the SUV?" Raelene pointed to the bedroom.

It was at over 50% when I parked it. But an over 2% loss per day? I thought as the Lexus warmed up.

*   *   *

An hour later I came back. "Where have you been?" Raelene asked in a slightly nagging tone. Reya was throwing a tantrum in front of the TV.

"Trying to find food." All of our usual restaurants were

closed. The Thai restaurant, the Cornish bake shop, Panera Bread, even Jack 'n the Box which was open 24 hours. Every single place to eat in the city was closed. A to-go order from Denny's wasn't even going to happen. Grocery stores were closed too. If we had a Waffle House here it would probably be closed just to piss me off and you know if Waffle House is closed, you know it's a true catastrophe.

Raelene looked through the plastic bags I set on the counter. "Tacos. Burritos. You could have done worse." I shot her a face that said *Really?* "Sorry. I didn't mean it to sound judgmental."

"Worse is in the other bag. I stopped at 7/11 because I thought I might not find anything else." She parted the plastic and pulled out a few Zero bars, off-brand beef jerky, a bruised apple, and some pumpkin spice flavored mini-donuts. It wasn't exaggerating to say that was all they had. Luckily, I found a taco truck parked near the levee work staging camp that planned to be there until at least midnight. The owner said I wasn't the only non-worker customer she had this evening.

"Ooh, the Zero bar. It's like the candy bar made to get around a trademark on tasting good." I laughed at Raelene's joke. "Reya, come eat your dinner," she called. "Daddy got you a bean burrito." Our tired, hungry, and red-eyed little girl came to the kitchen, climbed up on a stool, and sullenly started eating her burrito. "I tried to see if she would have some of Remy's Gerber toddler meals, but she said she wasn't a baby."

"TV dinners for kids," I said.

"They're more like Lunchables for babies."

"Remember on our first date when you wanted tacos

and ordered me the one made of tongue?"

"*Lengua*," she said with a smile. She laughed so hard when she told me what it was. The meat wasn't disgusting—a bit flavorless and chewy—but I never would have guessed. As kid I used to curiously poke the shrink-wrapped beef tongues in the meat cases at the grocery store until my mother shouted at me. I had no idea that was what they were used for.

"That's not the only kind of taco you've made me eat."

She slapped at my shoulder with her napkin. "Ross, don't talk like that; not in front of the girls!"

Day 1

French Toast People

Some time in the night I woke up because of a noise. I listened for a moment, hearing only the swish of warm air from the ceiling registers. I heard it again, so I got up and stepped out on to the balcony off the nursery/sitting area. Sound carried far in the freezing air. The thermometer out here read 32° exactly. What awakened me was gunfire. A long string of automatic shots carried across the river. *Is the National Guard shooting people?* More *pop pop pop* in return. Sirens.

Excluding a few stray shots, it quieted down and did not resume. The scanner app I had on my phone wasn't giving me any clues. It was possible I missed the call going out, but if the cops were involved there should be a lot of traffic as the officers fought back. If they weren't involved, I would think that automatic gunfire would generate a lot of attention. Ten minutes later there was no other shots and if the officers I heard talking on the radio were responding to the shooting, they didn't find anything.

So I went back to bed. Morning came and the temperature was comfortable once again when we woke. Raelene met me in the bathroom as I finished brushing my teeth. "The girls are still asleep. Want to have sex real quick before they wake up?" She was a lot more frisky in the mornings since she started being a stay-at-home-mom.

I gave her a kiss. "I'd love to, but I have that Zoom meeting at ten and I should probably run out and get groceries first-thing." She silently shrugged and left. I decided not to tell her about the gunfire last night. In the shower I wondered how many people had hot water. It shouldn't be many given all you need is water pressure and natural gas unless you went all electric or something.

It took me until after eight to find an open fast food restaurant which was the McDonalds off the Interstate on the edge of the city. The next one was thirty minutes away. The drive-thru was hopeless so I parked in the closed Taco Bell parking lot next door and walked over. The line was ten people deep and most of the seats were full. I hadn't seen a McDonalds this busy since the 1990s.

"Why so popular, even if this is the only place open in town?" I asked the cashier.

She laughed at me. "There's only two other McDonalds open in the entire county. My manager said that they diverted all the deliveries to just our stores so they can stay open without running out of food. We'd sell out in an hour if everybody got equal shipments."

I wanted to ask more but the manager was glaring and the guy behind me seemed impatient, so I ordered. While it took a bit longer than it should to get the food, they had a full menu and nothing was left out of the bag. All the way home I pondered the implications of McDonalds rationing.

"All this cost $50?" Raelene asked back in the kitchen.

"Inflation, baby. Twelve bucks per person plus tax. I didn't have to get the coffee and OJ or the extra hash browns, but why not?" A raise of the eyebrows and a crunch of a hash brown was her reply. Being a married man is kinda weird. I now found it sexy to see my extremely health conscious wife eating fast food.

"Sure you don't want me to take the kids and go to the grocery store?" she asked.

"No, they'd probably just whine about the cold and being in the car. I'll do it. I could use a couple hours away from my desk anyhow."

Sprouts, our normal grocery store of choice, was closed. Trader Joes was too. Albertsons had special hours that didn't begin until nine, so I tried the Kroger. If I wanted to go to a supermarket that looked like a hurricane was coming or going, I would have stayed in Florida.

"Is this what grocery stores in the Soviet Union looked like?" another shopper asked rhetorically. "Man alive." My own observation was that the taxi driver's statement about the "French toast people" was totally accurate.

The bread shelves were empty. The bakery had put out fresh bread, but it was all their white sandwich loaves. There were no bagels or donuts. Tortillas were gone except for the green-colored extra healthy ones that even we wouldn't eat. Condiments were plentiful but croutons non-existent; I figured people were eating those as snacks once the chips ran out. Peanut butter and all the quick school lunch snacks? Gone. If you wanted to snack on something it was pickles or jars of olives.

There was absolutely no meat of any kind, not even lunch meat. The cold cases were sold out of every kind of milk except the most expensive non-dairy kind. The girls would drink almond and oat milk, so I put some of that in the cart. Someone was moving inside the back of the milk case. As a kid, seeing the disembodied hands restocking the shelves from the darkness freaked me out. "Hey, what's the deal with the empty cases? Not even remaindered stuff here."

"We can't get anymore. Not until Friday, probably. We had to throw a lot of stuff out because of spoilage due to the power outages." He moved on. It was cold in there.

The frozen section was likewise decimated. Ice cream was the most plentiful item there was, probably because a frozen desert was the last thing all the people shivering in their houses wanted. I scored a few bags of unpopular vegetables, two straight Birdseye lima beans and a lima bean medley. Occasionally I'd make my mom's lima bean recipe, using stock instead of water, and bacon so they would taste like something, but there were no dried beans in the store.

Dried anything was gone. Two men were looking high and low in that aisle and grabbing the dented boxes and ripped bags that sat derelict. There was plenty of Hamburger Helper and other dinner mixes because there was no meat to go with them. I helped myself because we had a several large #10 cans of freeze-dried ground beef and chicken in the garage along with powdered milk.

Caught in the maw of indecision bred by ignorance, I stood in the bread aisle trying to Google the difference between the remaining cake and all-purpose flour (the expensive brands). As my fingers tapped away, the quiet was suddenly cleaved by the harsh crackle of raised voices. The two men who I thought were working together were fighting. Peeking around the end of the aisle, I witnessed a bizarre melee as they struggled over a large bag of dried beans.

One of the men fell down as the bag split, sending a spray of tiny red beans, casualties of the tug-of-war, everywhere. As the man hit the floor, he spat a series of expletives at the other guy and drew a pistol. I tried to backpedal away in slow motion. *Pop, pop!* The sharp report of two gunshots rang out, both misses. The remaining man retaliated swiftly, landing a brutal kick on the face of the shooter, and with remarkable tenacity, he pushed his shopping cart over his downed adversary.

I didn't see any more because I abandoned my own cart and bolted from the store, my heart pounding in sync with my footsteps. The lucky-to-be-alive guy passed me on my way out. Outside, about thirty of us huddled behind parked cars, our breaths held as we waited to witness the unfolding aftermath of the unexpected violence. The distant wail of police sirens grew closer, marking the arrival of the police.

For the first time in my life, I found my hand frantically patting my waist, seeking the cold comfort of a gun that wasn't there. Any psychologist would likely diagnose this as a subconscious wish that I had been armed. *Why didn't I bring the gun? Because I could never imagine a shootout over a busted bag of beans in a grocery store!*

It felt blindingly obvious now. Citywide food shortages, a major disaster, and hungry, scared people were apt to be dangerously anxious. What if that had been me? Sure, I wouldn't fight a guy over a bag of beans off the shelf but what if he had stolen out of my cart?

The cops showed up and interviewed me before anyone else because I saw everything firsthand. The shooter had run out the back and disappeared before they arrived. The officer told me that this was more likely to be a case of assault with a deadly weapon than attempted murder because the shooter had been pushed down. Regardless, without the identity of either party, there was no suspect to pursue or victim to press charges.

"This is wild. I could never imagine this happening here

on the island," I commented.

"You know that line from *Pirates of the Caribbean* about believing in nightmares because you're in one, or something like that? Well you're in one," the officer said. "Sprouts had a double homicide yesterday. A woman was fighting with another over a pineapple. So one of the women took her revolver out of her purse then shot the other woman and her daughter. That's just here. Across the river RCPD had a guy with one of those Glock auto switches shoot up the butcher's counter because there was no meat. He got dropped by an armed security guard."

"Seriously?"

"Yes, sir. During the first looting spree, we had two shootings in grocery stores or parking lots. RCPD had sixteen. Couple of people were hit by cars as thieves fled. That's not even getting into the fistfights, the shoplifting, or the organized crime."

"Organized crime?"

"That's what I said. Pricks send in a bunch of teenagers to load carts up with whatever they can grab. Maybe a dozen kids in total. Then someone else stages a fight or something. When the managers are distracted, the kids run out and the food is thrown into waiting cars, then they leave. Albertsons lost $900 of meat the morning their delivery arrived. Hence, stores won't say when they are getting deliveries anymore. The managers are calling the watch commander asking officers to standby when they unload the trailers."

"We saw a US Foods truck being hijacked last night on the freeway. I thought it was a riot thing."

"Nope. It's a hunger thing. This diesel shortage and trucker strike needs to end ASAP or it's gonna get ugly.

Starvation ugly."

Starvation? That seemed impossible here. "I saw on the news that independent truckers were being offered beaucoup bucks to take food into the hard-hit areas."

The officer looked up at me from his notepad. "Not here. You gotta remember other parts of the state are safer. We're the worst off of all the surrounding states. If you're a trucker and you have a choice of going to Fremont where the Metro cities are flooding and the National Guard is running convoys of delivery trucks or you can go to Kansas where you can buy fuel, get a burger, and sleep in a warm motel, what are you gonna choose? A 50% bonus isn't worth your life."

Albertsons was open by the time the officer was done with me. Only one of the entrance doors was in use and two armed security guards stood on either side. While security was common in some of the inner city stores across the river, it was like *The Twilight Zone* here. Only Walmart here had regular security. Albertsons' food situation was fairly similar to Kroger except the stocks seemed a bit deeper and the remaining brands better. This could probably be attributed to the chain sending deliveries from their more northerly distribution centers which ironically were less affected than the ones further south.

Trader Joes was still closed. Walmart was not only busy but there was a line out front. It looked like they were only letting in small groups of people, as they did when COVID started. Shopping carts and pallets of gardening soil formed a kind of cordon in front of the Home & Pharmacy entrance, which was the only one open. The grocery side had K-rail sections. I guess Bentonville was really serious about stopping looting mobs.

My last stop was Target. Something seemed off when I turned into the parking lot and saw the amount of cones and caution tape. The front entrance was entirely boarded up. Black soot stained the dun-colored stucco façade outside two emergency exit doors. "Closed" was unnecessarily spray painted on the plywood shielding. My wife wasn't going to like that. To her and many other suburban women Target was like Home Depot was to guys.

When I came back in the house, Raelene was on her cell phone. "Well I don't need a new car," she told the person on the other end. No, she didn't need a new car. She was driving *my* Lexus LX. It was supposed to be a temporary thing after she rear-ended somebody and trashed her Audi. When we couldn't get her a replacement in a timely manner (thanks car shortage) she took my new ride. And kept it. So I got the Tesla.

She said her goodbye and hung up. "What was that?" I asked.

Raelene set her phone on the countertop. "Contract recruiter. They're begging me to come in. $200 an hour." That was superlatively good money for a registered nurse.

"Wow!"

"I know, right? They're desperate." Inflation was pretty heavy right now, but even accounting for that, based on the 2020 crisis rates she earned as a travel nurse even $120 would be lucrative.

"You're not thinking about it, are you?"

"No," she said instantly. I felt relieved. "It isn't worth the stress. Besides, if Dr. P opens up the clinic to the public like he did with COVID or during the brushfires, I'll go."

Despite me begging her not to, she returned to work

not long after her maternity leave for Remy ended. A nanny and I were not a replacement for an infant's mother. Raelene would come home at the end of a long day (or night) and have maybe 30 minutes with the girls sometimes before crying herself to sleep. Finally in 2022 she had enough and quit.

For her, it hadn't been about the money, but helping sick and injured patients. She cared too much, saying it was her job to sacrifice to help these people. My concern was she would hear her friends' complaints of being overwhelmed at work and rush back to staff an ER out of a feeling of obligation. I'm sure it was the guilt of not being there for part of Remy's first year that balanced out her self-imposed sense of duty.

I put the groceries away and Raelene narrated as she got caught up on the NextDoor app. Others' grocery situation was as bleak as I experienced. If you wanted food, you went from store to store like a Soviet babushka everyday to buy whatever they had in stock that you could use. Trading with the neighbors was already beginning. How did an affluent community in America of all places fall into bartering like this in mere days?

There were reports of better stocks if you were willing to drive out of the Metro counties into the hill country that wasn't being flooded. "I suppose after your meeting we could take a ride up to the Walmart in Greenville," Raelene suggested.

"We better." I shook a box of Hamburger Helper. "Otherwise we're using that freeze dried ground beef in the survival buckets from the garage."

Raelene's mouth twisted into a wicked smile as she quoted a movie. "'I don't know why they call this stuff Hamburger Helper. It does just fine by itself!'" She laughed uproariously at her own joke.

Under the circumstances I didn't find it funny. How was it going to taste with reconstituted ground beef and milk? *Was this situation what we bought all the emergency food for?*

The Iron Giant

Being a department director was a great job for me. It provided *very* well for our family and took me away from the day-to-day drudgery of software coding. As a junior VP, the only person I had to report directly to was the senior VP of product development. A few more years learning about the corporate end of things and I'd be ready to slide into his spot. I had the freedom to solve the problems that I found interesting rather than mindlessly completing my small piece of the puzzle.

The downside was meetings. There was at least one meeting a day and several conference calls. For my birthday, Raelene gave me a mousepad that said, "I survived another meeting that could have been an email." If I saw an instant message that said, "Can I just call you?" one more time, I was going to scream. How about you learn to write what you want to say and email it to me? So here I was, the day after my vacation ended, not long after witnessing a violent crime, listening to people brainstorm out loud when it was clear they hadn't considered the problem at all until now.

I couldn't even think clearly about it because of all the *ums, wells, you-knows, how-abouts,* etc. An hour alone playing with the code and I might have a coherent answer for all this. The "cameras on" policy meant I couldn't multitask either. Worst of all, the customer experience VP was heading up the team working on the solution to our problem so I was as powerless as a spectator but had to actively participate.

Thankfully, God is merciful. The lights in the room went out and I felt the heat blowing out of the duct stop. Simultaneously the connection on my computer stuttered and froze. While the UPS (Uninterruptible Power Supply) kept my system going, it was useless if the fiber optic network that supplied the Internet connect was offline. It used to be that the old POTS phone system had its own 48 volt electrical current.

"Power's out!" Reya yelled from her bedroom, stating the obvious. Fifteen seconds after the outage began a boom came faintly through the windows. Something electrical exploded. The probable culprit was an underground transformer vault. Reya pushed open my study door and ran in. "Daddy, come look. There's blue lightning outside."

"Huh?" I stood up and followed her to her room. "I don't see anything."

"Look at the iron giant," she said. She was pointing at a high-tension power line tower, that she called an iron giant, after the children's movie. Reya's bedroom window had a partial view of the top of one such "pylon," as the English call them, about a mile away. It was such an inconspicuous part of the skyline that an adult would forget it was there.

"I still don't see anything honey."

"But Dad, there was blue lightning coming from the top."

"That was an electrical surge, sweetie. The power just went out and there was too much electricity so—"

The second boom shook the house. "Holy crap!" A large pall of gray smoke rose up in the direction of the city's major substation where the high voltage lines terminated. The smoke turned black quickly and there was tons of it. A few more spurts of gray smoke indicated secondary explosions.

"Ross, what's going on?" Raelene called. She ran up the stairs.

"Power outage. The substation is on fire."

"Great, just what we needed."

"I'm sure it appears worse than it is. We've been back almost a full day and haven't even had a brownout yet. Worst case scenario it takes them a day, a day and a half, to put the fire out and re-route the current."

She looked at me skeptically. "What about tonight? We need the heater."

"We'll run the generator." I had a 'quiet box' for the generator that dampened the sound to the level of a refrigerator. Only the immediate neighbors would hear anything.

"Do we have enough gas for it?"

"Five gallons. I can always siphon what's in the Lexus if we really have to but if we're gonna be on our own that long, I can go to the gas station."

"Alright. Since your meeting is over early why don't we go to Walmart?" It was the first time since I met her that she was excited to go to Walmart.

MLK Boulevard

For those who don't know, Walmart has the appellation of "Wally World," something it shares with a fictional amusement park from National Lampoon's *Vacation*. The real park is Magic Mountain in Valencia, California. There is a scene showing the Griswold family driving up through a deserted parking lot and finding the park closed, which made all the sacrifices and hardships of the road trip for naught. In case you forgot, Clark Griswold goes crazy because of it and takes a hostage at BB gun-point.

When we got back from Walmart, I felt like Clark. We got gas and we had hot food thanks to an open drive-thru but that was all I could say for the experience. It seems like everyone in the River City metro area drove up to Greenville to see if they had any food. The poor townspeople probably saw us as locusts descending to eat their crops.

On the way, we did see a few interesting things of note. The river was higher than it was yesterday. All the flood watches were not precautionary and rightfully set to go into flood warnings. Evacuations weren't being called for so we had to be safe. West River City was on an island in the upper river delta but we had very strong flood defenses that hadn't failed since they were built in the fifties and sixties.

The normally placid wetlands and bayous around West River City were no longer a sea of trees, reeds, and meadows. Instead, it was all a lake with treetops protruding out like broccoli florets standing in a deep dish of chocolate milk. The low-lying farmlands had also flooded submerging single story homes to their roofs. I understood why the Interstate going north out of town was built on an elevated causeway now.

"It's cold in here," Raelene said when we got home. She lifted Remy up and sniffed her butt. I disagreed with that particular method of checking diaper status.

"Do you need changed?"

"Nah-uh," Remy replied with her limited vocabulary.

"I don't think so, missy. Reya, go take off your jacket and put a sweater on while I change your sister. Ross, it's freezing in here. Can you get the generator going and make the heater work?"

"I'll try." My wife thought I was being funny. Though I had unboxed it and read the manual, I never ran the generator before. There had never been a need to, so why would I leave it full of oil that could congeal and gasoline that would turn to varnish? I wasn't much of a mechanic.

Wisely I did print and laminate each pertinent page of the manual and put them in a binder. Step 1: add engine oil. I had five quarts of 10W-30 for just this kinda thing. Step 2: add fuel. I poured five gallons in and it was nowhere near full. *Okay, read the instructions. 13 gallon capacity! Seven hours at full load with a full fuel tank. That's only two or three hours with one gas can's worth.* "Don't freak out," I said aloud to myself.

Step 3: plug in to generator tie in. This was a box on the side of the house with a heavy-duty outlet and a breaker arm. If you just use an extension cord plugged into an outlet the current can back feed the power lines and electrocute a lineman. This way we would be able to power the whole house instead of running extension cords to individual appliances. Step 4: start 'er up.

The generator fired up on the third tug of the cord. *Man, this thing is quiet.* I didn't even need the earplugs I had in my pocket. To be sure we didn't overload the generator, I flipped off the breakers for the upstairs, except my study, and all but the kitchen, garage, and utility room. In the garage I reset the breaker for the heater and it hummed to life. *Happy wife, happy life.*

As for the sound enclosure, I didn't think I need it but why not use it? The low frequency droning of the motor would get annoying and might attract unwanted attention. The enclosure itself was an easy, quick bolt-together kit that worked as advertised. The only way you would know it was a generator was if you knew what you were looking at, which wasn't hard because a in addition to the power cable running from it to the side of the house it had large branding on each side. I locked it down with a stout chain secured to an eyebolt I drilled into the sidewalk so thieves would have to have brought bolt cutters.

I popped my head in the house. "I'm getting more gas!" Easier said than done. The whole island was dark. None of the gas stations had emergency generators. Correction, none of them had standby generators. I found one where two employees were setting one up in a parking space and another who said they placed an order for the local equipment rental place to drop one off by evening.

So it was back over the bridge again. No Guardsmen were screening people going *into* River City proper. The power was working on the other side of the river, subject to rolling blackouts. Larger sections of the city were darker than I would have thought. Five gallons of gas and sixteen gas stations later, I was ready to head home. *This is stupid. I'll have to drive across the river every three hours to get more gas. This is why your brother told you to buy more than one gas can.*

"Well I can remedy that now," I said to no one in particular as I pulled into an AutoZone parking lot. Three minutes after entering the store I approached the counter. "Excuse me, you wouldn't happen to have any more gas cans in the back, would you?"

An expression worth a thousand words formed on the manager's face, all of which meant *You're not familiar with auto parts stores, are you?* Another way of putting it would be *You're an idiot.* "No sir," he said politely.

"You don't have more stock back there?"

"Just auto parts sir."

"Can you check the inventory of other stores to see if they have it?"

"Sir, I can tell you that it will be a miracle if any store, auto parts, Walmart, or a gas station has any gas cans at all. You're the third person this hour who asked for them."

I felt asinine for asking. I could have walked in, checked the shelf, and walked out without saying a word. "Thank for being cool about it. Do you have any suggestions?"

"Don't put any gas in a plastic bag or a bottle or anything that's not a gas can." That had been a PSA that the fire marshal delivered on the news last night. I wasn't that mechanically retarded. "You can try to go store-to-store to see if they have any that haven't been logged in, but I doubt it. People are selling them on Craigslist if you want to pay the price."

"Thanks." So I would be siphoning gas from the Lexus into the gas can and pouring it in the generator's tank. My five gallons and what was in the tank would get us through the night though it meant getting up in the wee hours. *Can you even siphon gas from modern tanks?* I wondered. Something to Google at home.

Everything was copacetic at the house. The generator took the additional gas without issue and nothing shorted out or caught on fire while I was gone. Using my phone as a hotspot, I went to find out if it was possible to siphon a Lexus LX. It was not and the procedure was to puncture the tank and drain it out, which clearly wasn't gonna happen. Out of curiosity I went to rivercity.craigslist.org.

In Silicon Valley in the late '90s and 2000s, Craigslist was still a pretty cool place to go. Things like Facebook Marketplace hadn't come along to supplant it yet so if you wanted secondhand stuff that's where you went.

Under "for sale" and "auto parts" I found what I was looking for. There were a few ads for different kinds of gas cans like Wavian and ones described as "NATO spec." The metal ones were $350 each. I had a catalog somewhere where they were only $89. At Walmart plastic cans were probably half that. On the second page I found a guy selling new plastic ones for $200 each, the lowest price for something that wasn't rusty or faded. I sent him a text.

While I waited for a reply, I went to some of the other pages. In each category, there was a LOT of "new!" items. New-in-box TVs, gaming consoles, exercise equipment (assembly required), furniture, and anything else but guns. My phone buzzed.

Cans 200$ each cash. Comes with the good filler neck. Take it or leave it.

The price is fine. I need a couple of them.

I got all you need.

He sent me the address and suggested I come now to

avoid curfew. The address was downtown, like "Ross, I don't want you going to that part of town," downtown. The major cross street was the exit where we saw the hijacked truck being looted. I would not be telling Raelene where I was going. It was ironic because she went to school in Berkeley and lived in a low-rent part of Oakland riding her bike to class and work for years. The world had changed significantly since the halcyon days of the Millennium.

Back over the bridge again. An Army Corps of Engineers boat (yes, the Army has boats; my brother confirmed it) was working its way through the floating debris in the river. The first Bank of America I went to had no power, so I hopped on the beltway and drove into the suburb of Southside to use their "super branch." The ATMs there were working and had no problem giving me $1,000 in fifties.

To call my gas tank vendor's neighborhood off MLK Boulevard "blighted" would be generous. A banner bearing RadCom's symbols, the "hammer, sickle, and circuit board" as my brother called it, hung from a freeway overpass. The pavement was poorly repaired. Parking strips were overgrown. Sidewalks buckled from tree roots. Weeds grew knee high in many places. Street signs, even stop signs, were missing. Nearly every yard was fenced off. Several had large, mean looking dogs in them.

Not a single house seemed to have been painted in this decade. Windows were barred. It was a rough part of town. The only reason I didn't get stares from groups on the street corners was the cold kept most everyone inside. I parked in front of the address I was given and sent a text that I arrived. Across the street, four men stood around a fire in a 55-gallon drum in the front yard and watching me as they drank beer.

My seller came out the front door and waved me to his detached garage. "Call me T."

"Is my car going to be okay there?"

T craned his neck to look and whistled. "Nice ride. You got balls driving down here in that thing."

"I couldn't take the Tesla."

T had a good laugh at that. He gestured towards the men across the street. "Don't worry, you're with me. They'll think you're a lawyer or something."

We went in a crooked side door that was warped with age and scraped as it opened. The garage was a narrow single bay made for a 1940s car. It was filled with all sorts of boxes, large and small. They were clean shipping boxes, not stored personal items. About fifty blue and red plastic gas cans were the only things I could obviously identify in the clutter. "How many you need?"

"Four. Two hundred each?"

"That's right. Eight hundred." I pulled out my "wad" and counted off a mix of hundreds and fifties. T counted it to be sure. "We good. See, they all got the good filler necks, not that California junk one."

Gooseneck nozzles were attached to each can. The labels and price tags were too. Either T was an exceptionally shrewd businessman who anticipated a run on gas cans or he was fencing looted goods. I didn't care. I wasn't a cop, I needed gas cans, and I had the cash.

"Grab two, I'll help you carry the others out," he said. "By the way, you got a gun?"

Uh oh. What do I say? Well you're in his home so you better tell the truth. "No. I thought it would be rude to bring a gun into a stranger's home."

T laughed again, this time harder. "You do own one, right?"

"Two. A pistol and a shotgun."

He smiled approvingly. "Man, either you stupid or you got some brass ones. Let me tell you, walking around with that kinda cash with all the craziness that's been going on, 'specially in this neighborhood and you better be packin'. Stay strapped or get clapped. Even at home." He reached down and lifted up his hoodie to expose the butt of a stainless steel revolver.

"My brother has something like that," I managed. My mouth was dry.

"He got good taste." We carried the cans out and put them in the back of my SUV. T slapped my hand goodbye and wished me luck.

I did the same to him and drove off. I made sure not to rev the engine too much or squeal the tires as I drove away, at least until I turned the corner. Stop signs? Red lights? I emulated our cab driver from last night and rolled through them all. Screw the directions that brought me here. I wasn't going back up MLK Boulevard. Truck hijacking or not, I got on the freeway as fast as I could and went all the way around downtown until I got back to the open gas station I went to earlier. With the four new cans, my old one, and the tank filled I headed back over the river.

Lingering smoke from the substation was visible from the bridge, but it was clear that the fire department had gotten everything under control. Mineral oil was used in the generators and when exposed to oxygen it burned really well. Smoke still hung in the air over the city, trapped by an inversion layer. The acrid smell of the smoke and tangy ozone came in the open window, mingling with the gasoline fumes inside. I made it back to the house with about an hour to spare before sunset.

I topped off the generator and noted that fuel consumption wasn't as bad as I expected. Only having the absolute bare minimum load on helped. The second biggest draw, the fridge, was packed with ice to lower the thermal load inside since we had to toss the spoiled food. The fuel would get us well into tomorrow and probably another day if we shut the heater down during the day.

"Everything go okay?" Raelene asked.

"Yeah, except finding a working ATM and gas station that had electricity. Southside was the only place with both electricity and fuel it seemed."

I gave her a hug. "You smell like gas. Did you hear the news?"

"What news?"

"The power outage. It was on AM radio. A cable under the river exploded because the flooding eroded the landing or something. The surge then caused the substation to catch on fire."

"Any ETA on getting the power back?"

"Nope." She looked at the package of Hamburger Helper. "Think I need to change any of the directions since I'm cooking with the prepper stuff?"

"Search me. Call my sister-in-law." Grant's wife Heather was the prepper chef of the family. "She'd know. I can cook dinner if you want."

"No Ross, you need to shower. And I tried. The phones were down. By the way, while you were gone there was a

43

drone flying around."

"And?"

"It was just odd, that's all. The girls ran outside and waved to it."

"Not like there's TV to watch. Might be that guy over on Park Avenue with the YouTube channel filming 'I Survived the Big Freeze' for his latest million-view video."

"How did we ever survive without the Internet?" she asked before turning back to dinner. Raelene and I were the last generation to grow up without the web. Of course we had it going into high school, but it was just a gimmick back then. Neither of us understood that it would shape our lives and our world.

Day 2

Handouts and Hunger Pains

At 4:30 in the morning I woke up to Raelene poking me. "Ross, wake up. It's cold in here."

"Get back in bed," I mumbled.

"I am in bed. The heater isn't working."

"Okay." *Man, it is cold*, I thought as I got out of bed. I was still cold after dressing in my socks, slippers, and long sleeve quilted shirt. Raelene came with me downstairs. The generator remained un-stolen and still hummed away outside the garage. The rest of the house had power. "Here's the problem." The breaker switch on the side of the furnace was broken.

"How can you tell?"

"No click. You should hear a click and the heater should start once I cycle this switch. Too many shorts and the trip coil failed. We'll need a new one."

"Does Home Depot sell them?"

"Guess we'll find out in the morning. Get the space heater."

"Reya broke it yesterday."

I swore. *How did she manage that?* "Guess we're gonna be cold then. Pile the blankets on the bed."

Neither of us could go back to sleep so we made some coffee and sat on the living room couch. The gas fireplace came in handy because with the generator going, we were able to ignite it (yes, electric ignition). Despite it being entirely decorative, in the cold it did throw a small circle of relative warmth. Too bad the room was large and the ceiling vaulted.

We cuddled and watched the 6 AM newscast on Raelene's laptop as the cable was out and we didn't have a TV antenna. A new segment of the daily news was the food supply update. Viewer reports fed the data used to indicate what the shopping situation was like. One station called it "Grocery Gaps," another "Shelf Report," and the last one gave the lurid sobriquet of "Pantry Panic." *A lot of file footage of bare shelves and long lines are going to come out of this*, I thought sardonically.

The grocery and drugstore chains were withholding the scheduled time for deliveries out of fear of robberies and flash mobs. Now trucks were arriving at random times, always in daylight, and accompanied by armed guards. Marked guard vehicles trailed the trucks and ranks of security officers, bagboys, and stockers stood guard while the pallets were taken inside. Shuddering cell phone video showed those same pallets moved right out on to the retail floor where customers stripped them bare in minutes.

Was that yesterday? That looks worse than what happened at Albertsons, minus the shooting. The situation had ironically improved a bit once people got used to not finding anything at stores. Instead of hearing that the roads had cleared and the stores were stocked, people just dropped in randomly throughout the day rather than beating down the doors as soon as the manager unlocked them. A trickle rather than a flood of customers helped keep things on the shelves for hours instead of minutes.

COVID was bad but then trucks were still coming. A scene from a store here now looked more like Venezuela or the Soviet Union than America. Even Amazon and the various food delivery services were suspending service. Nonperishables could be shipped in via FedEx, UPS, or the post office as long as one was willing to accept the delays from weather and the Teamsters. Forget Prime shipping, if anything was still in stock, it would be here when it got here, if at all. Ask me how I know.

That's how the press briefing later in the morning on the emergency food distribution centers became the most watched television program in the Metro counties. Even we would tune in to it once breakfast was finished.

Before the news piece aired, we got a commercial. Thankfully, it was not another political ad in the endless onslaught of them during campaign season. November 6 couldn't come fast enough. A montage of everyday Americans—factory workers, teachers, nurses, firefighters, and grocery store clerks played on the screen. A faceless female identifying person read the voiceover. "America—a land built by the many yet serving only a few. But it doesn't have to be this way."

The picture cut to images of homeless people, closed factories, and people being evicted. "We see the hardship, the struggle, the inequity. We understand the pain of a system that doesn't work for everyone. That's where RAISE steps in." A group of volunteers distributed food to a poor neighborhood.

"At RAISE, we believe in the power of unity, the strength of equality, and the necessity of social equity. We are a non-profit group, here to help those most forgotten by society, striving to help everyone realize the American Dream," the narrator continued over video clips of rallies, scenes of peaceful protests, and individuals helping others. "Your contribution to the RAISE Freedom Fund isn't just a donation. It's a lifeline. It provides legal defense and bail posting for those who could never afford it." Families were reuniting on screen after a loved one bailed out. "The RAISE Freedom Fund stands as a beacon of hope for those who have been marginalized and oppressed. Our mission is clear: to challenge systemic injustices, to seek reparations for victims of police brutality and to work tirelessly for the rights of BIPOC communities."

"You didn't bail Bert out, now did you?" I cursed at the screen. "He's Hispanic. There's your BIPOC right there." The RAISE fund existed to put rioters, looters, and radical anarchist activists back on the street. It was as if Hitler had a fundraising arm to pay for his lawyer and bail after the Beer Hall Putsch.

It cut to videos of diverse Americans pushing RAISE yard signs into their lawns and smoothing bumper stickers on their cars. The only white people in the commercial so far were a pair of green-haired lesbians who looked like their faces had been impaled with shrapnel from a jewelry store explosion. "A RAISE sign isn't just an object, it's a statement–a declaration that you stand for fairness, justice, and equality. It's a testament of your belief in a better, equitable America."

"No, it's frickin' extortion. 'Pay us money and put this in your yard and on your car or we'll break your windows.'" My wife nudged me. We had similar opinions on most topics but she detested it when I bitched at the TV.

The narrator went on: "It's time for change, and it begins with you. Join us in building an America where equity is not just an idea but a reality. Let's create a nation where everyone has a fair chance." The diverse people doing stuff in three-quarters speed changed to the RAISE logo on a black background. "Donate to the RAISE Freedom Fund today. Let's write the next chapter of American history together."

"That was utter bullshit."

"Language Ross," Raelene chastised. "I don't like it either but there's no need to constantly complain about it."

"Excuse me, let me rephase that. The narrative presented doesn't align with my understanding or perspective and I sincerely challenge the veracity of the claims made," I said. She groaned in reply.

Next a commercial for McDonalds played. Didn't anyone think to pull ads in this area where they had fewer stores open than they did in the 1970s? Following that, the news anchors came on again to cover the food story.

"Elements of FEMA and the National Guard will begin limited distribution of food to citizens. Regional distribution centers will be established centrally around the River City metropolitan area. Anyone seeking food will be required to use the distribution center in their area. You may not travel to centers outside of your area. Each center will be screening those seeking aid to confirm that they are indeed locals. Be sure to bring photo ID. No weapons will be permitted. Security will be established by the National Guard. Fresh fruit and vegetables will be handed out along with necessary vitamins.

"All distribution centers will open daily on the same day until the crisis is over. You may only return on the seventh day after each visit. Their locations will be announced on this station at 7:30 AM the day the centers open. Operating hours will be 8:00 AM to shortly before sunset each day. No camping or waiting before 7:30 AM will be permitted. No interference with the National Guard or FEMA will be tolerated."

"Why don't they announce the locations now?" Raelene asked.

"Security. Announcing the locations in advance gets you lines of people camping out like the mall before Black Friday. It might permit gangs or bandits to stake out the location. Plus everybody and their brother would mob it."

"Won't people see them setting up?"

"Of course they will, but word won't spread *that* easily." With a half-hour lead time, it would be very difficult for all but the closest residents to clog the place up." I got up.

"Where are you going?" Raelene asked.

"To get dressed so I'm ready to pickup our rations." The longer I waited to show up, the longer I'd be in line.

She acted as if I said something wrong. "We don't need their food. It's probably not very good food and there are other people who need it more than we do. It's not right."

Of course Raelene didn't feel it was right. We had money, some stored food, and thus no need to take handouts. My sensitive, bleeding heart wife was a very compassionate and considerate person but here she was wrong. This wasn't using my debit card so the restaurant owner didn't have to pay 3% to Visa (yes, she makes me do that because she hates credit card companies and likes small businesses), this was *food*.

The beautiful thing about having a feminine, kindhearted wife is she softened my selfish natural male tendencies. I didn't mind the volunteering or buying presents for impoverished kids at Christmas but our pantries were nearing empty. All the money in the bank couldn't fill our kitchen.

"Two things, they're giving it out to everybody. We also haven't done a proper grocery shopping since a week before our trip." Our venture to the despoiled Walmart out of town didn't count. Given how busy it was there, one could be forgiven in thinking that it was the day before Thanksgiving or the first of the month, when EBT cards got filled. Apparently all of River City and its suburbs had the same idea as us.

Anything worth eating in the store was gone. Produce was nil. Shoppers got down on all fours to retrieve broken packages of things that fell behind the shelves. The store was a disgusting, stinking mess of people. I guess had we been starving we could have bought some frozen pie crusts and salad dressing. We bought nothing. Probably the only redeeming thing that came from that trip was the girls got Happy Meals and Raelene got her own box of fries instead of mooching mine.

I shouldn't have to be convincing her of this. In college she went for days without eating, sometimes going on dates just for a free meal. Her sophomore year she shoplifted and snuck into the staff lounges to pinch bagels.

"Moreover, what if we run out of food? Unlikely but have you ever lived through a disaster like this? I don't want to miss an opportunity to get a little more, just in case, only to need it. There's no guarantee it doesn't get worse." I softened my voice. "Plus they said fresh vegetables. I'd eat celery at this point." Raelene still didn't approve but I got her to smile.

*   *   *

At exactly 7:30, the screen cut to the cheesy local government graphics. The local stations were all using the same feed from the public access channel. A bored and unprofessional voice read the instructions from earlier and gave out the locations. Anyone could look up their food center on a county webpage as well. Each location was shown on a map with the corresponding area it served highlighted. When our neighborhood popped up, it included the whole island so there was no ambiguity.

"See ya," I said and left without a kiss. I had fifteen minutes to get across town. There were only two bridges to get into the "old" town. West River City was split in two, creating the island by digging out what was originally a cut-off meander from the main river. Before WWII there was a huge defense depot and military base around here so a deep water ship channel was dug parallel to the river to accommodate the ship traffic this far inland. I think we were the furthest inland port not on the Mississippi, Columbia, or Great Lakes.

As I was backing the Lexus out, I noticed Mrs. Vargas, who lived diagonally across the cul-de-sac, getting into her car with a suit bag. Strange that she should be taking her husband Bert's suit out for cleaning. I didn't know any dry cleaners were open. I had no trouble getting over the river off the island using the old bridge instead of the newer freeway stub. Traffic was still stop-and-go at a few dark intersections, however.

The distribution point was at the city's biggest park in a large hall that was rented out for concerts, dances, and festivals. I parked on the curb across the street, choosing to stay out of the parking lot. Numerous bikes, wheelbarrows, wagons, carts, and even strollers lined the sidewalk behind their owners—cargo transport. The line was already 200 people deep.

I took my place at the back of the line. It slowly shuffled forward. After ten minutes, I imagined I covered not quite a quarter of the distance to the head of the line. I would probably be here at least an hour or so. I contented myself with listening to the idle chit-chat.

Small talk about the weather and generalities about the state of the world predominated. One complaint was about how the Internet and power outages were affecting binge watching of the latest big streaming hit shows. Someone else grumbled that their kids were home all day. It would be interesting to see if there was spike in divorces in the affected region like after COVID when the spouses realized going to work was a way to avoid each other.

"...and they took all the food. Just kicked the door down and took all my food," an elderly woman said. "Cleaned out the cupboards and the fridge. Left the milk cuz that was open but even took the condiments out the door. Didn't take nothing else, didn't lay a finger on me after they shoved past me."

"Did you call the police?" her companion asked.

"Police? Police took forever to show up back when things were normal. They lucky my grandson wasn't home."

Others in line shared similar stories. Most left the house and came back to find it burglarized and their food missing. One woman described how she turned her back to put a bag of groceries in her rear seat and someone ran up to wheel her cart full of food away. That was after she had people openly reaching into her cart in the grocery store grabbing what they wanted. A cardinal rule of the grocery store had always been once it was in somebody's cart, it was as good as theirs. That unspoken convention being violated was an indicator of other long-standing mores in danger of collapse.

"When did this happen?" I asked.

"Two days ago when the Kroger got a truck in."

I just nodded back. *Not going shopping may actually have been a good thing.* I never thought that going to market could be a hazardous chore. Downtown River City could be rough but West River City was a gentrified, if not a genteel, suburb. Only in the last two years did the retailers start locking things like razor blades up and put RFID tags on detergent like they did in low-income areas.

Half an hour later I was at the courtyard of the building. A simple barbed wire fence delineated the area that was under control of the National Guard. Armed guardsmen with deadly faces stood watch along the fence line and at each entrance, holding their weapons at low-ready. More guardsmen, probably MPs, walked the lines of assembled people keeping order. They wore reflective vests and carried only side arms.

A very large and stern sign stated: NO WEAPONS. I wasn't very comfortable with being illegally disarmed, even for the short walk to the distribution area. Despite the sign, I carried my pistol carefully concealed under my jacket. If I saw metal detectors, I would just walk away. To be honest I wasn't very comfortable carrying past the sign, either. I didn't have my brother's contempt for gun free zones. At least the guardsmen provided substantial overwatch. Cops stood guard in the parking lot against vultures preying on the unarmed carrying away their boxed food.

At the checkpoint, a senior NCO loudly turned away a man openly carrying an AR-15 slung over his shoulder. The censure he was turned away with was stern and seemed to consist entirely of four-letter words. The flanking guards had their rifles pointed at the man who quickly turned and walked away bristling with resentment. More than a quarter had walked. I wondered how far the man had walked and what he faced to get here that he felt a rifle was necessary.

A few days ago it would have seemed logical to keep guns out—separating the fuses from the dynamite if you will. Maybe in the old days, when everybody would have had a sense of community, it wouldn't have been an issue. Now it seemed criminal to make the desperate walk unarmed just so soldiers could feel a little safer.

I got a little nervous at the checkpoint. I had to remind myself that I was breaking no laws by having a gun. All the screeners did was give me a glance up and down, then nodded for me to proceed. In the city, a bearded, middle aged white man wasn't perceived as a threat by anyone even if he had a concealed pistol beneath his shirt. Okay, maybe if he had tattoos and very big arms (I did not). For some reason we were made to wave our hands beneath a UV light.

The inner line started in a typical queuing pattern constructed out of traffic delineator poles strung with wire supporting orange plastic fencing. I walked right up to this and was stopped by a civilian who broke up the line into different groups. There were three different paths, all separated by plywood walls six feet high. *Door number one, door number two, and door number three. Which one will it be? The Monty Hall problem*, I thought.

When it was my group's turn, we were sent through the small maze. Our small group of two women and five men walked through the looping queue until we reached the end of the line. Good queue management was always about keeping movement going and creating the impression you were near the end of the line. Whoever was in charge of setting this place up thought a lot about crowd control and keeping people from knowing how long they had to wait.

A fight broke out in the line back beyond the barbed wire. A gaggle of MPs ran towards the disturbance. There was a command to "Break it up!" shortly followed by the crackle of a Taser. Leaning so I could see, I saw two men pulled away from the crowd and forced prone. As they lay face down on the pavement, they were quickly searched and flex cuffed. One of the men rolled on to his side and spat at an MP. The MP swiftly kicked the man in the face and gave him a butt-stroke to the back with his rifle.

The crowd gasped and phones came up to record. Once the men had been pacified, they were hauled up by their arms and marched off to somewhere inside the enclosure. *Unnecessary roughness*, a zebra-striped referee in my head said and threw down a yellow flag. I'd have to ask my brother if the Army allowed such rough treatment. No way a regular cop could get away with that. On the other hand after going-on two weeks of hardcore rioting and lawlessness I don't think the authorities cared much anymore.

"Next!" a voice yelled. I spun around to see it was my turn. The line monitor waved me inside the building.

Once we made it inside the small lobby, everyone was made to stop at a table staffed with civilians, obviously emergency volunteers wearing their ICS Logistics Branch vests. "Photo ID," the woman said without looking up.

I put my driver license down on the table. The woman took it and began to type the information into the computer. When she was finished, she handed the license back and asked me to place my right thumb on a digital inkpad. "What is this for?"

"To make sure you aren't cheating and doubling up on food. You're the twentieth person to ask that. I need to put up a sign," she whinged.

"What if I object?"

"Then you don't get food and you get blacklisted."

Without a choice I put my thumb down. I doubted there was much they could do with it, even if they ran me through the FBI database. Besides, I made sure to smear my thumb. The computer didn't flag it and the woman didn't bother to examine the print.

"How much food do you have at home?"

I was momentarily taken aback by the question. "Usually one to three days' worth."

"How many in your household?"

"Four."

"Any children?"

"Two."

"Do you have a working vehicle?"

"Do roller blades count?" I said sarcastically.

No response. "Do you own any firearms?"

Why do they want to know that? Unconsciously, my hand checked to make sure my gun was still there. "Excuse me?"

"Do you own any firearms?" She held up her palm. "Don't ask me about it, it's on the list. I have to ask."

"No, they were all stolen." If I were Pinocchio, my nose would be as long as a broomstick.

"Do you or anyone in your household suffer from a chronic disease, disability, or is currently ill?"

"No."

"Thank you." She took a red plastic square the size of a playing card from a box and handed it to me. "Take this to Door Three on your left and you will receive your food ration. You will be directed from there."

The door was nothing more than a hinged plywood panel. I walked through a short plywood chute and popped out at a series of three tables behind a line of crowd-control barricades that separated the room in half. Most of the room was behind makeshift curtains suspended on a ten-foot tall rod. Through the gaps and the people coming and going I saw boxes of food and many figures in camouflage boxing it up. The mystery was just an illusion and to create some privacy for the "backstage" work.

A soldier took my plastic chit at the final table and stamped my hand. They were using invisible ink, impervious to light hand washing. This explained the UV scanners at the entry checkpoint. The ink would last 72-96 hours despite washing, he explained, and he imagined that most didn't have access to the alcohol swabs necessary to remove the stamp.

I was handed a 12-pack case of MREs in a box and another box with assorted fresh foods. The second box held a sealed plastic container which contained various vitamins, nutrition pills, and water purification tablets. The soldier, talking almost as fast as an auctioneer, warned me not to try to come back within seven days; there would be a record and the prohibition included anyone at my listed address.

Great service.

I couldn't complain. We had a week's worth of food at home, if we needed it, even if it was freeze dried. The point of this visit was reconnaissance and to obtain some fresh fruit.

The exit took me behind a row of trees that shielded those leaving from those queued up waiting for their turn. Soldiers kept watch along the fenced exit route. Tucked into a small grove, I caught sight of a cluster of tables and kerosene heaters.

My keen eyes saw at least a dozen men resting near the heaters. Each was wearing his full combat gear, minus helmets, which sat nearby. I counted at least four machine guns and saw several riot control grenade launchers and bean-bag shotguns. Two men armed with scoped rifles lounged on a raising platform that was currently collapsed, clearly marksmen. This would be the response force intended to crush any riot or suppress any attempt at robbing the stockpile.

The walk out to the street allowed a view of the waiting crowd. In the time I was in line and being processed, the amount of people seeking food swelled. I estimated that at least 300 people were waiting at the entrance to the building and the numbers in the line outside the perimeter had doubled or tripled. I had good timing. If it were not for the overwhelming and heavily armed military presence, the frustrated but calm atmosphere would quickly deteriorate into violence.

Cars were parked all on the street now blocking driveways and fire hydrants. None of the cops or soldiers that had been out earlier were around. Two lines of cars stretched away from the entrance in both directions as people idled and burned their precious gas waiting to park. Whoever organized this thing was stupid. All the COVID food banks kept people in their cars and used a drive-through system.

I forgot to mention that carrying two boxes with a

combined weight of over 20lbs was not fun. It wasn't heavy but it sure was awkward to bear the weight while balancing and trying to see over the top. The people who brought carts and stuff were smart. Though my field of vision was partially obstructed and my hands occupied, I wasn't oblivious to my surroundings. The dude who started following me must have thought he was the smartest guy around.

My first thought was that he was just heading the same way as me but it became a little odd when he followed me down the sidewalk. I parked far away from the entrance for a reason. There were no cars nearby when I parked so since he arrived after I did, he wasn't already going back to his car empty-handed. When I crossed the street, he did so shortly after me but a few car lengths behind. I grasped what he was doing.

Placing the boxes on the ground, I turned my head slightly to see him out of my peripheral vision. He was walking down the sidewalk faster now, trying to keep out of sight of traffic and be behind the line of parked cars. "Suspicious as hell" would be an understatement. This was a robbery seconds from unfolding and I was one step ahead of the guy, just barely.

My hands worked fast to unzip my jacket and untuck my shirt. When I had imagined something like this happening before, I assumed I'd be all thumbs. My CCW instructor said it was a common theme to have dreams where you couldn't draw your gun or the trigger pull was a thousand pounds.

Right as the mugger stepped across the parking strip and almost into the gap between the cars, he saw my pistol. Without a word he turned in a not-so nonchalant manner and did a 180° turn back down the sidewalk. Not a word was exchanged or my gun even drawn. Seeing that I was alert and an armed target stopped the whole thing before it started.

I kept my eyes on him until he moved out of sight. He was going to be somebody's problem but not mine. My heart pounded as I put the boxes in the trunk. That was exciting! The first time I used a gun to scare somebody away and I didn't even have to pull it out!

Neighbor Bert's Homecoming

I got home around 11:00. The food giveaway was not my only stop. There was gas to get, grocery stores to check, and ATMs to try. The Vargas' car pulled into their driveway two houses down as I was unloading the Lexus. Bert got out wearing a suit. I waved. He motioned for me to walk over. "Come inside," he beckoned, almost in a whisper. His head was on a swivel and his eyes darted in all directions.

"Whoa, what happened to the Camry?" With the way his car was parked on the side of the driveway facing the house I didn't notice the smashed windshield and dented hood earlier.

"Inside." We both followed Mrs. Vargas in. "Oh, it's good to be home." Bert immediately whipped off his coat, tossed it on the back of the couch, and pulled his tie loose. His wife handed him his slippers and he kicked off his still-tied dress shoes. "Much better."

This is strange. He wore a suit to work once or twice a year and never would just throw his clothes on the living room floor like this. "Bert, is everything okay?"

"Yeah Ross, just fine now." I followed him to the wet bar between the living room and the dining room. He poured himself three fingers of Scotch. "What's your poison?"

"It's a little early for me. Dude, what's going on?"

Bert knocked back half of the glass. "I just got out of jail Ross. Where have you been?"

"Jail? I've been in Florida and ever since we got back I felt like I landed in a parallel dimension like that old TV show *Sliders*. Why were you in jail?"

We sat down on the couch. "It was those damn rioters

downtown. You saw what they did to the car. I have a lawyer's bill in the ballpark of $15,000 but he got me off. The charges were dismissed with prejudice, thank God." Bert's glass of whiskey was half-gone.

Bert was a Nurse Anesthetist and worked at Downtown Memorial. Not the best hospital or the best part of town but the 10% incentive over market wages to work at the hardest hospital to staff was worth it to him. "Ross, I don't care what you saw on the news, it was worse than you could imagine once the snow stopped. When it got just warm enough for people to loot and riot, they did." The cold and rolling blackouts were the straw that broke the camel's back of a population already on the edge.

Social tensions in River City reached an all-time high this fall, in no small part due to the election. 2020, four years ago, began the unraveling of the city and Bert found himself caught in the long-overdue snapback. Thousands of angry and desperate people were stealing whatever they could get their hands on. Some were doing it to survive and others to profit. In the middle of this leftist groups were out in the street organizing protests over several high profile police shootings. Anarchists were burning buildings and committing acts of sabotage. It was the George Floyd riots on steroids.

Bert drove right into the middle of a protest organized by RAISE—Realize American Improvement by Social Equity—the polite acronym for the household name of RadCom. With the curfew in place there should have been no one protesting but the police were so busy dealing with the spike in crime, they were unable to contain the looting and riots. A mob of black-clad protesters marching down MLK Boulevard was not on their radar.

"They came around the corner when I was already halfway down the block," Bert said. "There's this raised median there so I couldn't make a U-turn. All these people just kept walking towards me. I tried to go as slow as possible. My turn to the hospital was just around the corner. The first people went by me; they made room! I thought these people were just looters or whatever."

He took another swig of whiskey and as he started to relive the memory he changed tenses. "As I get deeper into the crowd, they start yelling at me. 'Where are you going, asshole?' and all that. They start banging on the car and taking longer to get out of the way, like they want to get him. I'm going like five miles an hour here. Then finally they don't get out of the way. I'm totally surrounded, they're beating on the car and windows, and some dude is jumping up and down on the hood.

"So I call 9-1-1. Phone rings for over a minute before I get transferred to the state troopers. I told them I needed the River City cops. 'They're busy right now, blah blah blah.' I'm like 'Lady, they've got my car surrounded and I'm pretty sure they're gonna beat me to death.' That's when this guy who acts like he's in charge comes up. He tells the guy on the hood to get off and starts talking to me through the window.

"I cracked the window so I could talk to him. 'I'm just going to the hospital. I'm a nurse in the surgical trauma unit.' He gets shoved out of the way by some crazy looking dude, you know one of those homeless people who are so dirty they look like they have a tan? He tries to reach through the gap to reach me, can't so he starts pulling and hitting the window. I roll his fingers up in the damn thing.

"He starts howling so a couple of guys in all black and

ski masks rush over with a window punch and break the window. Now I've got a crazy guy's hands all over me grabbing for my neck. I've got one hand fighting him off and the other blasting on the horn, but nobody moves. So I just take my foot off the brake and let the car start rolling.

"People get out of the way as the car rolls into them but Crazy Dude is still grabbing at me. I give it more gas and honk but instead of getting out of the way the people are hitting the car and trying to get on the hood. Crazy Dude gets his hands around my neck and I panic. I just hit the gas. Knocked a couple of the people in the street down and the two hanging on to the hood jump for it.

"By now the idiots in front of me are scattering so I speed up. I'm getting desperate because Crazy Dude is trying to get his upper body in the car. He's spitting and slobbering everywhere and has his forearm wrapped around my throat. I don't know if he was choking me or if I was just freaking out but everything is graying out around the edges, you know?

"I make my turn at the corner and floor it. Finally Crazy Dude can't hang on anymore and releases. He goes tumbling down in the street behind me and I haul ass to the staff parking lot. Somebody on a smoke break sees me stumble out of the car having a panic attack and gets a gurney over to me.

"I find out when the cops turn up in my ER room that the crowd chased me down. Somebody had a drone that just followed me back to the hospital and filmed me wigging out until they got me on the gurney and inside."

The whole time Bert told me his story I was sitting on the edge of my seat, literally. I was breathing heavily like I was there. Maybe it was nerves from earlier with the guy who followed me at the food event or that I had driven downtown just yesterday, I'm not sure. I wasn't even there and his story bothered me. "Mind if I pour a drink now?"

"Not at all. Just bring the bottle in here."

I came back with my drink and Bert poured another finger's worth in his glass. "People were telling me it was bad but I thought they were exaggerating."

"No! We were doing non-stop surgeries; that's why I was going in. Dozens of trauma cases. We were cutting and stitching like it was a combat zone, one after another. I'd never done anything like it, even as a Navy Corpsman twenty years ago."

None of this felt right. Bert had his car surrounded by protesters and was attacked by them and a whacked-out guy. "Why were you arrested?"

Bert, now feeling the effects of his drink, laughed. "Why? Because 33 counts of assault with a deadly weapon— the car—felony hit and run, 33 counts of felony battery, in case the ADW charges didn't stick, and driving through a parade, That's why."

"A parade?"

"Yeah. The DA was trying to argue that stupid, weird law applied."

It wasn't even legal in this state to charge someone like Bert who drove through a protest like that. "What about that bill they passed in 2020 after the riots, the one with the funny name?"

"Plow 'em Down Act? That's what the liberals called it. Joint Bill 1. Saved my ass, plain and simple. Took them long enough to get to my preliminary hearing but boom, bang, charges dismissed with prejudice right there. 'Mr. Vargas, you're free to go. I'm sorry you had to go through this.'"

"That's it?"

"That's it. My lawyer made the claim that this was done in self-defense. Filed a preliminary pleading right after arraignment so the DA had to answer it at the evidentiary hearing or whatever. She plays the drone video and a bunch of cell phone video—I'm surprised you didn't see it on the news—that looks really bad."

I snapped my fingers. "We did! We had no idea it was you. It did look bad but you could still see that guy hanging out the window. Raelene and I thought he was trying to keep you from running people over."

"Well turns out she edited the drone video and gave the edited video to my lawyer in discovery. Except my lawyer found the full video on YouTube and downloaded it. Plus we had my dashcam that records me and the front view too. My lawyer said that if I hadn't pulled my car into secure parking the RadCom guys would have been sure to steal the camera to keep me from having my video at trial.

"My lawyer plays all of the unedited video and the judge is sitting there the whole time getting pissed and more pissed. He calls the DA to the bench and you could hear all this angry whispering. More legal stuff happens, I was in a complete daze, and the charges were all thrown out. The judge believed my self-defense claim. My lawyer didn't even have to push the stand-your-ground angle. The judge had no choice but to dismiss because that bill was so damn specific."

Bert explained that Joint Bill 1 required the state to basically prove that any preliminary claim of self-defense was unquestionably false, as long as the driver unintentionally drove into an unpermitted protest in a roadway. Dismissal with prejudice, meaning the charges couldn't ever be re-filed, was required. In the only other case dismissed under the law, the judge took weeks to decide, but Bert had a mountain of video to help expedite his adjudication.

"You shoulda seen the DA stomp out of the room. Didn't even look at me or apologize. My lawyer called on the way home and said the judge is going to be referring her for, like, malpractice or something."

"The actual district attorney or one of the deputies?"

"No Ross, the actual DA herself. That George Soros funded one, you know the reform lady. She refused to debate the last DA who's running against her to get his job back."

"Wow." I was glad we lived in another county. "Were you in jail the whole time?"

"Yep. No bail for me. Bondsmen wanted $100,000."

"But don't you have to put down only ten percent?" I asked.

"That was ten percent. I was held on a million dollar's bail. The judge reduced it from like $1.3 million or something." My mouth dropped open, aghast. "You were on vacation so you didn't see it but my wife was telling me the news was just terrible. Calling me a racist, a murderer, a terrorist. I'm going to have to sue a lot of people for slander. Boy did they ever shut up and drop the story when my lawyer gave them the full video." Bert started laughing again.

He was right. The unrest storyline was hot news for about three days and then it simply disappeared the day we flew home. The news of the riots in River City disappeared when the propaganda narrative had to change. Now it was a disaster/survival story again instead of mismanagement by our Republican governor and discrimination against the underprivileged. Raelene and I stopped watching the news midway through the trip and only turned on the Weather Channel.

"Did anyone try to attack you in jail?" I heard all the horror stories of the assassination threats against Kyle Rittenhouse, the kid from Kenosha who was chased down by Antifa, and how the guards in DC let the January 6th defendants get beaten up. If Bert was in jail on trumped up charges I could just see word getting around about who he was.

"Huh? No. The jail has been in lockdown since the Big Freeze got real. They gave me an orange wrist band and put me in a two-man cell with another guy who got arrested for doing the same thing. He didn't have any video so his fight will be a lot tougher. The deputies were pretty cool. I don't fault the actual cops. Except letting me drive right into it, but…"

"Aren't you pissed that they arrested you in the hospital?" I would be. I'd hate them forever if they put me through that.

"I wasn't. The cops interviewed me in the ER but the ones who arrested me were DA investigators. I didn't even know they had those. These four guys in suits came to the house two days after and handcuffed me. I thought it was the FBI." He sipped the last of the whiskey in his glass and hefted the bottle but didn't pour anymore. "Been going through hell this last week. I can't tell you how bad it feels to be the bad guy when you've done nothing wrong."

He leaned back on the couch and closed his eyes. In a few seconds, he started snoring. The poor guy must have been up all night agonizing about the hearing. I replaced the bottle in the bar and took the glasses to the kitchen sink. Mrs. Vargas came in. "How was your trip?" she said with her usual cheer.

"The kids loved it. Remy is too young to remember it but we took lots of good pictures. The way things are going they'll probably never get to go. How are you? I'm sorry we weren't home."

"I'm fine now that it's all over. Bert's vindicated. I knew he would be but you see all the stories where the jury gets intimidated or whatever and it worries you. The people coming by the house were just awful."

"People came by the house?"

"For a day or two after he was arrested and before the lawyer put out the video. Reporters and troublemakers. Someone keyed up our daughter's car in the night. Then when the truth came out it was like nothing ever happened."

I gave her a hug. "Well if you need anything, Raelene and I are just across the street."

Some time after noon we got reliable cell service or something like it. One to two bars and calls/SMS only. No data at all. I called my brother and started leaving him messages. No response. I didn't like it but I couldn't tell if the issue was on his end or due to the network issues down here.

"Did you try his house phone?" Raelene asked. He still had one of those.

"No."

I called. On the fourth ring Grant picked up. "We're happy with our long distance service, thank you," he said.

"Funny. Glad you guys are doing well enough to still have a sense of humor."

"Yo, dude. Laughing is about the only thing I can do right now. My stomach hurts a lot." He sounded relieved and drained at the same time. "Everything alright?"

This was not the time to complain because it was cold, the fridge was empty, and Uber Eats wasn't working here. "Relatively speaking, yes. What's up with your stomach? We're the ones with bad water. Are you pregnant?"

"No and it's not the water. It's bad up here Ross. I'm just tired of feeling like a prisoner in my own neighborhood. Not to take away from your situation." For days now angry mobs mixed with refugees and activists had picketed his street in particular. In Red Rock, with the police overwhelmed and the politicians browbeaten the next target was the average, bourgeois red-state American. Their fight was with the suburbs, not Wall Street. Grant had the hard luck to find himself rather unexpectedly and unintentionally in a hotspot.

"Of course. Consider it a positive that whatever you

did they let out with an ankle bracelet," I joked. I gave him the situation report with food in the least whiny way possible. "We're down to eating Mountain House and odds and ends. On the radio I heard that the National Guard shot a gang trying to break into a food distribution center at a school."

"I wish the Guard would shoot some people here," he said with a lilting tone that bordered on sarcasm and insolence. "I know you thought you were sitting pretty on the island there across the river from the animals but we've got them on our street. While you were on vacation we were living a repeating night of terror. We're pariahs. If eating Mountain House was my biggest problem I'd be delighted."

He repeated the same speech he had given me a dozen times before. *You need to get out of town, Ross. It's not safe there. You don't have any network you can depend on. Your preps are inadequate.* Had I not appreciated the stress of living in riot central, his nagging would have really pissed me off. He got out of "the city" and yet in his "based" smaller city the trouble found him anyway.

I heard his wife's voice in the background speaking to him sharply. Grant moved the phone away from his mouth, poorly covered up the receiver, and bickered back to her. "He's your brother! He's probably as worried and upset as you are. Being stressed is no excuse to talk to him that way," she said. "Show some sympathy."

He said a few more things to her and came back on. "Are you still there? Sorry, sorry. It's been very rough up here, like the worst of Iraq. We have the street barricaded and all the neighbors are taking turns guarding it." He sighed. "You have no idea how bad it can get. None."

So much for an older brother being a voice of strength

and tranquility. How bad could it be in Red Rock that he felt we had it better?

"Are you guys getting out of town? The capitol and Springfield are getting hit pretty hard and they say it's only going to get worse. The Cajun navy is already starting rescues from the people on low-lying ground." Neither of those cities had the flood defenses to the extent that the River City area did.

"That's what I wanted to talk to you about."

"Ross, it's not any better here," he said, reading my mind. "The police up and quit this morning."

"What?"

"Practically the whole department. They had a sick-out over all the crap so the mayor fired them all over the officers' unauthorized strike. We've got no cops and the neighbors are all taking turns guarding our street. You're always welcome, but I'm telling you, you might be going from the frying pan into the fire."

We hung up and I swore to myself. Raelene heard me and came in. "What's wrong?"

I gave her a sanitized run down. "But the good news is, he's got a neighborhood tactical team of off-duty cops and federal agents."

Her demeanor changed. "'Out of the frying pan and into the fire?' It doesn't sound much safer there. Only if we have to stay with your brother, Ross, only if we have to." She walked off to her exercise room. We were caught between a rock and a hard place; an insurgency and a flooding, rioting city. I couldn't blame her for being upset.

The Shotgun

It felt awkward carrying a pistol at home. People expected you to carry a gun in public, especially now. Home was supposed to be a safe place where you would have time to take the shotgun down from the top shelf of the closet, shout a warning, and rack the slide. Guys at the gun store called the racking of a shotgun in the dead of night the loudest sound in the world and one guaranteed to get all but the most stubborn burglar running. My brother called that something like "Fuddlore," whatever that meant.

In the garage, behind the Christmas tree box was a black four-foot Pelican case that was secured to an eyebolt in a stud with two lengths of chain and a combination lock. I got it down and opened it up on my work bench. *Crap.* There was supposed to be a Remington semi-automatic shotgun in here, a nice 1100 model that I used to bust clays with from all the way back in college. Dad got us into the hobby because he and all his fighter pilot squadron mates used to practice getting a lead on a target that way. Helped the reflexes when it came to dogfights, they explained.

I didn't shoot much anymore. I started getting into pistol shooting when I bought my Glock but COVID and the ammo shortage put a stop to that. I never really was much of a shooter, anymore than I golfed or fished. Raelene probably looked forward to our trap and skeet matches with my brother more than I did. Six months ago I took the shotgun up to his place and forgot I left it in his safe.

After some rummaging around in the cabinets, I found a box and a half of shells, just some cheap lead birdshot that I must have got on special at Walmart. The cardboard was dusty and slightly damp but the plastic cases seemed alright. With some pipe I knew could make a rudimentary shotgun but I didn't have a plumbing store, a welder, or the instructional videos at hand. Thinking of what my wife would say if I brought something like that upstairs made me laugh.

Raelene was sitting on the living room couch wrapped up like a burrito in one of our "summer weight" comforters. Her gloved hands protruded just enough to hold a copy of the *Ball Blue Book Guide to Preserving*.

"Hey Rae, don't get too upset but I left my shotgun at Grant's."

She folded the book over the armrest. "Are we really going to need a shotgun?" Her reaction was not what I expected it to be.

"I'd feel a lot better off with one. I know it's not some sort of magic talisman but I do feel better having the pistol with me."

"You know I trust your judgement, Ross." She tapped the seat for me to sit down, and when I did, she put her arm around me. "Be honest with me. What's going on? Are you afraid?" Her face grew concerned. If I was worried, then she should be too.

"Afraid, no." My dad was on my mind. *Don't ever be afraid, son.* "Just cautious. We shouldn't have laughed at my brother and all the times he told us that we needed to get out of the city." We sat in silence as she stroked my beard. He was right about how COVID would play out, the elections, inflation, the economy; everything. Our rebuttal had been that it seemed so far fetched that things would keep falling and not right themselves as they had for decades. Mom and Dad survived the '70s, right?

"Yeah," she said resignedly.

Grant told me after he came back from Iraq the last time he started watching the new TV show "Doomsday Preppers." Like our father, he would have scoffed at the notion that the sky was going to fall; nuclear war with the Soviets never happened, did it? Yet after Iraq he told me "These people may *be* crazy but their intent to prepare isn't." In Iraq he saw something like we were seeing now.

The two of us had now awoken to the changed world we lived in. The little details like me buying a pistol, Raelene buying heirloom seeds to tuck away, the canning equipment I bought her for her birthday, and the backyard garden were all examples of our changing outlooks. The homesteading channels we followed on YouTube weren't just entertainment, they were fantasies that had not yet turned into a desire.

"I'm going out to a gun store. I would feel a lot more comfortable with a shotgun here than nothing. A real shotgun, well, a combat shotgun. A riot gun they call them, not my bird gun. Is that a problem?"

She shook her head. "No, not if you think it's necessary."

Guys, if you want your wife to let you buy a new gun, no questions asked, tell her about it when the world is ending. It was like a free pass. "Do you want me to buy you a gun?"

She was silent for a moment as she considered it. "If you can. Something small." She tried to describe my sister-in-law's handgun. Honestly, I didn't know what she carried either. I was surprised that my wife recalled it well enough to describe it. Raelene never showed any interest in owning a gun before. She wasn't opposed to it; she just didn't feel the need. The only time she ever carried off-range was when we went camping in bear country and my brother lent her a .357 Magnum just in case she needed to shoot a grizzly in the face. "Be safe."

"I will."

I thought going out to buy a gun would be exciting but instead I felt nervous. It was a shock to see all the trees that had been elegantly losing their bright summer shade of green turn to a limpid and dull olive color so quickly. The freeze stole the normal poise with which autumn brought the yellow, orange, gold, and red hues to our deciduous trees. The colors peaked here in November just before Thanksgiving, followed by abscission that left them totally bare by the time Christmas rolled around.

Sickly green leaves were already littering the streets and branches were already bare. Severe thunderstorms often stripped trees naked but didn't rob the leaves of their dignity. The jaundiced trees looked like late-stage terminally ill patients. We would be skipping fall colors this year. I hated the cooler months here because it was so stark. The grass turned brown, the trees were bare, and it seemed like all was an ugly, brown, and dead world from December to March. I moved to California in mid-February and I remembered arriving and being slightly shocked, and offended, at how green the winter was in the Bay Area.

Raelene would take the harsh autumn and instant winter pretty hard. She was a kind soul, a kind of hippie in touch with nature who enjoyed long walks or jogs along the waterways. Autumn was a time for her to transition from the frenzy of summer activity to slow, indoor winter days. Each month to her had a color that mimicked the trees and different playlists to listen to. Decorating for Halloween, then

Thanksgiving, and Christmas (don't forget the tear-down) got a little tedious, as did my wife's predictable soundtrack of big band crooners, but it was endearing.

She explained to me once that the seasonal music to her was like eating candy or ice cream. Christmas music, and by extension her other autumnal music, took her to a deep emotional place that she couldn't reach any other way. It was nostalgia the happy memories of the past and, *fernweh* or farsickness, for a childhood or life that she never had.

I had to admit I kinda thought it was crazy when she first told me that being out in nature and just experiencing the natural world was what she lived for. Relating it to camping and hunting made me understand it a bit more. Looking at the rising moon one night—one of those picturesque scenes that the master painters strove to capture—she told me that sights like that broke her heart. It was literally so beautiful that she wished it was a pill that she could swallow and take with her always.

She taught me that perfect moments were total products of the present. Only in memory could they be remembered, imperfectly, so you had to be paying attention to the here and now. There was only one crack at experiencing it as it was, then it was gone, except for the lingering traces it left on your mind and soul.

"You dropped acid in college, didn't you?" I asked her after one such moment. What else could explain her insights?

"No," she squealed. "I just smoked pot a couple times. Just because I went to Berkeley doesn't mean I did LSD."

Mid-October, instead of seeing tinges of yellow, the riparian zones were all that cancerous green and brown; a metaphor for this year. I crossed the bridge over the end of the shipping channel where it met the river. The gates at the old locks were closed and holding back the torrent that surged down the main channel. The water was slightly less brown and turbulent than the river. It should've been a placid blue-green this time of year.

A few minutes later and I was on the freeway crossing over the river for the city. I stayed in the slow lane and looked down at the raging waters. It was worse than before. White crests of waves topped the disgusting mocha colored waters. Debris covered about a third of the channel. Tree trunks, reeds, and bits of buildings were headed for the sea. The world seemed like a dark and dismal place. It reminded me of the gritty films of the late '60s and early '70s when the whole world seemed to be a gloomy and dirty place.

The water ran from bank to bank. Near Confluence Park, a crew was building a berm of sandbags to keep the flood from spilling further into downtown. The kayak launching area was already submerged. The bike and walking trails that spanned the river were probably fully eroded by now and would be unrecoverable absent major work by the Army Corps of Engineers. Raelene would take that hard because it was her favorite place to go for a jog.

As I got off the freeway, I saw that the Department of Transportation had staged a huge amount of cones, barricades, and other sundry public works goodies in its lot by the off-ramp. A National Guard Humvee sat guard over the depot. Any more rain and that stuff would be needed.

I didn't see any cops in the city. It was early and this was the "good" side of downtown so I expected no trouble. The protests had fizzled out over the past days due to the cold and deprivation. I'm sure the police found that to be a big relief but could it really be considered a victory if the crisis shifted from riots and looting to burglaries and robberies?

My first stop was Big 5 Sporting Goods. The parking lot was deserted. The interior was dark and the gates shut. They were probably totally sold out. My next stop was Bass Pro Shops, a much bigger box sporting goods store. It was the Disneyland of its segment of the retail world. I would occasionally bring the girls there to marvel at all the taxidermized animal dioramas and aquariums.

The block Bass Pro sat on had power, although the store had only half of the lights on. Staff members were posted randomly, I guess, to deter looting. Every single one of them was openly carrying a handgun, a privilege usually reserved only for the staff behind the gun counter. Uniformed security officers from a large local company were posted at the door and in the firearms section.

My expectations were dashed. Using 2020 as my frame of reference multiple lines, one for picking up guns, another for looking at guns, and another for ammo, should have been stretching towards the door. "Where is everybody?" I asked one of the green-vested sentries.

"The past. Kinda hard to have lines when there's nothing to sell."

He was right. The walls were bare of all but multi-thousand dollar weapons that were impractical for self-defense. A nice Beretta over-under double-barreled shotgun was one of the few firearms for sale. I shot a much lower rent Ruger version of that when I was on the shooting team back in college. "What are the people here for?" I asked. A handful of people were waiting around the register, taking their turns with a clerk.

"Pick ups. Background check delays, folks who are having guns they ordered online delivered. FedEx is hit or miss with the deliveries, though they have been getting the guns here at least."

"What do you mean by background check delays?"

I knew that every over-the-counter gun sale from a federally licensed dealer required a background check which was recorded on a Form 4473. I filled out a couple in my life. The dealer always made a phone call right then and there to the FBI back east and sent me on my way with my gun. The one time I had to wait more than a few minutes was when I bought my semi-auto Remington in California due to their 10-day waiting period.

The employee explained that normally the background check was a few minutes, depending on the volume and hold times with the state call center. On a Saturday or holiday, it might be up to half an hour. But in 2020 and these past two weeks, the wait times had been ridiculous. Staff would call, hold for a few hours, and be permitted to run ten customers before being forced to start the process all over again. The phone queue would also close to new callers two hours before closing.

Many customers were forced to come back the next day. Even purchases at the end of the day couldn't have their background check phoned in until the next day. So much for the instant check that Congress promised. The final kicker was that if the store couldn't get a result back in three days, the sale was automatically approved, but the timer didn't start until the background check was started. Guys were waiting four or five days to pickup their guns.

Bad news for me. Our state was one that, if you had a

CCW permit, you could buy without the background check, the theory being that you already passed one and the sheriff would confiscate your permit if you became ineligible to own a gun. I didn't have a CCW because we became a permitless concealed carry, or "constitutional carry," state several years ago. I guess the best time to buy a gun was before you needed one.

"Any suggestions for someone late to the party like me?"

"Try the local gun shops, like all of them. One of them might have something, but I've been told it's a ghost town out there. Or you can call back in a few days to see if we're getting a shipment in from our distributor. Depends on the trucking situation though."

I thanked him and left. Finding a gun store was another matter. When I bought this pistol, we lived thirty miles away in the capitol. I knew where the gun stores were there, but not here. A lot of these places were discreetly tucked away in strip malls without big signs touting "Guns! Guns! Guns!" So I'd have to Google it.

Cell service here was non-existent. Due to the rolling blackouts, the cell towers were running low on fuel for their diesel generators. That meant a public hotspot for me. At a busy McDonalds I found a Wi-Fi signal and ordered a "sausage burger" off their handwritten special menu. That was a bad sign that probably meant they were both low on supplies and selling off whatever they had before closing the store.

The "sausage burger" turned out to be a cheeseburger but with a sausage patty instead of beef. It wasn't bad. Their sausage wasn't seasoned much to begin with and the pork flavor was unremarkable. Maybe it was something they sold in India? I browsed the Internet on my phone as I munched my strange lunch, using the back of the bag to doodle and put notes on.

Without a paper map and only screenshots of the mapped locations, I drove to three gun stores. The first two were closed. The second one had the front door boarded up and barricaded with concrete K-rail sections. Bits of broken glass and tire tracks told me someone drove through the façade to burglarize the store.

Finally towards the older section of town I found a venerable gun shop. Its front windows were boarded up but in a precautionary way. Heavy flowerpots and bollards protected the entrance. Someone planned ahead a long time ago. Inside it had a cozy, old-school kind of gun store feel. Instead of the latest high-tech tactical pants and accessories, the retail floor was hunting gear. I noticed one section of the wall had refurbished vintage camping gear on it. A teenage boy, probably the owner's son or other relative, set a green Coleman stove out and put a three hundred dollar price tag on it.

"My dad had one of those," I told him. Grant and I fought over it when Dad died. The three burner stove was dead reliable, if maintained, and could burn regular gasoline instead of Coleman stove fuel, if necessary.

"My hobby is restoring all this stuff. Just finished up this stove. Got it at a garage sale for $20. It was pretty rusty and whatnot."

"You did a good job."

"Thanks. Want to buy it? Lots of people looking for these right now since propane is so hard to find." Green one-pound bottles were sold out everywhere (I looked) and only the major propane suppliers had any gas left. Good luck getting an appointment to fill your barbecue bomb.

"Maybe, but not today." The price was too high.

The kid shrugged. "It'll be gone by tomorrow; I can tell you that. But once the electricity problems all get sorted out I'll probably pick it back up off of a panic buyer on Craigslist for a song."

Smart kid. Fixing other people's junk and selling it to those that recognized the value of old things. I wanted a stove like this and kept an eye out a garage sales for deals. We made do with a modern propane stove. I was at least smart enough to buy a dozen green bottles and a 20lb tank with an adaptor, just in case. Never know when bottled gas could be handy.

I let the kid go and strolled over to the counter. Apparently, asking if they had a time machine "back there" to last month was a hilarious answer to "How can I help you?"

"I need a couple of guns, apparently like the rest of the Metro area. A shotgun and a pistol for my wife."

"As you can see, our stock is extremely limited, but we do have a couple handguns in back. Do you know what your wife is looking for?"

"My wife wants something like—" I stopped. I didn't remember what gun she was referring to. Our sister-in-law had two pistols of her own, a long barreled .22 revolver that I knew of, probably a Smith and Wesson. I didn't remember what kind. The other was a little black gun, a semi-auto. "A Luger?"

The clerk's eyes narrowed just a tiny bit. "You mean a 9mm or a Luger, like the Germans had in World War Two? Perhaps a Ruger?" I could tell that he asked these questions everyday.

"No, I guess not a Luger then. 9mm sounds right but its very soft shooting. I'm not sure if it's a Ruger. Do you have any I could see?"

The clerk shook his head. "No, sorry. If you absolutely must have a handgun it's a very limited selection. You are going to be very hard pressed to find a single one on the shelf anywhere in the Metro area. Gun sales are going harder than in 2020. See here, all we have are the ones we can't sell."

He took a very large black pistol out and handed it to me. It was heavy and long. A Heckler and Koch, he said. It was a Mark 23 and made for Delta Force and the Navy SEALs. The price tag read $3,199.99. "Inflation," the clerk opined. "Couple of years ago you coulda had it for twenty-four hundred." There were several other guns that looked like they belonged in the Olympics, otherwise the case was cleaned out.

Rifles were the same way. Only hunting and sporting guns lined the wall. All the ARs and the cool-looking space guns were gone. "Can you sell me some ammo? Buckshot?"

He nodded. "I can sell you one box, $50."

He reached into a cardboard box on the back counter and set a green and yellow box of Remington shells in front of me. "Five shells?" That was ten dollars a shot. It was supply and demand. Sell the stuff at normal prices and it flies off the shelf with no possibility of being replaced. If what's sold can't be replaced, the store stops making money. Only by raising the prices could the store slow the depletion of its stock and make enough money to cover what they would lose due to the shortage. "Can I get two boxes?"

"No, sorry." He was genuinely sympathetic. "Guys are

scalping this stuff for a hundred dollars a box. It cost us $30 to buy it off a friend who had some he could spare so we could at least sell some ammo to customers who bought a gun. But..." he gestured towards the empty shelves. "Besides, how many people are you planning to shoot?"

His co-worker in the corner laughed. I had to as well. "Sold." I slid a fifty across the counter. "Do you have any suggestions where I can buy a shotgun, anywhere, at any price?"

The clerks exchanged a shocked look. "You don't have a shotgun?"

"Well, I do, but it's up in Red Rock City with my brother."

"Pal, a shotgun two hours away ain't gonna do you any good," the man in the corner said.

Your feet aren't going to have any answers Ross, my father's voice echoed in my memory. The pistol would have to do, and could do, if I only had one gun. Grant and one of his Army buddies went into a long discussion once about what weapon you could have if you could only have one. The consensus was a handgun because it was intended for self-defense against people, it could be easily carried and concealed, and was adequate to meet nearly all the realistic defensive scenarios. Hunting wasn't part of the discussion which I'm sure is where a lot of the advice to "just get yourself a shotgun" came from.

"Look pal," the man continued. "If you're hard up and willing to, I've got a friend who is liquidating his father's collection. You're not opposed to private sales, are you?"

A private gun sale was something I never experienced. I knew my dad did it all the time growing up, but since I spent most of my adulthood in California it was alien to me. If it wasn't for my dad and brother, I would be like most people who assumed that buying a gun that didn't involve a dealer, background check, and paperwork was the same as buying drugs. Even knowing it was perfectly legal in this state left me feeling a bit underhanded. Some gang member buying a Glock with one of those illegal fully-automatic switches from some dude's truck would laugh at me, I'm sure.

"No. I'm open to any remotely reasonable, legitimate offer."

"Let me place a call." The man took out his phone and dialed. "Josh? Phil here. We got a guy looking to buy a shotgun. You got anything? 12 gauge, that's right. Home defense. Okay, I'll send him over."

Five minutes later I was driving across the bridge into the big city itself. Everywhere I went had that ominous feeling from the depths of the 2020 lockdowns and riots. It felt like the end of the world then but wasn't; only in hindsight it was the start of something sinister. Now it felt like that unpropitious time had woken from its slumber.

"And what rough beast, its hour come round at last
Slouches towards Bethlehem to be born?"

*   *   *

Josh's house was a small one-story in an older, but very well-maintained area south of downtown. Raelene and I looked at houses here when we first moved upstate. The neighborhood was built right after WWII and looked like something straight out of a golden era Hollywood movie. Jimmy Stewart could pull up any minute by the looks of this place. A rise in the terrain, imperceptible after eighty years of urbanization, protected this area from flooding, although the power was out.

A few blinds shifted as I sat in the car debating whether or not I should leave my pistol in the car. It seemed like a major faux pas to bring a gun into someone else's house, even if it was concealed and you were buying another. On the other hand, if this was some sort of robbery setup, I'd want a gun. But then if I left my gun in the car, it would be vulnerable to thieves. I gave up and got out, keeping the Glock where it was. I'd never see this man again and it wasn't like he was going to frisk me.

I barely raised my hand to knock on the door when it opened up. "Hi, Ross?" a man in his late thirties said from behind the chain.

"That's me."

The man nodded. He shut the door partially to release the tension on the chain before opening it up all the way. "I'm Josh." We shook hands and he invited me in. "Come on back to the living room. It's warmest in there."

He led me down a short hall and I could feel the temperature rise over the ten foot distance. A roaring fire was built inside a wooden stove with an isinglass front. I stared as if it was the first time I had ever seen fire. After a few too many seconds I turned to catch Josh grinning out of the corner of his eye. "Don't have one of these at home?"

"I live across the river. In the marsh fields," I replied, using the long-time local's pejorative name for the suburbs of West River City. Maybe it would create some comradery. It implied all the low-effort cookie-cutter houses built by national developers in what was once reclaimed marshland and farmer's fields. It suggested a land of all electric appliances and gas fireplaces with fake logs.

"Ah. Well, here's what you come for." He whisked a blanket off some lumpy shapes on the kitchen table.

All four of the specimens were sub-par. The nicest shotgun was also the one I was least likely to buy. It was a bulky, black space gun with a pistol grip and a forward grip instead of a slide. It had two parallel tubes for shells and looked like something that would have been used in an Arnold Schwarzenegger movie in the '80s if it had been invented then. I knew it was a bullpup design because the pistol grip was in the middle instead of at the back, just where the stock should start, and I had the vague idea that it was a $1,000 gun.

The middle gun was also a modern design with black plastic furniture. It seemed tactical enough to do the job. "What about this one?" I asked.

"It's a 20 gauge. Do you have any 20 gauge shells?"

"Nope." That left the last contender. It was by far the most suitable but beat to crap. The finish had faded from a deep black bluing to an overall dingy gray that in many places was turning to bare metal. I looked carefully but didn't see any rust. The stock was dinged up in too many places to count showing the lighter color of the unstained wood beneath it.

I knew it was sound, at least as far as I could tell, but wondered if it would instill confidence in my wife. You wanted a gun to be impressive. It had to look serious and deadly, not like the trashed deal furniture of a by-the-hour motel room. Wood on a gun said "old" and "hunting." Not that my clay-busting gun was something you expected to see in the hands of the SWAT team, but I already owned that. My trip today was a mission to obtain a defensive weapon and I was afraid that if I came back like this, Raelene would take me for a failure.

Josh must have had an inkling at what was going through my head. "She's got some miles on her. Spent twenty years banging around a police car with a River City officer. When he retired, my dad bought it off him. This was Pop's home defense gun for a long time. Up until he bought that bullpup space gun."

"No rust," I commented.

"I know she looks rough. Despite all that, she's a good gun. The factory originally put the best parts in, all handpicked. Dad upgraded it with an extended safety button and slide release. All the springs are fresh in there too, I did that myself." He racked the slide. "Smooth as can be and reliable as all get out.

"Check this out." Josh pointed to the lower barrel, the one that held the shells, and indicated the portion that extended slightly past the barrel itself. "Know what this is?" I shook my head. "Magazine extender. Probably thought it was to mount a bayonet, like for riots, huh? Nah. Originally Remington didn't make police shotguns. What they did was modify their sporting models. You get an extra two rounds with this, six, instead of four. Plus one in the chamber of course.

"Rifle type sights, not your ribbing and bead." My shotgun had only a small gold bead at the tip of the barrel to aim with. "Those are so you can fire rifled slugs. Get a little more accuracy at up to 75, maybe, a hundred yards. Maybe." He touched an empty set of rings on the side of the body. "Sidesaddle. Holds five extra shells. The officer used to put slugs in there just in case the bad guy got some distance on him."

"How far will just buckshot go out to?"

"What kind?" I took the box out of my pocket. "This."

"Hm. Two and three-quarter inch shells, double-ought buckshot. Nine pellets. Fifty-fifty shot at hitting someone at fifty-yards. That's two or three houses down. It's dangerous out to a hundred yards against an area target like a crowd but you shouldn't be shooting that far with it. Inside the house or yard, it's gonna kill within 25 yards if you hit right." Josh's eyes narrowed. "You use a shotgun before?"

"Yeah, but never hunting. Just trap and skeet. Only ever did hunting with a rifle and that was when I was in high school." Just now, twenty-five years ago seemed very far away.

He seemed to approve. "'kay. You still have to aim with this, I don't care what distance you're at. None of that 'just point and shoot' business. Forget anything anybody told you about buckshot spreading out at an inch per yard. Maybe half an inch, if you're lucky, per yard once you get out to say seven yards away. That's like your driveway length." He put his hand over his chest. "This is how you want to aim. Your lead will hit an area like this. How much buckshot do you have."

"Just the one box," I admitted shamefully. "I've got plenty of birdshot at home. Do you have any to spare?"

He clucked his tongue. "Nothing to spare, sorry. Already gave what I could out to friends. It's not all bad. I would have told you if you had more buckshot to take it out to a field somewhere and pattern it. That's shooting a few shells at a paper target to get an average idea of where the pellets will land. Each shotgun is different. Nevermind. Close enough for government work. Those double-ought pellets are .36" in diameter, somewhere between a .32 pistol bullet and a 9mm. One in the right spot should be effective and if you aim right, you're gonna get many more, if not all nine, in the target. You good at hitting those clays?"

"Good enough." It may take me a second shot, but I hadn't let one hit the ground intact in years.

"Then you should do just fine with what you've got. Let me tell you what you can do with that birdshot. First off, make your last round in the magazine, the first one you load, birdshot. That way you have five buckshot shells behind it. Well, this holds six so put two birdshot shells in first. Then four buck, rack the slide to chamber a round, then the fifth buckshot."

"Shouldn't I leave the chamber empty? You know, for safety and to scare the bad guy?"

"Heavens no. I mean do what you gotta do for safety, if it makes you feel comfortable if you got curious kids or something but keep it ready to go. You're gonna be panicking and all butter fingers in an emergency anyway. Getting the safety off—which you should always keep on if the chamber is loaded—is going to be hard enough."

He explained something called "cruiser carry" which was where you made sure the chamber was empty and then pulled the trigger. That would drop the hammer so the safety could be left off. In an emergency, there would be no fumbling for the safety or the slide release, just shuck the slide and pull the trigger. Safe as could be, as long as the chamber really was empty when the hammer fell.

"You don't need to add an extra step if you aren't scared of cruiser carry. Believe me, first time we were in contact in Iraq I literally forgot how to flip the safety on my M16 I was so scared. As for the bad guy? Forget that stuff. He might not even know what the 'shuck-shuck' sound was. If somebody is in your house and isn't scared off by you pointing a gun at him, racking the slide won't scare him. Just shoot him."

I nodded. I wasn't going to be shooting anybody. This was an expensive precaution and security blanket such as the extended warranties that RadioShack would try to add on to anything, no matter how cheap. "How much?"

"Six hundred." The price was still $150 less than a comparable gun being sold by the creeps on the local gun forum trying to profit on the emergency. Inflation hadn't helped either. My hand dug into my pocket and I counted off six crisp hundreds without a word. Inwardly, I winced a little. This was a three hundred dollar gun and only that much because it was a "vintage" model of the kind that old guys who like their shotguns the same way that gearheads like old cars.

Money, other than the temporary difficulties getting cash, was not what bothered me. The hole in our finances wouldn't even be noticed. It was my pride that stung. Here I was trying to buy a gun at the last minute after everyone else had totally cleaned up the market. I felt like a guy trying to buy his kid a doll at 8 PM on Christmas Eve. Perhaps it could be a good thing and this gun would forever be a reminder to pull my head out of the sand and plan for even outside contingencies.

"Before you go, don't get any ideas about cut shells

with your birdshot," Josh said.

"Cut shells? What's that?"

"A Great Depression-era trick. The idea is to turn a birdshot shell into a slug by cutting through the outer hull of the shell without cutting into the wad. You know what the wad is, right?" I nodded. The wad separated the powder from the shot and served as a gas check until it all left the barrel. "You perforate the hull just enough that when it fires, the thing splits. The lead travels downrange in a cup from the separated hull." The crimped top of a shell was supposed to open up and let the shot out. "So you get this mass of lead that stays together until it hits the target. The idea being that if concentrated it applies more force and penetrates more.

"Not true. Once that little cup you made hits, the shot bursts out and is no more dangerous than it normally would be. Only real advantage is a tighter pattern, possibly, but it's not worth the risks."

"Which are?" I asked.

"Mainly having the cartridge separate in the gun and causing a jam. Or worse plugging your barrel and having it explode."

"I saw that once. Looked like a peeled banana of steel." One of my dad's buddies put his shotgun muzzle down in the mud and didn't notice the barrel was obstructed. When he went to shoot, the gas had nowhere to go so the barrel failed. His gun was ruined but no one was hurt.

"So you know then. Good. Birdshot will kill up close. Definitely will take the fight out of somebody inside a house. Outside, well, use that buckshot."

"Gotcha."

"Good luck."

Looting

I was in the living room when we heard it—the screeching of tires against asphalt like fingernails down a chalkboard. Looking out the window, I saw in our quiet cul-de-sac, a tricked-out Honda spinning wildly, leaving dark donuts of rubber in its wake. The driver was no stranger. He was a local teen with a misdemeanor record aspiring to felonies and a knack for ruffling feathers in the neighborhood. Raelene appeared at my side, her lips pressed into a thin line of displeasure.

"That jackass," she muttered, more to herself than to me. "He's back." I watched as she made her way towards the front door, a storm brewing in eyes.

She had always been the fiercer one between us. She'd confronted the kid before when his late-night shenanigans had disturbed our peace. I would call the cops but she would throw open the window and yell. East Coast women are just made different. He was evicted from his dead grandmother's place by the deputies a while ago, or so we thought. Now, he was back, uninvited, and clearly unapologetic.

Raelene was on the front porch now, her hands resting defiantly on her hips. "Hey!" she yelled, her voice slicing through the cacophony. The car skidded to a halt, the driver's side window rolled down, and the smirking face of the teen peered out. A cold ripple of unease ran down my spine. Without any regard for if the girls were listening, Raelene shouted, "Do that shit somewhere else!" her words echoing across the quiet street.

The jackass simply shrugged, his smirk never leaving his

face. His dark eyes flicked to me, a sinister glint in them, before he brazenly flipped Raelene off and hit the gas. The Honda roared to life, burning out as it took off, leaving behind a heavy trail of acrid smoke. Raelene watched the car speed away, her expression vicious. I could tell she was both upset and annoyed; even more than the time I forgot to put the toilet seat down and she sat in the water at night.

I couldn't shake off the feeling that there was more to this incident than a simple act of juvenile rebellion. There was no reason for him to come back, and his bold show of disrespect hinted at an underlying bitterness that was deeply unsettling. We stood there, watching as the last traces of exhaust dissipated. The sound of screeching tires echoed off the houses as he departed the tract, a spiteful reminder of the unwanted interruption. Our tranquil neighborhood felt tainted by his inexplicable return. I found myself wondering if we would be seeing him again soon.

"What a little prick," Raelene bitched.

"I don't see why you let it bother you so much."

"Try being a little more aggressive, Ross," she said before walking away.

Hey, I was the one who wanted to snip his tire valve stems in the middle of the night but you said no! Oh well, there was no point in arguing. It was probably just her inner nag coming out. As for the kid, it must be nice to be able to waste gas like that.

Speaking of, the time for the daily gas run was here. Earlier in the morning I checked the grocery stores and balked at the lines. Why wait around when there was probably nothing worth waiting for? I'd give it a day or two for the trucks to catch up before wasting my time. On the way over the river, I caught a bit of the news.

"Confidential sources within the police department are telling me that over half of the officers scheduled today have called in sick. While this appears to be unrelated to the incidents in Red Rock one cannot help but think that officers across the state may be in solidarity with each other. Union president Luis Ocampo said that many officers are actually physically and mentally unable to continuing working. Excessive shifts, sometimes 16 hours long, and no days off since the Big Freeze has taken its toll, he says."

Angry callers phoned the radio station to express how angry they were that the police weren't answering their calls. Burglary and theft victims were told to fill out reports online (most had no Internet) and hot calls were taking up to an hour for officers to get to, if they responded at all. Many were saying how they simply weren't bothering to call 9-1-1, whatever that meant. You know that some out there were taking matters into their own hands. Did this mean I could string a line of caltrops across our cul-de-sac without having to worry about the cops saying I couldn't do that?

Finding an open gas station—one with gas, not that the mini-mart was operating—was eating into my MPG. The social media of some of the local radio stations were pretty good at updating listeners' reports about what stations got fuel deliveries, but they could be outdated by the time they were posted. So I went from place to place hoping there wasn't a miserably long line or a sign that said, "no gas." Again, if the Internet was properly functional I could build an app no problem or even just make a map of the most fuel-efficient routes for manually checking gas stations rather than this wasteful circuit I was making.

In the parking lot of a grocery store, I saw several camouflaged vehicles parked. On a hunch I swung in the lot only to see that the store was closed and deserted. *Rats.* A small unit of National Guard soldiers huddled around a propane heater on the back of one of the Humvees in the corner of the lot. I slowly drove up with the front windows down and waved as the SUV approached. None of the soldiers seemed to react much.

"Excuse me, are you guys with the 925th Engineer Battalion?" I called out to the sentry who stood with his rifle slung.

"No, two of the 875th Infantry. Why?" a sentry responded.

"My brother was their commander a few years ago."

"Oh. Well, hooah to the colonel then."

"Know of any open grocery stores by chance?" I asked. "And sorry, I didn't mean to frighten you driving up like that," I said.

"Frighten us?" a sergeant, who was my age, asked.

"I dunno, you might think it could be drive-by."

All the guardsmen started laughing. "Sir, a white dude in a six-figure Lexus isn't gonna intimidate infantrymen with M16s."

"Point taken. How about those grocery stores?"

"Yes sir, but you gotta drive to California," a teenage private said. His sergeant lightly backhanded him in the shoulder.

"I thought this place was open when I saw you guys here. You know, guarding it."

"We were supposed to," the sergeant replied. "No delivery."

"Is it true what they're saying about the police?"

"'Fraid so, sir. We've got it easier than they do. They go call-to-call and we just stand around looking mean, for the most part."

"But we can't call in sick. Or quit. We don't have a union, neither," the private said.

"Write your congressman," the sergeant snapped. "Folks gonna have to look out for themselves," he said to me. "You got a gun, right sir?"

"Yeah. Well, thank you guys for being here." The sergeant gave a half-hearted wave as I backed up to pull away. It was hard to see what kind of deterrent effect these guys were having sitting in an office complex parking lot. At least they were not wasting diesel driving around aimlessly.

What I was quickly coming to learn was that in a major disaster, fuel was life. Gas made it possible for you to get places and if there were shortages, you had to go to a lot of different places just to get enough of what you needed (if you could). Generators needed gas too and a lot of it. Refueling once or twice a day was a royal pain but vital if we wanted to have some semblance of normal life. Efficiency was not part of the survival game.

The gas station I found had an entirely different atmosphere today. It was as busy as it had been but now cars were being routed in through a line of cones. Four employees or volunteer friends/family members in orange vests were working the lot. Two people with holstered handguns directed traffic while two others with rifles stood watch.

When it was our turn at the pump, a mousy woman and I were pointed to two pumps. "Bizarre that they have men with guns out but the Muzak is still playing, right?" I asked. The woman flashed a nervous smile and turned away from me. Everyone but the guys with guns seemed on edge.

Ordinarily thousands of people moved around each other in their own bubbles, each going their own way. Now people on the streets moved around like cockroaches caught with the light on. One would think with such artificial desolation that encountering another person would be reassuring instead of a thing to be avoided. Emptiness was preferable to others of our species. Comfort was in solitude, not the company of the crowd.

Here and there trucks loaded with goods moved openly through the streets. It was hard to tell if they were moving, evacuating, or looting. As one neared downtown, these sightings became more frequent. Traffic became more reckless. I watched a car stop at a dark intersection, treating it as a four-way stop, only to be rear-ended by a someone doing probably sixty. The speeding driver abandoned his wrecked vehicle and ran. I waited for several minutes but heard no sirens. There was nothing I could do so I went home.

Hugo, the guy immediately next door, had his garage open and a fire burning in a metal barrel in the driveway. TV sounds drifted across the cul-de-sac. Two other neighbors stood inside watching, so I headed over.

"You guys wouldn't believe how weird it is in the city. Like a ghost town but you can see the ghosts moving around."

None of them replied to me, just nods from two half-turned heads. Hugo's garage TV was plugged into a portable battery system and an antenna cable snaked along the way to the outside. It was a local news station, but they were filming with an extreme zoom lens from the top of one of the skyscrapers downtown. On the screen I saw a line of Walmart semi-trucks on the Interstate. There were twenty or so of them stopped going back well over a quarter of a mile. They were being looted with apparent impunity.

The picture switched and the main shot became one at ground level, much closer up. The cameraman was clearly on his belly filming through some small hole or gap of a bridge. The convoy had been escorted by several private security cars. Their windshields were now opaque from being shot and bullet holes marred the body and door panels. Guards lay slumped and probably dead inside.

The camera moved around and showed the remains of a spike-strip in the road and shredded tires. *So that's how they stopped them.* In front of these was a line of box trucks stopped so as to block the entire freeway as both a roadblock and as receptacles for the hijacked loads. The scene was so surreal I reacted the same way as if it was happening in another country, not twenty minutes away.

The camera angle prevented us from seeing the back but the doors must have been rolled up because men were carrying goods up to them. Men ran, towing and pushing pallet jacks full of food or whatever, down the freeway to the box trucks. One such pair went right past the body of a dead guard who lay sprawled on the concrete.

Near the retaining wall, the truck drivers kneeled facing the wall with their hands on the backs of their heads. Riflemen with masks on stood guard. Probably two-dozen non-descript vans were parked parallel to the trucks being unloaded; transportation for the bandits. "There's gotta be one or two hundred people involved in this," Hugo said.

In the smaller picture within the picture the building camera panned to show a lone state trooper blocking traffic at an exit a mile down the freeway. Cars were still getting on at the next ramp but kept moving unmolested. At the far end of this mass-hijacking, more gunmen in pickup trucks held traffic at bay.

"Where are the helicopters?" asked the neighbor who's name I didn't know.

"Did you hear the voiceover? Someone is shooting at the helicopters as they try to takeoff."

"Nobody has the resources for this kind of operation," I said.

"Except the cartels," Hugo replied.

"How? This isn't Mexico. They sell drugs, not food."

"Just how much drugs do you think they're selling around here right now? Way I see it, this is a way for them to get food and butt wipe. They need that too. They can sell that food too."

I could scarcely believe what I was seeing. A large armed group had stopped and seized a massive delivery convoy that had been guarded by no less than a half-dozen vehicles, armed I assumed. Walmart planned this out fairly well and spent serious money on the security arrangements, but not enough.

Pandemonium erupted. Men who seemed to be in leadership roles began shouting and whistling. Fingers circled in the air in the universal sign for "let's go." Arm loads of things were dropped. Pallets were left in traffic lanes. Within a minute everyone was in a vehicle. The new convoy of escort and spoil vehicles fanned out via the next two exits. The feed from the cameraman on the ground went dark after a burst of machine gunfire was heard.

The building camera tried to track the vehicles as they split up. The camera panned around, looking for signs of where each vehicle went but given the oblique angle of the shot the buildings got in the way. Finally in the far distance we saw a Stryker armored vehicle drive the wrong way up an off-ramp. Traffic was light enough that no one hit it and its three companions followed it up. By the time the soldiers got to the scene of the crime, it was too late. Everyone but the hijacked truck drivers were gone.

The four of us stood in silence watching the soldiers clearing the area and setting up perimeter security. "Where were the cops?" Darin asked.

"Smart enough to stay away," Hugo replied. "They probably had more guys robbing that convoy than the police have working an entire shift right now. What would even a dozen cops do? Re-enact the shootout from *Heat* on the freeway. They'd be slaughtered."

The coordination to pull this off was amazing. I had no idea that the cartel had so many people in the city. As bad as River City was, this was the first time that something that happened in Mexico happened here. Walmart's corporate security was clearly compromised. To plan this in advance would require knowledge of when the convoy would leave. Trucks and vehicles would have to be stolen and the shooters and labor rounded up. From there, the convoy could be easily tracked as it got closer and closer to the city.

The second order effect of this would be that deliveries would cease for a while until new security measures could be implemented. Hiring a couple armed guards who were used to checking out alarm calls and transporting stacks of cash wouldn't cut it against real *sicarios*. Whoever was in charge of the emergency response should have put those idle infantrymen I met to use. Soon they would have to if they wanted food to move.

Day 3

The Gunfight

"What's that?" Raelene whispered. It had been the eek-eek of worn brakes in the cold. A mundane sound that the mind could ignore in the in-between stages of sleep. "Ross, are you awake?"

"Yeah." As long as I didn't move I was warm. I had my wife spooned up against me and my back to the cold. Lucky she had Reya and the baby on her side. I took my watch off the nightstand and saw it was almost 5:30 AM. The sky would begin to lighten soon.

A car door shut down the street. Footsteps.

In the cold, silent night of an electricity-less city even someone walking on asphalt coming through double-pained windows was an incredibly loud sound. Without a word I got out of bed, ignoring the chill. I was already wearing a t-shirt and pajama bottoms so all I needed were slippers. As I peeked through the blinds, I saw the top of a hoodie disappear underneath the eave of the garage.

"Call 9-1-1." I ran and opened the bedroom drawer to punch in the combination for the quick-action pistol safe. My motions were automatic without conscious commands or deliberation. Despite this, I was mentally calm, to my surprise, as the wild river of hormones drowned thought and fear, leaving only raw action.

"What's going on?"

"Raelene, call 9-1-1. Prowlers. A burglary in progress. Tell them I'm going to check things out with my gun."

"Okay." She rolled over the kids and grabbed her phone. The light of the screen lit up her face in the darkness. Even in the wee hours, sleepy and frightened, she still looked beautiful. One of those disturbing stray thoughts that is a product of our fears and anxieties crossed my mind. Would this be the last time I saw her again? I couldn't imagine life without her. *Stop being dramatic.* It was a stupid thought. I'd yell at the prowlers, they would realize that we weren't still on vacation, and they'd run.

"Take this," I said, handing her the pistol. She took it. Next we heard the back gate rattling.

The dispatcher's voice came muffled through Raelene's phone. "Yes hi, my husband and I heard a noise. He thinks it's prowlers or burglars." She sounded polite, as if she was bothering the dispatcher. Outside, the gate rattled.

"They're inside the yard," I whispered harshly. "They're wearing hoodies. Tell her to get the officers here *now*." My heart was pounding. I was in the clutch now, my turn at the plate holding the bat and watching the pitcher wind up. This was really happening.

I grabbed the shotgun from its case in the closet, its cold metal providing a desperate reassurance, as I left the safety of our bedroom. With trembling hands, I locked the door behind me, sealing my family off from the unknown horrors that awaited me. The beat of my heart thundered in my chest, a relentless drumming that echoed the ceaseless doubts, questions, and fears that crossed my mind. Where do I go first? *Do I start yelling now or wait until downstairs?*

As I got to the kitchen it was decided for me. There was a clatter and cussing from the garage as the intruders stumbled on something. *How did they get in the door? I didn't hear them kick it or anything.* I proceeded down the hallway, inching closer to the barrier that separated me from them—the laundry/garage room door.

State law permitted use of deadly force against someone entered a residence in a "surreptitious manner" and anyone in the process of breaking in. The only purpose of burglarizing a house, during a disaster when everybody would be home, in the pre-dawn hours could only be doing it to harm those inside. I was entirely within my rights to kill them and if they went any further than the garage, I would.

I listened on the other side of the door as a fireman might check a knob to see if it was hot. The voices were still muffled, so they were still in the garage. Opening the laundry room door would be safe. It had no lock anyhow. I slowly lowered the handle and let it back up once it unlatched. The nice thing about an expensive, well-built house was nothing was cheap or old enough to creak.

No bet on the tables of Las Vegas had ever felt so nerve-wracking. No performance, interview, or anything could match the weight of this moment. I had one chance to succeed, pass or fail, with life-altering consequences if I didn't come through. Buck fever had nothing on this moment. *This is how Dad felt going over Hanoi.* The only time he told me about a Route Package Six mission, in detail, he described something like this. His entire life was distilled into a single moment.

Except rather than bombarding communists, my heroic act would probably go no further than yelling at a burglar. I had no idea what to say. My throat was tight. I felt like I was in a dream, the ones where you couldn't shout and anything that did come out was all wrong. *What do I say? 'Fuck off!*

Wanna die?' No, you'll probably screw up and shout out 'Wanna fuck?' then your wife will start asking questions...

I resolved to use "Hey!" because that always was what I could manage in my nightmares. Only thing was I forgot to lock the inside garage door that led to the laundry room. There would be no warning shouted from behind the relative safety of a locked fire door.

The door opened. I saw an indistinct face with a blue surgical mask on beneath a dark gray hoodie. I snapped the shotgun to my shoulder the same way I would have when "Pull!" was called on the range. I put the white front dot of the front sight over the face of the burglar. *This is just like shooting clays*, I thought, except not in words. All my reflexes and instincts were working the same. *Chest!* At the last moment, I lowered the muzzle to aim at the center of mass and fired.

The fight unfolded in vivid slow motion; no that's not the right way to describe it. With the adrenaline flooding my endocrine system, a tidal wave of sharpened awareness washed over me—heart pounding like a war drum, breath quickening, muscles coiled and ready to spring. The world was honed to a razor's edge, sounds amplified, and every detail magnified. I can only describe it like a nerd: in survival mode, my brain was capturing more information, the way a very fast computer might display a game at 240 frames per second instead of 60.

As I lowered the gun, I saw the burglar realize what was happening. I saw the pistol held at the low ready in his right hand. The door opened wider to see a second accomplice. The trigger pull was normal in every respect, not like in my nightmares where I pull and pull until belatedly the hammer drops.

The gun roared. A huge flash of flame lit up the night. Remembering lessons from my youth, I used the recoil of the shot to help cycle the slide backwards and chamber a new shell. The burglar was turning just then but still the pattern caught him in his chest, though he was angled about 45° to me. He fell straight down when hit. He wasn't blown back nor did he dramatically clutch his chest and stagger towards me, moaning apologies. He just collapsed like the World Trade Center.

His two partners who were a bit faster had already turned and started running. The first dashed around the corner into the side yard. I saw the left hand of the slower accomplice flutter up towards his back as he dashed towards the open side garage door. *Should I shoot him? In the back?!* It didn't matter. The second burglar crumpled just as he made it outside and didn't move after he fell. A lucky pellet must have penetrated his posterior thoracic wall and hit him in the heart. That was the only way to get a near-instant kill like that, according to the trauma nurse upstairs.

I lowered the muzzle again to the first guy and saw that he was clearly dead. His pistol had skittered along the floor and was somewhere in the darkness. The body jammed the door open. My ears were ringing badly although I didn't notice any pain. A throbbing sound came from behind the tinnitus. Dust, smoke, unburnt powder, and particles from the drywall made the hallway air hazy. Five seconds had elapsed but it seemed like minutes.

You gotta shut the gate and the doors, I thought. The cops weren't just minutes away, like I always thought they would be if I shot someone. Even I knew enough that I shouldn't disturb a crime scene by moving bodies or altering the points of entry. It could make me look guilty. In this case, the cops *weren't* coming, at least not right away. If there were more burglars, I'd be screwed.

My dad always said in flying the priorities were "Aviate, navigate, communicate." Not crashing the plane was the first priority and talking to air traffic control was last. Safety came first, not worrying that a detective might get ticked off that I moved a corpse so I could shut the door. Secure the entrances and worry about legalities when everyone is safe.

With the courage to step over the first body worked up, I entered the garage. Clumsily I scanned the darkness while holding the shotgun at the ready. *One of those mounted flashlights sure would be nice.*

The garage was empty except for the dead. From there, I had to clear the side yard. For a second I wondered if I should lower the shotgun as I went through the door because having it straight out and leading the way might make it easy for a bad guy hiding beside the doorway to grab it. I decided that anyone there would have to be really disciplined not to scream, attack, or try to help his fallen buddy.

Wait, I thought. *Fire one, load one*, came the thought from a blog or something. I stuffed a new shell in the magazine tube from the side saddle. In spite of all the stress I didn't fumble at all. Reloading shotguns under time pressure on the skeet range *did* have a tactical benefit after all.

Everything that was happening to me seemed as if it was transpiring as part of a realistic nightmare. None of my dreams involved the confusion of whether or not to vomit or crap my pants though. I breathed a sigh of relief when I saw the side yard was clear. "Dude, you okay?" a voice inquired.

Thank God for neighbors, I thought.

It wasn't a neighbor. Another hoodie wearing burglar came around the corner holding a silver revolver in his hand. I instinctively raised the gun and shot right as he dodged. *Missed!* The buckshot hit the fence two feet from the burglar's face and ripped a hole in the wood the size of a softball. The burglar at least flinched and ducked, but he brought his gun up. I missed at three yards and was going to die for the mistake! I even neglected to cycle the slide instinctively.

I shucked the slide fast and aimed on reflex, this time not using the sights and only putting the dark muzzle over the bad guy's face. I pulled the trigger at the same time he had the muzzle on me. He died, I didn't. A splotchy pattern like bloody freckles surrounding a central wound appeared on his face. *Birdshot, dammit!*

I had used birdshot when I reloaded, so naturally following my miss the next shot would be the tiny bird pellets. Shotgun tubes loaded on a first in, first out principle so that's why topping off with the birdshot made it the next one up. I cycled the gun again and knew that in addition to the buckshot now in the chamber, I had two buck shells left in the tube followed by birdshot as the last round.

Through the open gate I saw one of the burglars jump into the driver's seat of a car that was parallel to the driveway in the street. Muzzle flashes came from the passenger window. I took cover against the stuccoed corner of the garage. Splinters of wood from the fence told me they were shooting blind.

They're shooting at me; I can shoot back. I didn't stop to consider whether my shots would be effective or what was behind my target, only caring that I knew it was legal to return fire on a car that had someone in it who was trying to kill me.

I fired the last three shells into the car. Glass shattered so I knew the pellets hit but not if I got anyone. The car floored it and burned rubber in a loud, screeching retreat out of the cul-de-sac. I cycled the slide, forgetting I had already done that automatically, this time, and a live birdshot shell fell to the ground. No matter. With a tremble the second time, I took the rest of the shells out of the side saddle and put them into the shotgun.

Once more, I did not fumble as I reloaded. The car squealed away into the gloaming leaving the street deathly silent. No sirens howled in the distance; no reactions came from the neighbors. I also could have been half-deaf.

I didn't know what to do with the handguns but I didn't want to leave them out, so I gingerly picked them up by the trigger guard like on TV and threw them in the trash. What burglar would look for a gun in the trash? *What is the prosecutor going to say about that? "Were you worried that the burglars you shot were zombies?"* my mind doubted, going a million miles an hour. The ability to think extraneous thoughts in a time like this was far-out and astonishing simultaneously.

While the bodies outside didn't block anything, the inner garage door couldn't be closed because of the dead burglar's legs lying across the threshold. I used his arm to drag him far enough away to shut and lock the door. That throbbing noise I heard above my tinnitus was the smoke detector. It was an optical model and all the gun gas and dust set it off. I pulled it off the wall and ripped out the battery.

"I'm okay!" I yelled from downstairs. Out of nowhere

my stomach made a backflip. I ran into the bathroom and knocked up the lid of the toilet. Nothing came up. The dry heaves and retches were violent, abdomen shaking contractions. The urge abated as quickly as it had come. *I'm okay, I'm okay. You managed not to puke or soil yourself.*

As I went back upstairs, I yelled "It's me. Raelene, it's me. Can I come in?"

"Yes," she said breathlessly.

My wife was wild-eyed and teary. She was clutching the grip of the pistol so hard her hand was red. I helped her slip it back into the holster. Raelene kissed me. It was a hard, passionate kiss with wide lips, not one of her usual, delicate pecks. We knelt, mid-kiss, and hugged as Reya and Remy wrapped their arms around me. Reya was sobbing hard which made her sister cry.

"Did you scare the bad guys away?" Reya managed to ask in between sobs.

Raelene gave me that knowing stare. "I told her that you were just scaring the bad guys away with your gun."

"That's right. They're gone." *Someplace warm where they won't need their hoodies.* A powerful urge hit me mid-hug. I pried Reya's pincer-like grip away from my neck. "I gotta poop!" I ran into the bathroom, slamming the door behind me. So much for thinking I escaped *that*.

The garbage can held the butt of the shotgun nicely so it propped itself up in the corner as I fiddled with my pants. I made it just in time, expelling what felt like everything I ate in my lifetime in one quick second. I hoped that the door dulled enough sound to shield my family somewhat from my embarrassing toilet noises.

There is nothing in the fatherhood manual on how to

calm down a terrified family after you've shot several burglars. There is no such manual but someone should write one. The girls didn't know exactly what was wrong but they knew it was *bad* and scary. Listening to their terrified wails was as painful as listening to them cry when they were sick and there was nothing you could do to ease their pain.

Fifteen minutes after the shooting, the police arrived— fifteen minutes in a town that used to pride itself in a sub-five minute response time. We knew it was them because we heard their sirens and saw two black and whites pull up out front. Though with the adrenaline spent, it took all my effort to make my way downstairs and opened the front door with hands still trembling.

"Show me your hands! What's your name?" the first officer asked. His gun was aimed at my face, the light beneath the barrel shining in my eyes.

"Ross. My wife is Raelene. She called."

"Keep your hands up in the air," the officer said. "Turn around." He stepped inside, grabbed my fingers and pinched them together tightly. "Any weapons on you?"

"No, they're all upstairs." His left foot spread my legs apart and he swiftly patted me down.

"Is there anyone else here? Any family, any bad guys?"

"My wife and kids, upstairs. I think the bad guys are all dead or gone."

"Is this your ID?" His hand was over my pajama pocket.

"Yeah." He took it out and looked at my license.

"Okay, cool," he said before handing it back to me. "16-Adam-49, Code 4, with the homeowner now. Suspect vehicle gone on arrival." I had trouble slipping my license back in the pocket. The officer watched me scrabble with it and then as I inexplicably dropped the card on the floor. I swayed as I picked it up. "Sir, you gotta sit down." He led me into the living room and towards my recliner. My legs started to go weak and I staggered. "Kyle, help!"

His partner came running over. "I got it, I got it," I said. "I'm just tired all of a sudden." We made it to the chair. I fell into it and felt the whole world swoon before my eyes. That's when I noticed how fast my heart was beating and how hard it was to breathe. My head drooped.

"16-Adam-49, we need an ambulance at our location for the homeowner."

"I'm okay, I'm okay," I told the officer. "No ambulance."

Raelene came halfway down the stairs. The girls were peeking between the balusters at the top. "What's going on? Ross, are you okay?"

"I think he's having some kind of medical emergency, ma'am," the officer said.

"I'm a nurse, let me get my bag." Raelene came charging down and slipped a blood pressure cuff on my arm. "Your BP is way, way up."

"Obviously," I gasped.

She snapped the pulse oximeter off my finger. "159 BPM." I jerked when she put the cold stethoscope diaphragm against my chest. "Sorry. Your heart sounds normal." She popped the earpieces out. "Ross, you're having a panic attack. Calm down. You're alright."

"I know I'm alright. You're alright, I'm alright. This is my subconscious, not me," I wheezed. I felt like I just ran a marathon. Here I was, in front of my wife, two cops, and my terrified children having a panic attack after shooting burglars. I wasn't so much embarrassed as I was pissed off. Why should I be the one freaking out at the arrival of the cops for heaven's sake? Those bastards came here to steal from us and the Lord only knows what else!

"I'm going to get him an aspirin," Raelene said. That was just in the off case I actually was having a heart attack. She moved off to the kitchen.

The paramedics, who were stationed just outside our tract, arrived. A sergeant walked in behind them. He had gray hair, carried a side-handled baton, and wore a very old jacket with new patches sewn on. Clearly he was an old salt and in a way, his presence was reassuring to me. The sergeant stood back and watched the medics work.

The senior medic had a quick confab with my wife and I got hooked up to a portable EKG and oxygen. They ran a tape or whatever it was called. "Cardiac rhythm looks normal even with that heart rate. Blood pressure is concerning. 140 over 88. Ma'am, is your husband hypertensive?"

"No, he's usually quite stable," Raelene replied.

"Propranolol?" the younger medic asked the other.

"That's not indicated for this," Raelene interjected, slightly irritated. "Excluding the palpitations, which are transient, there is no cardiac arrhythmia. He's already down about ten systolic and his heart rate is normalizing. If he were that bad off, labetalol and nicardipine would be indicated for emergency use. Hell, a Xanax would be better."

I had no idea what they were talking about. The older of the two held up his hand. "Ma'am, I agree with you completely. It was just a suggestion in case things got out of control. We are out of everything else."

"Out?"

He nodded. "The whole region has been having problems with medication resupply. Whoever is in charge made the decision to push what does come into hospitals, not us on the front lines." Raelene cussed in response. She knew that the minutes it took for the paramedics to get a patient stabilized for transport might make the difference of survival. When someone had a life-threatening emergency, getting them to the hospital alive was half the battle.

"Yep," the younger medic said. "You're right. But look here." He tapped the monitor. "The O_2 has been helping. Do you feel better?" he asked me.

I merely nodded and swallowed the aspirin Raelene gave me. "This is embarrassing. You never see the heroes in the movies have panic attacks."

The older medic gave me a disappointed look. "Sir, this is nothing to be ashamed of. It's a natural, normal reaction to the adrenaline dump you get in a life-threatening situation. You can't help what your mind and body decide to do on their own, only how you consciously choose to deal with what happens from here." The sergeant who stood watching this whole time raised his eyebrows in silent agreement.

Ten minutes later, I had calmed down enough for the medics to leave. The police left me alone for about another twenty minutes while they investigated. A detective, Kimbrough, came after that and took my statement. He looked to be in the same age range as the patrol sergeant and ran through his questions like a pro. He sounded bored, like he was going down a checklist. Being able to tell someone who understood violence what happened and how I felt acted like a catharsis.

I knew that I probably should have asked for an

attorney, just in case, but I didn't care. I did nothing wrong. What did I have to hide? I gladly signed his Miranda waiver and the consent forms to "gather evidence from the premises" as he put it.

Tired, but functional, I led Kimbrough to my office after the interview. "How do your cameras have power?" he asked in surprise. The whole city was still in a blackout.

I pointed to a cabinet built into the desk. "I have an uninterruptible power supply. Three, actually. In my line of work I can't afford to lose hours of code because Fremont Energy decides to replace a transformer at 10 AM on a Wednesday. The Wi-Fi router will run indefinitely, which means the cameras will still record to the server here, but I can't watch them over my phone without Internet access. I'd have to build an app but I haven't had the time yet." It felt so good to talk about something normal like tech.

I had to break it down and explain how I built my own HTML interface to better display the raw camera feeds. It wasn't much more complicated (for me) than building a website from scratch. The result was a secure system set up the way I wanted to, not the way some Chinese software engineer thought it should be. Detective Kimbrough was in awe that such a thing was possible. "If you could build such an app, I know a lot of cops that might be interested in such a system."

We reviewed the video together. Was this normal procedure? I didn't know. The incident started with three men in hoodies walking down the center of the street and up the driveway. One peeked in the front windows to make sure no one was downstairs. He waited by the front door just in case I tried to come out that way. A second climbed the gate and used a cheap shim to pop the padlock so his partner could enter—the guy who died in the side yard.

The car I shot up stopped in front of the driveway. The driver got out and walked up to the gate while the cheap knob lock on the side door was picked. We couldn't see the exact details from this angle. However he did it, it was swift. At this point, one of them got out of the car and sent one of the others to go be a lookout. I got chills remembering what happened next.

I cycled the feed to the garage. The detective tried not to chuckle when the first burglar tripped over some stuff in front of the door. The guy who tripped got cussed out. Not far from the camera, they whispered to each other. The three prowlers looked like ghosts in the green and white footage. "Wait, what did they say?" Kimbrough asked.

I ran the video back and turned up the volume. All either of us could make out was, "...man, I don't wanna rape no little girl. We can double up on the mom."

My body went cold and rigid as my head took a roller coaster ride. I felt the detective's hands steadying me. "It's alright, they're dead. They can't hurt anyone now." I didn't remember any more of the video. I saw the movements and heard the shots while Kimbrough played everything a few times from each camera. I was dumbfounded. I thought it was a random burglary for our generator. If they knew about Raelene and the girls, they must have known us, but how?

"It's not unheard of for other motives to crop up as a crime is planned or committed," Kimbrough said, his words very far off from where my mind was.

I made a snap assessment. Discretion and when to withhold certain things is something a good husband and father must learn. *Raelene must never know.* My wife wasn't new to the dangers of the world. In high school, she was walking alone one evening when a would-be rapist attacked her. She was nearly six feet tall and beat the guy's ass but, still... She was upstairs, afraid of this very thing happening, and it almost did.

I would insulate her from her fear. A secret like this would have to burn inside me, a confidential pain that I would have to bear alone unless I wanted to worry her. My brother, I could always tell him. But never my wife. All she needed to know was that I fought the wolves, not how close they came to her. A man doesn't have to bear up alone or without rest or comfort. Women make bearing the burden easier and soothe the pain, but a man must shoulder the weight that is his to bear.

As Kimbrough played the videos over, the face of the driver who got away was all I could focus on. He was the one who seemed to have made the horrible suggestion of what to do to my family. Other than being a bald guy with tattoos on his face, there was nothing special about him other than the utter emptiness in his eyes. "Excuse me?" I asked, snapping back to reality. The detective had said something that I didn't hear.

"The DA will have to review as a formality, but I will tell you right now my report will state that this was a self-defense shooting and that no criminal charges should be filed." This was Fremont after all. I would have been within my rights to shoot them for simply stealing my generator. He put the thumb drive of the videos in his pocket. "Normally I don't say that kind of thing but 'normal' has left the building." I started to wonder if Kimbrough had been so busy lately that he simply was out of shits to give to stick to what I assumed was a policy of ambiguity regarding suspicions of guilt.

"Thank you. I...just thank you."

"Good shooting, sir. You handled your gun very well, better than some of the guys on the range. Were you prior service or law enforcement?"

I shook my head. "No. Just a lot of trap and skeet shooting when I was younger." It surprised me he was being so casual. Compared to what happened to Bert I figured I'd be in a dingy interrogation room right now. Maybe the rumors were right: the cops just didn't care anymore.

"Those skills counted for something today," he said. "We will have to impound your shotgun as evidence. Do you have another weapon?"

"I have a pistol."

"Good. Get yourself another shotgun or an AR or something, ASAP. Lightning usually doesn't strike twice, but it can't hurt to have something. Might be up to six months before you can get your scattergun back." He departed, saying he wanted to get back to the station to get the video uploaded and a draft report written before he went home for some sleep. This was his third shooting of the night.

Once Kimbrough was gone, I chatted with one of the patrol officers, Collins, who was waiting for the coroner to show up. "Three shootings last night; are things really that bad?" I asked.

"You have no idea. I've been on the department for six years. My dad was a captain here for three decades. He saw one home defense shooting in all his time. I've seen three, four now, myself plus reports of a dozen more defensive brandishings or shots fired and missed in the last two weeks. I made more felony arrests since all this started than in my entire career and you gotta remember that West River City has consistently been in the top five on the FBI's list of safest cities over 100,000 people for as long as I can remember."

The sergeant stuck his head inside the front door. "Hey Collins, the wagon is almost here. Go out front and show them in."

"Sure thing, Sarge." Collins excused himself.

I watched from the kitchen hall as the medical examiner and the evidence tech did their thing. More photos and samples were taken as each body was removed. Something about the process made me sick so I stepped into the backyard. *I wonder if its normal to allow the…the…victim, the defendant, or whatever I am, to watch.* The fresh air made me feel better. I took several deep breaths in to convince myself that I wasn't smelling that coppery blood smell. I smelt smoke.

One of the men from the mortuary under contract with the coroner's office was smoking a cigarette as he waited for the okay to remove the last corpse. "You alright, sir?" he asked.

"I'm feeling better. I think I'll be fine. I didn't do anything wrong, right?" I said, trying to force humor into my rhetorical question.

The attendant shrugged. He was probably in his late fifties, fit, but weathered. "I guess if you did do something wrong, you'd be downtown right now. But the DA is cool, you know." He took a long drag on his cigarette. "If you shot a couple burglars you should be okay. Nothing from what I saw or heard was negative. The ME—," the medical examiner, "— is a bit gabby."

"Have you seen a lot of shootings like this?"

"Oh yeah. This is my part-time job. Spent thirty-three years across the River working for city PD."

"Small world." I replied. "Have you ever shot anybody before, I mean, what do they train you about killing someone, even when it's necessary, and how it affects you?"

"I have killed someone," he said with a grave nod. "A suicidal man murdered his family and was taking potshots at cars on the road. I wondered for years if I could have done more, perhaps had traffic blocked off and been more patient. Ridiculous thoughts, really. That guy was going to shoot at whoever he needed to because he was brave enough to murder yet too much of a coward to take his own life.

"Those were different times, of course. No less-lethal shotguns, no Tasers, no Crisis Intervention Training. Still, yesterday or today, that man chose to kill and die and die he did. It's natural for the human mind to try and punish itself for killing. Despite our violent ways from time to time, I suppose it still goes against our inner nature, at least until we become so depraved that part of our conscience is seared.

"I know I did the right thing. The only thing. In the face of all that, I still wake up at night with this random thought, 'You killed a man,' that pops into my head. You're gonna be involuntarily replaying this incident for a long time, my friend. Not a damn thing you can do to stop it, either so don't make the mistake of thinking drugs or alcohol can fix it. Maybe a shrink can give you something but don't self-medicate. It'll fade over time.

"You're alive and your family is safe. You did the right thing. That's all that matters. Talk to somebody, not your wife, a pro. Don't bottle it all up. I can't stress this enough, get professional psychological help, even if you feel fine." He stood up. "Now I'm not supposed to give advice like that, so if you tell anyone I did, I'll have to call you a liar." The attendant winked. He rubbed out his butt in the dirt and pitched it in the garbage can before heading out to collect the last body.

It was late morning when the evidence tech released the scene. He gave me a list of crime scene cleanup companies. The police and coroner's office doesn't clean up the mess, the tech explained. He didn't sound optimistic about someone being able to come out today or even tomorrow so he gave me some basic cleanup supplies. Watching his van drive away was a very anticlimactic for the end of what was easily the most important event in my life.

About twenty minutes after the bodies were gone and everyone left, one of the patrolmen called my phone. They had the suspect vehicle stopped near the old bridge and wanted me to identify it. *That's a happy ending*, I thought. Raelene didn't want me to go, understandably. I didn't want to go myself, but if it meant that these jerks would be going to jail for burglary and felony murder charges, I'd do my part.

One officer waited at the house while I went with the second who gave me the run-down. The driver got into a verbal altercation with a DOT crew manning a road closure on the south end of the island. He was begging to be let through because he needed to get his friend to a hospital in the capitol, an hour south. When they wouldn't let him through (the road was physically impassible) he cussed them out, flashed a gun, and tried to speed away only to hydroplane off the road. The DOT crew called the state troopers.

Now the car was on the back of a tow truck at barricade on the old bridge, on the north end of the island, which was closed because the flooding made the low span unsafe. For whatever reason, they didn't want to go across the freeway bridge into downtown River City. So the driver was in the middle of moving the cones and barricades when the trooper arrived. He ran, went down the embankment, and disappeared into the brush that lined the riverbank. With no backup, no helicopter, and no canine, the trooper was unable to prevent the suspect's escape.

"The passenger is at the hospital," the officer said as he rolled by the scene. "Can you identify the vehicle?" He explained this was called a 'field show up' identification although normally it involved people, not a car.

"It certainly is a match to the one I saw." It was a gray late-2000s Acura, like I described in my statement to the detective. The paint on the hood was faded and the right rear quarter panel had been repainted in a primer that matched the overall gray color but not the texture. "I know that car." And not just from the other night. It was that dumbass donut kid's car.

It belonged to the teenage ne'er-do-well that lived around the corner until a few weeks ago when the bank finally foreclosed. I always saw him and his friends out on the street skateboarding, drinking, and smoking pot. Every time he would come down our cul-de-sac and do donuts, it provoked the wrath of my wife as it did yesterday. Did they target us because Raelene wasn't afraid to cuss him out?

The officer relayed my confirmation to a detective in the hospital.

"Do you know anyone by the name of 'Uncle P' or

have you heard that before?"

"No."

"The registered owner, Kevin Galvez, is apparently one of the people you shot. From what the guy you winged said, the driver was the dead kid's dirtbag parolee uncle who recruited them all to commit some burglaries. All we know is the survivor was told to call him Uncle P, so who knows if this is Galvez's actual uncle or what."

"Just burglaries?"

"I don't know about that. Whatever they set out to do, he's wanted for murder among other charges. He'll be lucky if the DA gives him a plea bargain for life," he said. On our side of the river, our county was far tougher on crime than the one who tried to railroad Bert.

"Once you catch him."

"Yes, once we catch him." That was the caveat. Until then, the man responsible for what could have been a monstrous outrage on my family was in the wind.

Confessions and Consequences

I called my boss. Not the executive vice president, but the actual CEO and owner, Simon Price. Price was a tough and shrewd electrical engineer-turned-entrepreneur who got his start in IT during the Silicon Prairie days in Texas. He was a Texan, through and through, and wouldn't recoil in horror at the mention of guns the same way my direct-report, Sukhjinder 'Sunny' Das, would. It was time to put the number one man's "open door" policy to the test.

Price didn't even say hello when he answered. "Ross, you're finally calling me to say you want to move to Austin," he said pleasantly. He'd been needling me to move to Austin ever since the pandemic took the company almost fully remote.

"Simon, that's not why I called."

"We could use you. Right now, at the data center I've got the backup diesel generator alternating with a pair of two megawatt portable gensets I had flown in on one of those 747 freighters with the nose that lifts up. Ungodly expensive but if we can't communicate with the backup servers in Iceland, we lose a million a day. With the natural gas supply being cutoff to industrial customers, we're having to Shanghai diesel shipments from all over the country at an effective price of $15 a gallon. Anyhow, what can I do you for?"

"I shot someone this morning."

Simon was silent for a few seconds longer than was normal. "What, like on accident? Did you get drunk at a bar?" he said, his tone shifting slightly towards disapproval. I imagined he was thinking back to his days in college drinking at rural bars where that kind of thing happened regularly in the '80s.

"No, at home. There were burglars."

"Were you or your family hurt? Did they catch the bastards?" he said, concern growing in his voice.

"We're all okay. I got four of them. Three are dead, one's in the hospital." Price whistled in admiration of that. I launched into the story. He interrupted me part way through.

"Ross, you gotta clam up fella. You gotta be careful what you say and who you say it to. You didn't talk to the police, did you?" I admitted I did. Instead of swearing, he held the receiver away from his face and made some indistinct noises. When he calmed down, he said "Okay, it's probably fine. You're in Fremont, after all. Look, you need to talk to a lawyer pronto. You've worked with Doug, haven't you?"

"Yeah." Douglas Taylor was our corporate counsel.

"I'm gonna give him a call. He's got a ranch not far south of you. I want you to see him as soon as possible and talk to him. Get a real lawyer's opinion and a recommendation from him to a good defense attorney, if it comes to that."

"Thank you. Look, about telling Sukhjinder..."

"I'm just gonna tell him there was a burglary, that's all he needs to know," Price said softly. "Sunny doesn't understand our culture. I'll tell him you got cell phone trouble and couldn't reach him in California so he don't get no hurt feelings that he didn't get called first."

"I appreciate it Simon, I really do."

"Ross my boy, it's my pleasure to help you out. Now you talk to Doug and watch after your family. Getting damn squirrely all over the country. You wanna get out of that city and buy yourself a ranch I'll make sure you can afford it."

I thanked him again and we said goodbye. Quitting Google to come work for Simon Price had probably been the best decision of my life. Next I called my brother.

The relief in Grant's voice was audible after he picked up. "I got Raelene's text and then I didn't hear anything. You got me worried but I didn't see your name in the news. The phones have been iffy lately. Everything okay, considering?"

"I'm truly kinda shocked at how normal I feel. Now that the physiological reactions are over, it's oddly calm. Can't stay keyed up forever."

He agreed. "How bad is the house?"

"Minimal. Some blood and I shot a hole in the fence. They jiggled the lock or something on the side garage door. One of the neighbors is a contractor and he's going to help me shore it up this afternoon."

"The cops are letting you do that?"

"They don't have the manpower to mess around like cutting out a doorframe for evidence. CSI is already gone. Guy was decent enough to give me some stuff to clean up the blood in the garage."

"Saved you a few bucks from having to call the crime scene clean up guys," he said. After the coroner had gone, the pool of blood that congealed in the refrigerator-cold out in the garage came up easily. That still left the odd spattering of blood in random places around the garage that I'd have to search out and find, lest the wife or kids find them. I would have to pressure wash the side yard and driveway too.

"How are you getting along up there?"

"Today seems less stupid than it has been. Got some good sleep, but you should talk. I thought you'd be tied up with a lawyer and detectives right now. How are you dealing with it?"

I ran him through the whole incident. We dissected it and he gave me a lot of praise for how I performed. I wanted to tell him that's not what I needed. What I wanted was my shotgun back or maybe an AR and a pistol for Raelene. Four more guys with guns would be nice too but I'd settle for just my brother watching my "six." He gave me a generic, brotherly speech about dealing with combat stress. He handled what he saw and went through in Iraq pretty well, so coming from the same DNA, why shouldn't I be the same way?

Mopping Up a Nightmare

My grandfather rarely threw things away. His garage was a collection of old tools and random junk that all had a purpose. My grandmother would point to something and complain about it, but Grandpa would say that the dish drainer with the peeled enamel would be tacked to the fence and used as an arbor for the new grapevines. Used paint trays became drip pans when it was time to change the oil in the Buick.

I was nowhere near that much of a...collective saver...but a plastic paint scraper could be washed and reused. So could Tyvek coveralls. The 99¢ tool and COVID supplies that coulda been chucked out came in handy today. With the scraper the congealed blood had come up like peeling spilled jelly off a countertop. The coagulating or thickening agent the CSI guy gave me worked well in the cold.

The gelatinous substance was deposited into a, you guessed it, paint tray (unused) and into a trash bag. Only a thin layer of rusty streaks remained on the concrete. I scrubbed that away with hot water and Simple Green. To avoid fouling any more of my shop towels, I used a squeegee to push the remaining water into the floor drain.

Now for the blood spatters. There were a few I could see, but less I couldn't. I wiped down the obvious ones on the case of the washer and dryer. A blacklight was what I needed. Since neither my wife or I conducted nightly news exposés of poorly cleaned hotel rooms, we didn't have one and the usual options of Amazon or a store were not available. Where would I find a blacklight?

It was October. *Halloween decorations.* All ours were harvest themed—the girls were scared of the spooky stuff—but Bert made a haunted house every year. Without changing I jogged across the street and knocked. Mrs. Vargas peeked out through the crack in the door. "Ross?" She was straining to recognize me.

"Does Bert have a second?"

"Yes. Why are you dressed up in a space suit?"

Oh crap. I'd forgotten how odd I looked. "I'm cleaning up from, you know, earlier this morning." I plucked at the plastic sleeve with my rubber-gloved fingers. "Old COVID supplies."

"Ah. Just a sec." She closed the door. I didn't blame her. It was cold and the neighbor who just shot a guy and now was wearing a biohazard suit might not be the kind of guest you wanted to invite in.

Bert came to the door. He looked me up and down. "Hey buddy, you doing okay?" There was some concern in his eyes.

"Yeah, I'm just cleaning. I didn't go crazy or anything. Yet."

He laughed. "Okay. Just wanna make sure. I thought you'd still be talking to the cops."

I shook my head. "I thought so too, but they're really busy I guess."

"Well, I don't know what your lawyer said, but if you need an ear, I'm willing to return the favor for you listening to me."

"I appreciate it buddy, but what I need is a black light." This would help make the blood spots show up as fluorescent spots on whatever surface they impacted. "Can I talk you into digging through the Halloween supplies?"

"Absolutely. Doesn't look like we'll be decorating this year." He yelled back into the house to tell his wife what he was doing. We walked around to the side garage door and went in. Bert got up into the rafters and handed me down a couple boxes of Christmas lights. "Hopefully we'll get to put these up this year."

"I hope so. I have the weird feeling that last year might have been the last good Christmas." With the banking crisis, the signs of a faltering economy, rumors of wars, and knowledge that the election this year was going to be interesting, Raelene and I wanted to make sure the holidays were really special and enjoyable. We really pulled out all the stops so, should hard times come, the girls might have one last opportunity to enjoy the same Yuletide prosperity their parents did growing up.

"The police weren't over long. Did your lawyer make an appointment for an interview tomorrow or something?"

"No, I talked to them. I had nothing to hide."

Bert gave me a displeased look. "Man..."

"I know, I know. I heard it from my boss and from my brother. But it's all on video. Plus all the cops were cool. They told me 'Don't worry about it.' Even said they don't usually say stuff like that. I got the feeling they were being straight with me."

He was still skeptical. "That's what I thought about the cops across the river." It was the DA's office that jammed him up vs the city police.

"Different county, different DA."

"I'll keep my fingers crossed for you Ross. You don't want to go through what I did." He handed down a lamp.

"Here you go. I've got a spare bulb in case that one doesn't work. That is an old-fashioned incandescent. Don't let the EPA know I still have one around, okay?" he teased to lighten things up. "And talk to a lawyer."

"Mum's the word." I swore that I would follow through on the appointment with Doug.

In the dark garage I found out that blood doesn't fluoresce. Though it took a while with the slow Internet, I learned I needed both a special dye sold only by forensic supply companies and an entirely different wavelength of UV light. Stupid TV lied to me. So it was on my hands and knees to scrub every possible surface.

An hour later, the garage was cleaner than it had been twenty-four hours ago. I'd love to see the look on the salesman's face if he only knew just how stain resistant the epoxy concrete sealant was. The only lasting damage was from an errant buckshot pellet that penetrated the bottom of the Tesla's front bumper, but the car insurance would cover that. The lack of overpenetration from the shotgun was a saving grace.

The side yard was something else. When the sun finally hit it about midday, I hooked the electric pressure washer up to the generator and started blasting. The residual blood quickly came up and I used the fan of the water to "sweep" it into the grass. Except for the hole in the fence where I missed, there was no unpleasant reminder of the incident.

Around three, my neighbor Hugo, the contractor showed up. I showed him the side door which had no indications of being forced or pried. "See the problem here is you have no deadbolt, just the latch on the knob." Kneeling with great difficulty, he stuck a screwdriver between the door and the weather stripping to depress the latch. "See how easy it is to jimmy that open?"

"I've got the long screws in the latch plate and hinges that go into the studs."

"That's great, but they bypassed all that with just a screwdriver in the right place. Without a bolt, the door fails there or with a single kick. You can block the door if you want, but let's reinforce it. I'll be right back."

He walked home and came back with a cart full of tools and bag of parts. "I've got a deadbolt and latch protector I salvaged from a house we flipped." He took it out of the bag and tested the pair of keys that came with it. "Sorry it doesn't match the rest of the house."

"Better than putting a trash can filled with rocks behind the door."

Hugo thought that was funny. He attached a clamp-type jig to the door that was the size of the deadbolt housing and cut a hole with a circular cutter on his drill. Next he used a drill and a chisel to cut the mortises for the new lock plates. In addition, he attached a badly painted over anti-pry plate. It took him about twenty minutes in total. "So now they'll definitely have to donkey kick it. You got a 2x4 laying around?"

"No."

"Hmm. I've got one in the scrap pile. Let's put some brackets on the inside so you can slide a two-by behind it." That took him about two minutes to do. "In a pinch, you could have just done this but it might be nice to be able to unlock the door with a key instead of having to go around to remove the bar, you know?"

"Hugo, thank you for doing this."

"Sure thing, pal." He put his arm on my shoulder. "I'm glad you guys are okay. That was the right way to deal with scum."

"Thanks." I didn't share his enthusiasm. I wish it had never happened.

A Sleepless Night's Vigil

Reya did not want to go to bed. She seemed cheerful enough all afternoon and into the evening, but when eight o'clock came, the fight was on. We agreed to let her watch a video with her sister as they both fell asleep. Half an hour later the baby was out and Reya was still wide-awake. Any parent knows what followed next. The back-and-forth continued for ten minutes, escalating to angry tears, threatening to wake the baby.

"Raelene, she wants to stay up until we go to bed. We'll be in soon enough."

"She needs to get her rest. She was up early yesterday and didn't nap today. See how cranky she is?"

"I'm NOT cranky!" Reya screamed, her arms held rigidly down by her sides, her hands balled into fists.

"Okay young lady, that's it. You *cannot* behave that way," her mother scolded. I bowed out of the fight. *Let her stay awake. She'll crash eventually,* I thought. From my study I heard Raelene negotiating with her. At some point a detente was achieved and celebrated with a glass of juice.

"Sugar before bedtime?" I asked Raelene when she came in to my study report.

"It's got children's Benadryl in it. I'm a terrible mother," she said without meaning it.

I shrugged. "She had a rough day. You're a nurse and gave her medicine. This way she won't have any nightmares?"

"Do you want some to help you sleep?"

"No thanks. I might drink that last glass of wine in the bottle and call it a night pretty soon."

Sleep came easily enough that night. As it was, having a two year old in your forties is exhausting and a grid-down lifestyle plus cleaning up a crime scene put me over the top. Maintaining sleep was another matter. At first, I woke up with a physical jolt and a fact, not so much spoken but known, violently came to mind. *You shot four people today. They tried to break into your house*, not so much in those words, but that was the gist of the thought.

"Everything okay?" Raelene asked.

"Yeah," I lied. "Myoclonic jerk." That's where as you are falling asleep your leg randomly jerks.

"Okay."

I checked my watch. It had been only a half an hour after I closed my eyes. Everything was quiet. The pistol was in its nightstand safe. I would have liked to put it on the nightstand but with the kids around the risk was too great.

My eyes had been closed for a minute or two when I began to drift off again. In that twilight stage of sleep, I wasn't quite dreaming but the conscious restraint on thoughts was loosened. I heard the whispers in the garage. In my semi-dream the burglar's descriptions of what they were going to do were more vivid. I saw the garage door open. Snapshots of the dead bodies on the ground and the muzzle flashes from the car followed.

I snapped back awake again. *This is going to be a long night*. Lying there with my eyes closed and thinking about a software project helped keep my mind from wandering. Nonetheless the constant reminder of what happened played under my thoughts. Eventually I nodded off. The replay began again.

I rolled over, pushing the seven year old away against

her mother. Raelene woke up a bit and adjusted herself in the bed. I tried again, thinking of different ways of getting around a problem we were having with some code—the software engineer's version of counting sheep. Sleep eventually came but some inconsiderate asshole made one hell of a racket and I was instantly up and out of bed.

"Shh! You'll wake the neighbors," someone said outside. "You couldn't wait until morning to do that?" Peering out the blinds I saw it was the adult kids of the people to our right doing something with a metal trash can in the driveway.

"Everything okay?" Raelene asked again.

"If our dumbass neighbors' kids count as okay."

I got back in bed. My heart was racing. I had that strange tingling sensation of the fading adrenaline rush. While I hadn't killed anyone before, I had nights like this. The topic was much more trivial and even laughable now.

It was the night I learned about sex. Sleep was impossible to come by with that information fresh in my brain. I had been vaguely aware of the concept of sex since the time I read about it in the encyclopedia. I must have been about nine or ten then. Even now, I'm still astonished that in the same set of books I read about nuclear war evacuation plans, I found the phrase "the man puts his penis in the woman's vagina, and they have sexual intercourse."

My father, who was probably the real cause of my disturbed sleep then, told me the details that the encyclopedia didn't tell me, such as the gyrations that led to the sensation of pleasure and eventual production of children. He was roughly that clinical about it, minus the big words. Sometimes I wonder if someone had told me about sex, and to avoid the trauma of that memory, I subconsciously changed the details to something more...encyclopedic.

Lying in bed, my mind wanted to be anywhere other than on the couch with my father an hour earlier. My father would never have let me watch a horror film, much less watch it right before bed. So why would he tell me about sex when I was in my pajamas? What kind of perverted bedtime story is that? Nonetheless, it was necessary and only disturbing because of my father's statement "Everyone has sex, son. Everyone." I knew who "everyone" meant. Western culture does not like to dwell on, or even admit, that parents have sex, or ever did so, even just for procreation.

My preferred method for repressing unwanted thoughts was to read, using the steady stream of words parading through my head to drown out what might try to crop up. I couldn't read and try to fall asleep, so I built a house in my head, nail by nail, board by board. It was rather crude in its construction, but I managed to frame the one-room structure before blessed sleep finally came to get me. Over the next few months, this evolved from building simple houses to distract me, to full-on fantasy worlds.

There was no fantasy tonight to get my brain off what happened. Why was this happening to me? Hadn't I done everything right? I killed the bad guys, protected my family, and even the cops told me not to worry. Okay, I should have called an attorney before giving a statement but no jury in this state would convict me of anything. Maybe the DA wouldn't even bother referring it to the grand jury for a perfunctory review.

You'll never hear the end of it from your brother, though. 'Why didn't you get a lawyer? What have I told you?'

What was this? Why should I be suffering a sleepless night? All four of us were alive and I did nothing wrong. For an hour, I tried to fall asleep. I tossed and turned. Reya woke briefly. The baby emitted a few cries as she woke up a bit.

Raelene leaned over and whispered to me. "Ross, I really love you, but you're disturbing the girls."

"What do you want me to do?"

"Go lie down next door. You'll be right there."

"What about the gun?"

"Take it. If anything happens you'll be a few feet away." I looked at her skeptically in the darkness. She couldn't see me but probably knew. "We'll be fine."

In the dark, I got angry at how Raelene could sleep so well. Probably the lack of caffeine, all the exercise, and clean eating. Her fear wasn't being killed by a burglar, not the same way I feared it happening to her. She knew she was safe with me and that was the end of it. I envied the presence of mind, and utter trust, she had in me. What if I failed? Oh how I wanted her to be sleepless with me, parting the blinds in paranoia. Only if she doubted me as well could I confide my fears to her.

She could sleep in peace, but not me. The only time she ever had trouble sleeping was when I wasn't home. The one time I got pissed off at her and stormed out the door, I returned the next morning to find her exhausted and wild-eyed. Her biggest fear was being abandoned by the man she loved. After all, she had been abandoned by her father and the guy before me, Reya's bio dad.

Reluctantly I got up and laid down in Reya's twin bed. It was her "big girl" bed. It seemed absurdly small to me. Thankfully we didn't have a son. Instead of a princess themed bed it would probably be cars. No way my "big and tall" frame could fit in a race-car shaped bed.

Notwithstanding the hypervigilance and "what ifs" I felt normal. I did not feel bad for taking human lives. It was a sense of "Oh, I did kill someone, didn't I?" You know what? It felt kind of exhilarating to have shot those men and be unharmed. It was the ultimate power trip; the power of life-and-death over someone and I chose to kill. *Does that make me a psychopath? Aren't you supposed to feel bad for taking a life?*

Twice during my tortured night I got up to patrol the house, pistol in hand. All was quiet and safe. Was this what my brother was going through with the riots in Red Rock? Or how about the people across the river in the city? We probably should have had a neighborhood patrol or watch like Grant had going. I still wouldn't be able to sleep but at least I would feel better knowing there were eyes and guns on the street.

D a y 4

The Little Dutch Boy

I woke up sometime after dawn. Judging by the light it was eight o'clock. Reya's bed was uncomfortably firm. We'd have to ask her if she wanted a new mattress. My breath fogged as I trooped off to the hall bathroom for the usual morning functions. My new companion tinnitus came with me. Now I knew why guys used silencers on their home defense guns.

"What the heck?" The toilet was refilling with brown water indicating the city water supply was compromised. *Glad I didn't see that before I sat down.* The sink was doing the same thing and the water pressure was low. I tapped on the bedroom door and looked in. Reya looked up at me from her mom's iPad and looked back down. Her sister slept peacefully under the covers. "Raelene?"

"In here," she said softly from the exercise room. She was looking out the back window and sipping a cup of tea. "The golf course is flooded." Through the gap in the houses a brown pond stood where the turf should be. A bank of dying grass and dirty snow separated the new water hazard from the houses on the course itself.

"It's supposed to do that, babe. It was designed to absorb excess rainfall and serve as a catch basin in major flood events."

"There's your major flood event right there," she said sarcastically, gesturing with her cup and without taking her eyes off the view. Had I not been exhausted and traumatized I would have laughed.

"Let's check what the city is saying."

"The generator is off, again, no Internet, and no cell service."

"No cellular?"

"That's what I said."

"Guess we'll be listening to the radio then."

She turned around, undid two buttons of my flannel shirt, and stuck her hands in where it was warm. Raelene was always cold. Being so thin it was no surprise and I'd become accustomed to chilly feet in bed or finding her hands in my pockets. "There's a problem with the water."

"I know. We have plenty of bottled water and the big blue plastic cans in the garage."

She looked me in the eye. "Ross, I'm worried and I'm scared." She had sad eyes. Raelene was a fairly stoic woman who didn't often show very passionate emotions but when she got scared or depressed I could see it in her eyes. Eye contact was her way of seeking reassurance, that her man was there, the same way I might yearn for a touch of her hand when I felt blue.

Drivel about gender roles aside, I was her protector. Emotionally, if not physically. When this woman stuck her hand out for help you had better take it. She didn't often do it and when she did she was asking for something she couldn't provide herself. I met a totally self-reliant Raelene, a wreck of a thing under a veneer of an independent woman who embodied all the things feminism said she should be. In reality she was a half searching for her other piece to make a whole. Someone who could unpack and repair all the hidden and broken things that had to be stuffed away to function.

People these days forget that couples are

complimentary to each other. I was her strength so she didn't have to be. She was my spot of softness in a harsh world. Some guys knew it better than I did but it gets tiresome being strong all by yourself. To me, she and the kids were something to live for. All through my thirties until we met I hadn't changed much since I graduated college. What did I need a woman for? I could get girls easily enough and when I got tired of them, or they got tired of me, we went our separate ways. Companionship was a thing I did with my buddies.

With Raelene I found out that love was more than just the butterflies that a pretty girl gave you or sex on near-demand. It was mutual obligation and responsibility to someone. Once our relationship blossomed I strove to be a better person, to be someone worthy of getting this amazing woman to settle down with me.

"Did you sleep?" she asked.

"A bit. I think I went out after four o'clock."

She put her head on my shoulder. "Sorry. I know PTSD can be rough."

"Doesn't that take a while to develop?"

"Yeah, weeks to months, but you had an initial stress reaction to a traumatic event." She looked me in the eyes, sensing my apprehension. "Don't worry. If it happens we'll get through it. It's not at all like most people think." I wondered how she knew so much about PTSD. It wasn't the kind of thing trauma and ER nurses dealt with. "You saved our lives and we're all safe."

The baby started crying from the bedroom. "Mom, she needs changed," Reya called.

"I'll go do it," I volunteered.

"No," Raelene said. "I will. You go cook breakfast. I

don't want dirty hands on the food." Handwashing would now be of the camping variety.

"Cook? You mean tear open Foil Pouch. Add boiling water to Foil Pouch. Stir contents of Foil Pouch. Consume freeze dried goodness."

She wagged her finger in my face. "Hey, just be happy we have Foil Pouch," she said, and started laughing.

I went downstairs as Raelene tended to the kids. Reya let out a loud "Ew! Somebody didn't flush the toilet," as she discovered our latest hardship. Brown water meant that there was either an open water main somewhere that was sucking in dirt or the water treatment plant flooded and failed. I was betting on the latter. Jackson, Mississippi, had its municipal water system fail totally and it was down for months. Without any serious, structural damage I figured we would be without clean tap water for a few weeks.

My brother told me that the National Guard had plans for a large water system outage—that's what his battalion did. The city would be trucking in drinking water for the public but for cooking and hygiene needs everyone would have to collect it from big water tanks. 5,000 gallon "water buffalos" would be filled daily by water treatment specialists, its own specialty Army job, and placed around town. Instead of showers, we would have sponge baths.

A shower, even if the water went clear again, wouldn't be safe if there were contaminants in the water. You might get away with scrubbing up in a river while camping but the water after a flood was going to be filled with all sorts of nasty chemicals and diseases. Imagine rubbing some obscure little germ into a shaving nick. The girls might not mind missing a proper bath at their age but Raelene and I would. With my beard I didn't have to shave. My wife had very fine hair so if she didn't shave her legs it wasn't noticeable. Either way, two or three weeks of *yuck* on your skin was no way to go.

The water system failing didn't bode well for us. Ordinarily we would just skip town but an area the size of western Europe was affected by the freeze. A short-term disaster was compounding in to a crisis. None of these things seemed to happen when I was a kid. The Midwest floods were over in a week or two and LA was back up and running in a few days after the earthquake. Katrina was an aberration. We needed news. Information in an emergency was as vital as supplies.

The Internet was a much faster and comprehensive way of gathering intelligence, as I was starting to think of it, than waiting for mainstream TV news to give it to you. Internet depended on the utility grid, which was failing. The fiber optic to the neighborhood needed mains power and a working regional hub. The major central office for our telecom company was in a big building downtown; a relic of the 1950s when it physically needed to be there. It wasn't in a materially robust location that was insensitive to power interruptions. Short of something like Starlink or some miracle we had gone back to the 1970s without the older infrastructure still in place.

We were within an easy line of sight of the tall buildings of downtown where the TV transmitters were. Getting a clear signal was no problem. Except in our 21st century, upper middle class household, all our TVs were smart TVs and those no longer shipped with integral antennas. You needed an external unit that wired into the back with a coaxial cable. Since we had a dish and all the streaming services, we had no need to slap a digital version of rabbit ears on our wall. We weren't living in Section 8 housing.

Buy a portable TV went down on my mental to do list. That left the emergency AM/FM radio that followed me in my disaster kit since moving to Silicon Valley ages ago. It sat in its emergency case ignored for years. Upon examination, I found the single AA battery inside all crusty with alkaline leakage. I raided a remote control for a battery rather than dig through a drawer for a fresh one.

Happily the radio's electronics weren't damaged. The big clear-channel AM station was coming in strong. Apparently I tuned in during the middle of an emergency press conference. "The flood control works are doing their job and absorbing the overflow. At current water levels it is expected that the basins will fill completely but will do their job."

"About that current water level..." a reporter began.

"Yeah. As you know the river is at sixteen feet above flood stage. Fluctuations in the flow or other factors are causing about a foot variance which is what is causing the overspill, along with some combined seepage and backflow from various drains and whatnot."

"How are the levees holding up?"

There was a shuffle at the microphone. "The levees are doing fine at the moment. We have engineers constantly monitoring them."

Must be the Corps of Engineers. The metro area was all protected by levees. Flooding was a historical problem and only after about a century of land reclamation was the area really considered safe from floods. The last major incident was well over fifty years ago and the entire modern flood control system resulted from that.

"It's overcast today, but we've had no rain, thank goodness, but it did rain upstream. What impacts are you expecting?"

Another shuffle. "I'm Caitlin McGee, National Weather Service. Yes, we are monitoring the impact of the rain in the mountains near the headwaters of the river. We're working with our partners in the USGS to calculate the volume of the actual runoff that is expected to arrive."

"Do you anticipate further flooding?"

"Uh...well, more water when the river is already full is not a good thing, so I'd have to say yes. Rain falling on snow melts the snow at an accelerated rate. The ground across the entire state is saturated so it's going to have to go somewhere. The issue is exactly how much that's going to be and I don't have those numbers right now."

There was an interruption. Footsteps on the dais. Microphone noises. "We do expect some additional flooding but given that, the exact timing and nature isn't known," a man said.

The meteorologist was still speaking in the background. "...peak in 20 to 30 hours after the event..."

"Thank you Ms. McGee! Nothing is certain at this point," a slightly-off-mic male voice said. Another shuffle at the mic was happening. "We expect further flooding, we don't know how much or exactly when. We're working out the impacts at this point."

"Sir," a reporter said, "confidential sources have reported that you do know but are working on mitigating the information before it is released."

"Mitigating the impact," he said. "Flood mitigation measures." The reporter accused the flood control director of a cover up and he was trying to deny it.

"Two more feet by tomorrow morning!" someone in the back yelled. "Springfield has already ordered evacuations! There's seepage at the Pine Valley Dam too!" The room erupted in a jumble of excited voices and reporters shouting questions.

"Quiet! Order! Get that guy out of here. Be quiet!" an entirely new person said.

The radio news anchor came on. "I'm watching the TV feed from Channel Six and that's the sheriff trying to calm things down. The camera is panning around and there are deputies escorting a few individuals from the room."

Finally the flood control director came up to the mic. "We got ahead of ourselves here. Yes, we do expect the river to rise. Maybe two feet. We're not sure yet. The exact impact is being worked out this morning now that the field survey units can work in daylight. We'll have better numbers by midday. The takeaway is that more flooding is to be expected but we believe that the engineering will work. Just barely, but it will."

He went on. The problem was that the sloughs, bayous, and the low-lying farmlands that were intended to flood first had already filled up. The only place for the water to go was downstream and to spread out. I sighed. What did that mean for us?

We lived on an island surrounded by levees. Our local flood control elements were already filling with water. Would we be proverbially under water as the river overtopped the levees? Our house was on one of the higher parts of the island but still not out of danger should the levees fail, which they hadn't been concerned about yet.

I stopped stirring the Mountain House bag and sealed it

up. It struck me how screwed we would be without those plastic tubs and the stored water. We were living on a tenuous edge. Was it even safe to be here anymore? The flood control guy was preaching reassurance and faith in the engineering works, but was he correct to do so? I had my family to think of. Local government had been failing in the good-faith department lately.

The kids came downstairs followed by my beautiful wife. Raelene opened Foil Pouch and emptied it into a bowl. "Smells okay." She sampled the breakfast skillet. "Oh, that's awful," but she swallowed anyway. "You're not feeing the kids that."

Why did you say that? I thought. In a survival situation, you ate what you had. By calling it disgusting she was programming the girls to automatically dislike it. The freeze dried eggs were bland but not inedible. I bit my tongue and slid a second Foil Pouch over. "Granola in rice milk and dried berries. I added extra water so it would be softer for the girls. And we have some canned peaches."

She squinted at me. "Acceptable. Under the circumstances." I found it cute so I slapped her butt. She giggled.

"Why did you spank Mommy?" Reya asked.

Whoops. "Nevermind. Buckle your sister into the high chair, would you?" I handed Raelene another warm Foil Pouch. "Biscuits and gravy. We tried this one before, remember? It's okay."

"Acceptable. Under the circumstances," she repeated with a flirtatious squint again. "We probably should have sampled these before the world ended." She served the kids their reconstituted breakfast and the girls ate without hesitation. "They seem to be enjoying it but still…"

"I agree that we may have been a little behind the power curve on this whole prepping thing. I need to apologize to my brother for rebuffing all his advice on this kind of stuff."

"You didn't do too bad. We're way better off than most people. We have a generator. There's plenty of water in the garage and enough dried food to get us through. Yesterday morning you kicked butt, as well." That earned me a kiss.

After breakfast, I got dressed and unboxed the water filtration equipment we had. The backpacking purifier was already staged in the kitchen; we hardly put any mileage on it since our last trip years ago. It would be suitable for drinking/cooking water but for washing it was inefficient to pump gallons through it by hand.

The system I bought was basically two buckets stacked on top of each other. The top bucket was the prefilter that got the worst of the particles and sedimentation out while the second held the clean water and the nano filter. It was relatively cheap and simple to use, being gravity fed. Pour a bucket of brown water in the top and a few minutes later out came clean water from the spigot, or so the instructions said.

Assembly was not difficult. Like I said, it was one bucket on top of another, basically. I set the whole thing on top of the washing machine, filled a third bucket from the utility sink, and poured the water in. The solid contaminants in the dirty water were well dissolved like iced tea rather than chunky like runny mud. Only a very faint trace of grit remained in the pouring bucket. Clean water streamed out of the tap, just as advertised, into a used gallon water jug. It had a faint, lake-water like smell.

I dug out an emergency preparedness book that dated from the '80s and was all tattered to pieces. It recommended 6 drops of 8.25% bleach—pure sodium hypochlorite—for one gallon. Okay, we had just plain bleach that was still fresh and hadn't degraded to salt water nor did it have extra additives in it, but how much was a drop? The book didn't say that. We didn't have a suitable water purification bleach dropper lying around the house either. I stuck my head back in the garage door.

"Raelene, how much is a drop?" I yelled.

"I don't know," she yelled back.

So much for that. Upstairs in the bathroom trash can I found what I was looking for, an empty travel sized eyedrop bottle. Bleach got poured into a clean container out of the recycle bin and I sucked it in to the dropper. Eight drops later (oops, it was supposed to be six) I shook the jug up and sniffed it. *Smells like a swimming pool.* We now had a way to clean water to wash ourselves an dishes with. I just needed to empty this into one of our two five-gallon camping water jugs and do it nine more times, then we could have wash water in the kitchen and master bath.

After that, it was time to finally go see someone I should have talked to a lot sooner. I didn't simply walk out the front door like a stroll before. Each angle of the camera was checked along with a playback of all motion events. I peeked out the front window too. No one was hiding behind the dying hydrangea bush.

I saw some curtains move in the house windows along the street as I walked up the cul-de-sac but not one person came out to talk to me. Kill three burglars in the dawn twilight and suddenly everyone avoids you like a leper. Curious enough to talk to the cops but not enough to come to me directly. Bunch of caring, neighborly people these were. Okay, that was a bit harsh. The Bert and Hugo didn't scorn me.

When we moved in to the neighborhood, a house on the corner had a lawn sign that said, "Join CERT: Community Emergency Response Team." It sat out there for the good part of a year before it faded too much and was thrown away. At the annual block party, I met the owner, Jim (I forgot his last name), and we cooperated a few times for block Halloween and Christmas events. He worked in the city planning office and was a volunteer for the fire department's version of the citizen's patrol. In our little neighbor's-only chat group he was by far the most active sharer of information.

Jim had just gotten home from his shift at the city Emergency Operations Center (EOC). I caught him in the garage. "Ross, how's it going?" he said warmly.

"Could be worse. Literally."

"Yeah." He gave me one of those handshake-hug combinations. "You, Raelene, and the kids doing alright after last night?"

"We are. Lightning doesn't strike the same place twice, you know," I said.

"Right. Did the officers say why they picked your house?"

"No. You know that idiot kid that did donuts in the cul-de-sac?" Jim nodded. "It was him, his convict uncle, and some friends. If I had to guess, part of it was revenge for Raelene and me yelling at him for driving like a jackass. It wasn't just theft." I told him about the whispers in the garage.

"That kid used to cut our grass before he got into drugs or whatever. It could have been any of us." Jim shivered. It could have been the cold but it was much warmer today. "Sorry it had to come to that buddy, but you got the ball to the end zone. They won't be hurting anyone anymore."

I nodded. "Hey, uh, I feel bad coming down here to ask you this, considering I blew off all your invitations to join CERT, but what's going on? I heard the joint press conference and they were not helpful."

He laughed. "That was a mess, wasn't it? Truth is, they're panicked. The river is going to rise over the levees for sure, and not just the little splashes and leaks now. One to two feet deep spilling over the top. The question is exactly where and for how long?"

The overspill was even more dangerous because the top of the levees weren't concreted over everywhere so the water could erode the soil. The continuous process of erosion would worsen as the flow of water increased, thus widening the breach. Something similar happened in New Orleans.

He explained that the bend of a river was particularly dangerous since the water tended to "pile up" there. That meant the northside of the cities were badly exposed. Downtown West River City would get part of that. On the island we were slightly better off because the river channel was straight so there was less resistance, so to speak. The Corps of Engineers was also planning to open the locks and divert some of the water down the ship channel.

"But even with all that it's not good news. We can take an hour, maybe two, of the water coming over the levees and filling up all the parkland and basins at the base." Open spaces had been set aside all around the edges of the island to act as a buffer from the homes and absorb any floodwaters. "Half a night's or day's worth of flooding? Forget it."

"How bad?"

"Low lying areas will flood. The mayor is going to proclaim a voluntary evacuation of Zone A this afternoon." Zone A was the lowest part of the city. "1-3 feet is the prediction and it'll stand around until the pumping stations are back on line."

"The pumping stations are off-line?"

"Well yeah buddy, where do you think all the extra standing water in the canal and on the golf course came from? The generators will only last so long without diesel and with the trucker strike the city can't put in a diesel order from the refinery down south. Don't you worry. We're in Zone AH. We'll be alright."

"One foot or less."

"In Zone AH, yes. That's over the curb but not past the doorstep. Park your car in the driveway," he said with a nervous laugh. "Zone A is up to six feet. Knee to waist high inside the house."

"You remember when that happened a few years ago in Houston? Fish were swimming in people's living room."

"Easy to catch," Jim said with false cheer. "As long as they get the pumping stations back we'll be okay."

"And if they don't?"

"Pray the little Dutch boy keeps his finger in the dike. If the overflow starts to cut through a berm, the levees will fail and the island will fill up to the level of the river. Assuming the flooding keeps up."

The level of the river in flood was approximately our

second floor.　　　"Where's your family?" I asked. The other two cars were gone.

Jim grew a bit serious. "Oh, they went out-of-state to visit my wife's parents." He knew I knew he was lying.

"Jim, please level with me."

His face went from serious to guilty. "Two thirds of that statement is true." He sighed. "I don't have authority to be telling people any of this stuff I just told you. You can't tell the neighbors."

"Pinky swear." I trudged back home and let the guy get some sleep. Today was going to be a busy night in the EOC and we needed guys like Jim in charge.

River View Heights

Raelene didn't take so well to the idea of me visiting Douglas Taylor by myself. "River View Heights? That's halfway to the capitol," she objected.

Getting out of the house felt to me like a bit of a reprieve from doing nothing other than freezing inside the house and I was looking forward to it. "There are some things that you can't do over a video chat. Talking to a lawyer about," I lowered my voice to a whisper, "killing people is one of them. It has to be done."

"I'm not staying here on my own with the kids if you're going to be over an hour away."

"Well you can't hang out at Doug's."

"I'll take the girls into town for breakfast. I'll wait in the car if I have to, but we're not staying here, home alone, with you gone for half the day." And that was how the family road trip came to be.

I couldn't believe how excited I was. I was positively giddy to be getting out of the house and away from here. Clear, blue skies was a tall order but I'd take the change of scenery. We could all use it. Raelene would drop me at Doug's ranch and take the kids out to breakfast in town while he and I discussed what an idiot I was.

The chances we would be stranded somewhere were low, but not impossible. We had no bug-out-bags but we did have camping gear. Short of an EMP that was bad enough to disable the cars (unlikely), I could not think of a single realistic scenario that would require us and our two children to hoof it out of town. A house fire or tornado was the biggest sudden danger that might deprive us of a home meaning a change of clothes, some photocopied documents, and a cell phone charge would be of more use to us than a tent.

I figured that any disaster bad enough to put us out of the house would put us with my brother or in a hotel. Currently, if we got stuck due to flooding there would be no hotels but only god-awful Red Cross shelters. I'd rather sleep in the car. So to that end, I got blankets. The girls would each take their own "blankies" and I grabbed the two large, heavy wool ones we spread over the bed. After a second thought, I threw in two sleeping bags.

For warmth, the blankets and the car heater would work, but cooking might be an issue. I dug around the camping gear and found our ultralight Jetboil stove. *When was the last time we went backpacking, 2019?* It hadn't been recently. So heating and cooking was taken care of. For water, I'd use the half-opened case of bottles that were left over from the summer. Since the heat caused the plastic to leach into the water, giving it a chemical taste, I'd been using these for cooking.

Raelene would flip out if she knew we were using these. Though the leached amounts of acetaldehyde was too minimal to cause any harm, she had us all drinking out of stainless steel bottles filled from an ungodly expensive under-sink filtration system. A package of Crystal Lite singles added to the girls' water would keep them from mentioning any off-taste to Mommy.

With the generator shut down and locked in the garage, I put the empty gas cans in the cargo area too. These I wrapped in trash bags to help keep any lingering fumes down. I should have strapped them to the roof but empty plastic cans were pretty light and made too obvious a target for some brave, but dangerous fool who might think they were full. *Low profile, in a $120,000 vehicle. Yeah right.*

I understood why people drove large pickups now despite having no need for them in a suburb. Hauling stuff on the weekend meant not having to rent one from Home Depot. The gas cans wouldn't be inside the passenger compartment reeking. The high-end truck packages were nearly as luxurious as the Lexus without standing out too much. Even a Ford F-250 Limited pickup with all the trimmings didn't shout affluence the same way this thing did. Only a Mercedes could have been worse. If we went for an SUV, it would be a Suburban or a Tahoe next time, for sure.

I followed the state highway out of town. It was one of those old-farm-to-market roads graded in the thirties and expanded as the population grew. In the direction we were headed, it led nowhere in particular, finally dwindling down to two lanes from four outside city limits. We were surrounded by hay fields that would be eventually built up if suburban expansion continued, which I doubted given the recession. Until very recently, I was never one to believe the Zerohedge-types that the economy was going to collapse.

The fastest route to River View was a toss-up between the Interstate, for speed, and the way I was going, for straight-line distance. Without traffic or cops running radar to worry about, the scenic route would washout about even, plus we could avoid the city, which I was eager to do because of recent events. The caveat was, with the ferry crossing closed, we would overshoot the city and have to go further south of it to reach the Interstate to cross the channel.

We passed over a slough that was once a barge canal from the 19th century. This marked the transition from the higher island land to the even lower floodplain country. The crops here were mostly rice and other plants adapted to high water tables.

"Hey, that's where we took the family photos," Raelene said. She pointed at a field of sunflowers behind a fruit stand. That was a happy day. The girls entertained themselves by playing hide-and-seek in the thick rows of flowers. Now all of the tall stalks had broken or fallen over under the wind and snow, leaving a tangled, faded green mess. No matter what happened to that field, fallow or flooded, we would remember it as it was that warm, sunny summer afternoon.

Raelene slipped her hand into mine. I only needed one to drive with. Why did this woman marry me? She was the kind of woman that a man might date once in a lifetime and many never at all. She was model hot, extremely smart, and at the same time a traditional wife. I honestly never thought she would take my last name. Of all the guys she could have settled for, she picked me, a guy in his late-thirties whose gut showed the signs of a desk job and used a beard to conceal the bulge of fat beneath his chin.

There were so many times my self-doubt nearly caused me to shoot myself in the foot. I figured that she was the best I had done in ten years so I might as well take advantage of her foolishness to date somebody like me. Once, after we slept together she called me "sexy." I got mad, stood up, and told her not to kid around like that.

"You think this is 'sexy'?" I said, jiggling my chubby belly. "When I lose 50 pounds, then you can call me sexy." Did she understand how hard it was for me to keep from putting on weight? "If you're gonna tease me like that, go home."

Men too suffered from negative body image.

She got out of bed and put her arms around me. "I don't want to go home. I wasn't teasing you." Raelene looked at me with wide, sad eyes. "I love you." A past girlfriend used those three words as a manipulative tool. A younger version of me would have thrown Raelene out for saying something like that in this moment, but I believed her.

Silently, she took me by the hand and led me into the bathroom. In the mirror, I saw a pudgy, soft guy who got uncomfortable when he wore his pants around his natural waist. Tucking my shirt in without a coat on made me self-conscious. Raelene pinched my arms. "Your arms are huge."

"That's fat."

"Flex." I did and definition showed. Okay, so what if I did do fifteen minutes of weights every morning? I did that to keep my arms strong so I wouldn't develop carpal tunnel or something. She went over every part of my body, describing what she liked and why. For whatever reason, she liked guys who were large-statured and to her body fat, as long as it wasn't excessive, wasn't an issue. "You're my big, strong bear." She compared it to guys who liked curvy women.

"They don't have porn categories for BBM, big beautiful men," I said.

"I think they do in gay porn," she said, "but I think they call it something else." In spite of myself, I laughed. She turned to me and looked me in the eyes. "I've dated shredded guys before. My last boyfriend, before I moved here, was one of those sub-ten percent body fat bodybuilders. He was so self-obsessed and narcissistic. Plus it's not comfortable having sex with those guys. It's like fucking a rock."

The great part of dating a woman with an IQ in the

'gifted' range was she could articulate why she liked dudes with meat on their bones. Like how men tended to subconsciously find curvy women to be more fertile, dad-bod was hyper-masculine. Size projected strength and the excess adipose tissue meant that we likely had outside interests beyond ourselves, unlike her gym-rat meathead ex-boyfriend. I only understood it intellectually but then again, as a straight male, I'd never understand what women saw in us.

I felt good hearing what she had to say. Not only did she truly compliment me, but she brought the receipts. That evening we laid the groundwork for overcoming difficulties in our relationship. Communication was key. The two of us had to dig deep to understand what caused us to become upset and explore the roots of the problem. Talk it out until the answer was found. In reflection, the level of wisdom and emotional maturity required was huge.

As the memory faded, I squeezed her hand. "What are you thinking about?" she asked.

"The first time you said, 'I love you.'"

She flashed her real smile, the one that was hard to capture in a photo without telling a joke. "It's still true." She started to say something more, but instead let go of my hand. "Look out!"

My eyes instantly went back to the road. An idiot on a dirt bike had wandered across the double-yellow into our lane because he was looking down at his cell phone. I hit the brakes and swerved over until the tires were on the fog line. Reya grunted as she was pressed into her locked seatbelt, then tossed back against the seat.

"Sorry," I said to the ladies as we passed the idiot. He briefly looked up and maneuvered his bike just barely far enough over to avoid the sideview mirror. "Dumbass."

"Ooh, Daddy said a bad word."

Remy laughed at her sister and then attempted to approximate the new word she heard. "Ross, watch your language in front of the kids," Raelene admonished. "I don't want a two year-old who knows how to swear."

"I coulda said 'asshole' and then we'd really be fucked," I mumbled to myself. Raelene gave me that special disgusted look of disapproval wives have. She knew I said something inappropriate but it was too quiet for anyone to hear. Without being able to prove what I said, all she could do was be annoyed. *A perfect moment ruined by a dumbass—an asshole—on a dirt bike.*

I might have been half-a-standard deviation less smart than my wife, but something was out of place with that guy. It was mid-day and in the 40s, not dirt biking weather and that guy was underdressed in what looked like a hoody. Even with something on underneath, at speed he had to be freezing. And where did he come from? The people who lived out here could be counted on the digits of an amputee.

After another mile we began to see flooded fields. Water in the rice paddies was not unusual but all we were seeing was sheets of water with equipment poking out of it. Only berms and lines of electric poles broke the still waters. Something down here wasn't right. "Probably letting this area flood to relieve the pressure upstream," I thought aloud.

"Detour ahead," Raelene, my copilot, announced. As wonderful as she was she still did the wife stuff like that. There was no missing the digital message board or the barricade across the road. A hundred yards beyond it, the highway descended into the water. *So much for Plan A.* The detour would be a backtrack through the hamlet of Hunter's Landing and to the Interstate. We'd have to go east, away from our destination, for about twenty minutes.

Hunter's Landing was one of those small rural communities that was the backbone of America up until a century ago. Now it was a place that catered to the road trippers, boaters, and weekend tourists looking for a BnB outside the city. It was a great place for a date. Today it looked like it had been totally abandoned.

Businesses were boarded up. Doors had sandbags lining them. A few homes were already surrounded by low walls of sandbags. In the parking lot of the fire station, two groups were filling the bags from a huge pile of sand and throwing them into pickups. Dirt bikes, motorcycles, and four-wheelers zoomed all around us. Where were all these people coming from and why were they riding exposed like that in the cold? Many wore thick jackets, others only long sleeves. A solitary deputy sat inside his SUV and watched a bunch of them roll right through a stop sign.

"Isn't he going to do something?" Raelene asked.

"What? He might get one, maybe two to stop. Then what?"

"What are they doing anyway? They don't look like they're from around here and I don't think they're helping with the flood preparations."

"Dunno." I turned out through a gap in the traffic and drove towards the bridge. This was the only crossing on this part of the island that wasn't flooded. The traffic was thicker near the center of town. Most of it was turning north, to follow the eastern highway up towards West River City. I stopped at the traffic light, which meant, inexplicably, the electricity here was working. I looked right, straight down the bridge over the river and was astonished at what I saw.

A dozen or so dirt-bikers were riding in circles, doing wheelies and other stunts, in both lanes of the bridge. Behind them, a pickup truck straddling the center line followed with its hazard lights on. Past that, there was a huge convoy of more ATVs, dirt bikes, and cars pouring across. Rap music blared from stereos, sending a rhythmic thumping down the corridor of iron girders. "What is this?" I asked.

A siren chirped behind us. A deputy came up around us with his lights on and turned down the bridge. He made a funky turn a few car lengths over the abutment and parked sideways to obstruct the lanes. Seeing this, the vanguard on dirt bikes hit the gas and roared past the Ford. The lead vehicles in the automotive wave stopped as did most of the bikes and ATVs. Those who could get by did. Others were now approaching the deputy and yelling at him.

"I don't like this," Raelene said.

"Neither do I." I looked in the mirror. The girls were still deeply entranced with the iPad, poking away at some kind of game together.

The biker and four-wheeler traffic that had gone into town was turning around now. They zoomed past us and seemed to be getting thicker. *This is not good.* A confrontation was brewing and we were in the middle of it. A helmet-less dirt bike rider stopped next to the car. My hand unconsciously reach down to brush my holstered pistol in reassurance. Reya looked up. "Hey, a motorcycle," she said.

"Reya, put your head down. Don't wave," I said. I didn't want to attract the rider's attention which was focused elsewhere. Luckily, he was watching for a break and pulled out, flying across the intersection going north.

Two pickup trucks came up the dirt alley between the businesses on our left. Several farm boys with rifles got out. "I don't want to be here," Raelene said.

"We're gone," I replied. This had all the hallmarks of something very nasty about to happen. I did not want the girls, or my wife to see it, nor be a witness myself. With no one behind us, I shifted into reverse and backed up almost half a block before I could safely turn around. *Damn, now we have to backtrack through the city.* I heard a loud pop behind us. I didn't even look but reflexively turned the radio on, then up. The sounds of Top 40 filled the car.

"Ross, where are you going?" Raelene asked loudly. Our turn went by us on the right, but I was going south, the opposite direction from home.

"I don't know. Away."

She turned off the radio. The popping noises were pretty loud even half a mile away inside our luxury vehicle; however the girls didn't notice. *Where am I going?* Off the x and away from the danger, but where? I didn't fail to turn left out of panic as my copilot probably assumed. *Ignore the fear, think!*

Okay, I knew where I wanted to go now. The tri-city cross-state trail went through here, following the old right-of-way of the Fremont Central. There was a railroad bridge across the river that was turned into a bike path at the south end of town across from the old depot. The old depot was the community center for the town park now. It was rented out for some church function we went to once before Remy was born.

"What are we doing here?" Raelene asked when we

reached the park.

"Hold on," was my reply. The sign which read 'Authorized Vehicles Only' held no authority as I drove into the park. One bit of self-critique was I took the curb too hard. All of us bounced.

Raelene said the s-word, Reya dropped the iPad, and Remy said something like "Daddy hurt."

"You can't drive here," my wife protested as we drove into the park. "Look at what you're doing to the grass." The Lexus was leaving tire tracks about four inches deep in the sodden ground. I was personally more worried about getting mired than I was about what the county Parks and Rec landscapers would have to deal with.

"Remember when I told you that if there was an active shooter at the mall, you should take the employee-only doors into the back corridors and go out the delivery and trash doors? That's what I'm doing here." She instantly understood.

The bridge itself was protected by a single bollard locked with a cheap padlock. There were several ways I could break the lock off. I got out and dug into the cargo area. I found a claw hammer. What it was doing there I didn't know but it was handy. "Ross, what are you doing?"

"Rae, you know what that sound is?" The gunfire was echoing all across town in the cold air. "I'm getting us across the river." My voice cracked a bit like I was in one of those dreams where you're struggling to yell.

"What sound Daddy?" Reya asked. "It sounds like fireworks."

I didn't hear what Raelene said to her. The claw of the hammer went between the shackle of the lock. I used the top of the head as the fulcrum and pulled backwards. Without too much effort the shackle broke free and I tossed the lock aside. The bollard wasn't heavy and I lifted it off its short pedestal and threw it on the grass. My wife was done protesting. She fully understood what I was doing and why now. That didn't stop her from asking "Did you see the weight limit sign? How much does this car weigh?"

"Babe, this thing weighs two tons, tops. Besides, this bridge was built to have fully loaded trains cross it."

It sounded a lot more reassuring to say when we weren't twenty feet high over the center of a river. I was old enough to remember watching the news coverage of the 1989 Loma Prieta earthquake and seeing the cars hanging off the collapsed Bay Bridge. I knew the bridge itself might easily bear our weight but it was the decking that would snap, sending us plunging through, unless we got hung up on a girder. It was not a comfortable crossing and hearing twenty questions coming from the back seat about why Daddy was driving here wasn't helping.

We reached the other side safely and the padlock here snapped just as easily as its counterpart. I stayed on the bike path for a few miles until we reached a farm road and followed that. Raelene took the iPad away from the girls. I was so thankful that Reya was too naïve and confused to understand what was going on and that Remy was two. "Movie time. How about *The Little Mermaid*?"

"Yes, yes, yes!" Reya said.

"Stop bouncing in your seat!"

Reya didn't listen. I had to smile at her excitement and Remy's toddler-speak trying to say "Ariel." What a weird juxtaposition it was to be speeding away from a shootout after an action-hero escape and find your daughters' innocence to be adorable. This is why Dad had to keep his cool; if he freaked out and started yelling the kids would get scared. By playing it cool, the girls just thought the adults were being weird.

Once the movie started, Raelene looked at me. "What?" I inquired. She was staring with a mixture of adoration and fading fear. Once more, her valiant, bear had come to the rescue. "Why are you looking at me that way?"

"That was so brave."

"Rae, please not now. I don't want to think about what just happened until we're all some where safe." My arms were trembling slightly on the steering wheel. *The shakes.*

"Okay, sorry." She saw my hands and rubbed my shoulder. Irritated, I shrugged her away. Tenderness in the midst of danger was not what I needed right now. It was confusing to me. Didn't she understand that until we were on the Interstate the bikes and quads could be back at any time? Those hoodlums would scatter like rats off a sinking ship in every direction.

My heart was pounding and my chest grew tight again. I tried something I saw on YouTube which was to take two breaths through my nose. The first was a full deep breath without exhaling and the second a shorter one. I let it all out and did it again. The deliberate double breathing mechanism had the same effect as when a sobbing child did that double-gasp thing involuntarily. It activates the body's parasympathetic nervous system to stimulate the body's relaxation mechanism and helps stop hyperventilation.

By the time we got on the freeway, I recovered. *Didn't feel the urge to vomit or soil myself, that's an improvement.* I supposed it was also some sort of major achievement that one could get his family away from ground zero of a massacre alive with the only emotional outcome being excitement for a Disney flick and an annoyed wife.

Attorney-Client Privilege

We finally made it across the river into River View Heights. It was a distinct realm a world apart from the River City metro. The traffic flowed moderately. The bridge deposited us directly in the heart of downtown, where many businesses were doing brisk trade. Outside the restaurants, lines formed defying the chill of the October day, resembling a Sunday morning. My attention was snagged by the functioning signal lights, a luxury they possessed here. I hadn't thought of them that way before.

The city housed only thirty thousand souls if one accounted for the unincorporated outskirts. It served as a quasi-resort for those of us confined to the inland reaches of the state. Raelene and I used it as a weekend getaway more than on the rare occasion we could get someone to watch the girls. The economy was primarily retail and service-based with any industrial activity limited to the construction and boating sectors. What was once a port and agricultural town had become a haven for retirees and the work-from-home crowd.

Nothing at all seemed amiss. A blessing from Hunter's Landing. I counted at least two patrol cars parked in the main business area. Another pair of cops walked a foot beat up the sidewalk, turning in at the arcade. That was a reassuring sign. "We moved to the wrong town," I said.

"Their hospital sucks," Raelene said. All the money in the world couldn't make a travel nurse go full-time in a toxic work environment.

"Mommy said a bad word," Reya said. I thought she hadn't been paying attention.

"Watch your movie honey," she replied. "Ross, you didn't like the drive to the airport from here."

"Well, I was wrong. Way wrong."

"I'm starting to agree with you and with your brother," Raelene chuckled.

Ever since we got married my brother had been urging us to "get out of the city." When we bought the house on the island, he went on this five minute diatribe of how West River City was still River City and being one bridge away from a one-million person population center was *not* out of the city. Back then, I still had to go into our satellite office. Pre-COVID, "work from home" meant you weren't coming on Friday.

"So where does this Doug live? Up by the golf course?"

"In the ranchettes just outside of town." A large dairy farm sold its land decades back and the developer subdivided it into four-acre lots. It was horse country set in the gently rolling hills that marked the start of the hill country. We last looked at this area in late 2020 and decided the prices were too steep for us. As great as our salaries were, we couldn't compete with California retirees walking in with half-a-million in cash.

Raelene commented that she thought a lawyer who wanted out of the city would be in a gated community. I replied that a place like that might just be offering an illusion of security. "Being out here, even if it is town-adjacent, is another level of security. Look at the eucalyptus tree right there. Knock that across the road and no cars are getting through."

"I guess you're right, but wouldn't you need some barbed wire or something over the top to keep people from just climbing it?"

"Who are you?" I said with a laugh. "Next you'll want a

militia to guard it."

She laughed too, then got somber. "Like in Hunter's Landing. I wonder how that worked out."

"Probably best not to know right now."

Doug's home sat behind two low hills with the driveway threading through the gap. The perimeter fence was five-strand barbed wire about waist high, fairly typical for cattle country. It didn't stand out here. His gate was palisade-style and flanked by another section of the same type on each side of the driveway. The base of each was set in concrete with a recovered brick facia two feet high. Each end of the gate itself was braced by a decorated steel I-beam for ramming protection.

I pulled up to the call box and rang. There was an antenna for a remote control mounted on a pole with a camera behind the gate. Another camera was inside the call box and a third was at license-plate height. There was no hiding from the camera nor could an ambusher hide behind the gateposts with the fence's open design.

A face looking into a cell phone appeared on the call box screen. "Hi Ross, I'll buzz you in," Doug said. The house appeared not far up the drive. The twin rises made it seem like the house was further in than it was.

"I don't know how long I'll be. Probably an hour or two. Why don't you get the girls some breakfast and do a little shopping? I'll text you when we're about done."

"I don't want to be alone," Raelene said.

"I'll leave you the gun."

"That doesn't change anything."

I put my hand on her shoulder. "Raelene, you'll be fine. Things are safe here. You'll feel better once you've eaten and done normal things. You really don't want to wait at the bottom of the driveway in the car listening to a Jamaican crab sing 'Under the Sea,' do you?"

Yes, I was pressuring her. I wasn't going to ask Doug to make his wife entertain my wife and kids, nor embarrass myself by having them wait in the car in front of his house. Besides, it would do them all some good to get out and forget about the freezing nightmare back home.

"Okay," Raelene acquiesced. We got out and she walked around to the driver's side. "Gun?"

"Right." The holster I was using just clipped over the belt, so I loosened the buckle, lifted the clasp, and pulled the holster free. Raelene pulled up her sweater and tucked the pistol directly over her appendix. She did it so naturally it almost seemed sexual. I felt slightly jealous that she could do that with her flat abdomen. Some feminist literature professor would probably say it was entirely expected for a man to find a woman putting a gun in her pants to be arousing.

Doug met me as Raelene drove away. "Your family was welcome to wait here."

I shrugged. "I really didn't want them overhearing anything I said."

"I get it."

"By the way, can she get out?"

"Yep. There's a magnetic sensor out there." He led me into his study that looked out over a small grove of oak trees at the bottom of his sloping property. In the distance ran the river. I'm sure it was a lovely sight on a clear day. "Long before I worked for Simon I was w public defender down in Springfield. Anything we discuss is privileged, so don't hold back." And with that we launched into it.

Doug listened patiently to my verbal diarrhea. It seemed more like a therapy session than giving a legal account of a self-defense shooting. The words just flowed, like they did in front of the officers. I told him about how afraid I was for my family, the internal mental recriminations, and how I felt afterwards. He scribbled notes the whole time. Once that was done, he watched the security camera video several times before asking me questions.

But we weren't done yet. We had the police interview recording to listen to, twice, once for Doug to listen and the next so he could ask me questions. It was painful listening to my quavering voice, falsetto with adrenaline, recount to the officers what happened. Finally, after it was all over, Doug jotted down a few notes, and thought for a few minutes.

"Consider yourself lucky that your wife had the presence of mind to record the interview. I wish she wasn't so shaken up herself that she could shut you up, but here we are." I didn't even notice that Raelene nonchalantly switched on the recording app and left her phone out on the table. "If she hadn't done that, I'd be wondering for a few months what exactly you said waiting to get a copy through DA discovery." The police did not release their interview recordings, even to defense attorneys, and certainly not the day after the incident.

"All in all, not bad," Doug said. "Your fear comes across clearly in the tapes."

"I babbled."

"Yes, but you babbled in a good way. You sounded like a man who was truly in fear for his life. Going on and on about your family was something a proper defense attorney would have recommended." Doug was trying to be reassuring but I didn't feel much better. "There's nothing incriminating in this interview. 'No, I'm so glad I killed those bastards,' or anything like that. That's a normal feeling to have but not the kind of thing you want a prosecutor to have questions about."

"So?"

"So what? Do I think you'll be indicted?" He paused unnecessarily. "No. Armed nighttime burglary, with the intent to commit rape and probably murder. Not even the most progressive George Soros prosecutor and blue-pilled liberal jury in the state could make this case against you."

I breathed a huge sigh of relief. "Thank God." Talking to the police, even though there was zero way I was legally or morally guilty of anything had been a poor decision. Doug explained that a lot of well-meaning people talked themselves into trouble by offering too much detail or making inappropriate 'off the cuff' statements. Those of marginal innocence or who had mitigating factors in their favor often shot themselves in the foot by saying the wrong things or by saying the right things in the wrong way.

Unscrupulous cops could twist these little statements into criminal charges if the subject rubbed them the wrong way. Iffy cases that might be politically sensitive have been turned into show trials by DAs who wanted to show how good a comrade they might be or to try and placate the leftist lynch mobs. Doug told me about a Lyft driver in Austin, Texas, who had an Antifa goon point an AK-47 at him after unintentionally coming up on a roadblock in the middle of a so-called "peaceful" protest.

The driver, Daniel Perry, was railroaded by a radical prosecutor and put in front of a jury from a deep blue city that was guaranteed to convict. Exculpatory evidence was withheld and 'off the cuff' text messages were deliberately misconstrued to push the murder charge. Perry initially cooperated and spoke freely to the police, who also felt he acted in lawful self-defense, because he thought he was the good guy in all of this. Not in Moscow-on-the-Colorado, as Austin had become with the influx of tech jobs and Californians.

In this case, the far-left prosecutor probably—no one can say for sure—was sending a message that violence against the communist revolutionaries wouldn't be tolerated. Comply or else you'll catch a murder charge. "Do I need to go on about George Zimmerman, that cop in Minnesota, or Kyle Rittenhouse?"

I shook my head. "I understand. I'm stupid."

"No, you aren't stupid but you did a stupid thing. Just be thankful you live on this side of the river." Our DA might be a registered Democrat but he was a levelheaded, old school prosecutor who wouldn't cave to any political pressure. It also helped that the guys I shot were white or Hispanic—I wasn't sure—and I was inside the house. Nobody could get upset about a father who didn't even go outside looking for trouble.

He went on to add that it would help that the detective was probably tired and overwhelmed with the homicide cases going on recently. This case, as clear an incident of self-defense as there was, would get the least attention. Because it would be so low-priority, the case would languish well into next year before it was finally dispositioned.

"The cops will refer the case to the DA's office, who may send it to the grand jury. The practice in the last decade has been to refer every case but given the overwhelming evidence in your favor there is no way short of alien brain parasites you'll be indicted." Doug explained that in Fremont, if the grand jury declined to indict citing self-defense, the case was dismissed with prejudice, meaning I could not be charged for the incident in the future.

The grand jury in this case wasn't a bad thing. In most states even a clean shoot theoretically had the lifetime possibility of being turned into a murder charge upon new evidence as murder didn't have a statute of limitations. Several states that had fallen under solid progressive control were using this as a Sword of Damocles tactic in politically sensitive cases. A solid DA who refused to file charges could be overruled in the next election cycle should they lose to a radical candidate. The only way to ensure no conviction in those places was to stand trial and be acquitted; freedom on the flip of a coin.

Doug said I did do some smart things. First was using the shotgun instead of the pistol. While a handgun may have been more maneuverable in close quarters, it wasn't seized as evidence. I could tote the handgun around if I needed to, like today. A shotgun wasn't so handy. Even with open carry being legal, carrying around long-guns made people uncomfortable. Seeing the neighborhood watch folks with their slung AR-15s and shotguns certainly gave me a moment's pause.

Second was I didn't "breach my perimeter" by going outside the house or into the garage to investigate (initially). He told me stories about guys stepping outside and being ambushed or killed when they would have been fine had they not gone out. The cameras with their panoramic coverage of the property and inside the garage was another brilliant stroke. Not only did it capture valuable evidence to backup my story but it allowed me to see what was going on without leaving safety.

However, if the side and inner garage doors had been reinforced with stronger frames and high-quality deadlocks, they never would have made it inside. Stopping the casual burglar was not hard to do with just a locked door, but determined killers was tougher. Doug suggested adding some solar/battery motion lights and perhaps indicator lights to imply that the cameras were operating. Had the power been on, the burglars would have likely assumed that cameras were on and stayed away. Instead, they thought they would be disabled if the mains electricity was out.

I sent Raelene a text that we were about finished up and she replied instantly that she was on her way. *Must be on her phone.*

"I'm going to make some calls to a few friends in the city for you," Doug said. "All good, high-class defense attorneys."

"Billionaire murders his wife, those kind of attorneys."

Doug grinned. He knew what high profile lawyer I was referring to. "Yes, he's one of my friends, but I have another pair in mind that are probably better suited to something like this." He stood up, opened up his globe, which was a small bar, and poured two glasses of whiskey.

"My wife likes bourbon," I said. Despite being born in Maryland, Raelene had southern blood in her. When I did drink it, it was always with water and ice, never neat, but Doug didn't give it to me for sipping. I knocked the glass back. I managed not to grimace at the medicinal taste.

"Will you be staying in the city?"

"In the long term, I doubt it. This week has been one hell of a wake-up-call. We seriously considered Red Rock after COVID, but with the airlines cutting regional flights I was concerned about the two-hour drive to the airport."

"And how many times have you flown anywhere for business since then?"

"Exactly twice a year," I said. "Funny how we adapted to remote work when pushed into it."

"If you do move, Simon will probably be willing to send a jet to you in Red Rock if he needs you that badly."

"I'm not that valuable anymore. I'm just the coach now, not the star quarterback."

Doug finished his glass and walked me back to the front door. As we got to the foyer I noticed that there were two sets of doors; the second windowless pair folded back against the portico walls. He saw me looking at them. Usually this kind of setup was found in houses in far northern climates to separate the interior from the winter chill.

"Good eye. Both doors are bulletproof but these are in case the front door is breached. Should law and order break down, well locally, no insult intended to you up there in the city, we can seal off the front door."

"Like something out of Rhodesia or South Africa."

"Right. We've got something similar in the bedroom wing. Say someone gets a package, but the deliveryman is really a robber. Well, with the inner doors closed he can't get into the house." The back doors on the house, sliding glass, were all covered by tough rolling shutters with their housings concealed in the soffits. Our back door had a cheaper version that rolled up into an ugly box. Doug's house was much more than it appeared to be.

Powder Keg in the Restaurant

The girls were dozing in the back seat when I left Doug's and got into the car. The Benadryl from last night was still in their systems or something. "So how'd it go?" Raelene asked flatly.

"Not bad. He told me I wasn't a total idiot. I said all the right things to the cops and nothing that *should* get me indicted. Good thing we bought on the right side of the river." I went through the play-by-play of Doug's assessment as she drove us back into town oblivious to the fact she was still upset I left her alone with the kids and the car.

A few moments passed and I realize she wasn't paying attention. Her worries about me being put on trial relieved, she tuned out. When she got quiet, she was mad. I shut up. The only leverage I had was to let her become uncomfortable in the awkward silence. She would impute her emotions and behavior onto me, assuming I was also upset, so she would feel forced to say something to break the ice. If I responded reasonably, so would she until she slowly normalized. This was a much better way than the always-ineffective *What's wrong?/Nothing* dialectic.

As we entered town, I exaggerated a lean forward to look at the dash. This was a ploy to solicit her to say something. The fuel gauge was full and I could smell the fumes coming from the jerry cans in the back.

"I went to the gas station," Raelene said.

It's working. "Oh, thanks babe."

"I filled up the gas cans and wrapped them in the bags too. Doesn't help with the smell though."

"Nope," I said pleasantly, as if nothing was awkward

between us.

She was silent for half a minute more. "The girls fell asleep after the candy store so I didn't have a chance to feed them. Do you think we should get something to eat now before we leave?" This was Raelene speak for *I'm hungry*, the same way *Can I try some of your burger?* actually meant *I'm going to eat half of it.*

"That's a good idea. I'm already tired of Foil Pouch." This made her laugh. *Score one for jerkass husband. I'm outta the doghouse now.* "Will the girls be cranky if we wake them up now?"

"No, they should be coming out of it soon."

"Were you able to do any shopping?"

"Nope," she said, popping the 'p.' "Both the grocery store and Walmart are closed except for pickup. They're using online orders to prevent out-of-towners like us from stripping the places bare."

"Wow."

"Yeah. Smart of them but there were a lot of angry people. Cops were standing by at each store."

"Like fights? Looters?" I asked.

"No, just there to keep the peace or whatever. A deterrent. Armed security guards too. It looked like all those videos of security contractors in Iraq."

"I'm surprised they even had food at all, what with the governor commandeering rural deliveries too."

"A woman I was talking to outside the candy shop said the selection is really limited. Some staples and other totally random things. Like they might have one-pound bags of flour and some yeast, but since so few people know how to bake anymore, the deliveries are all weighted towards packaged sandwich loafs and cinnamon rolls. Unusual things are being sent as well. Like there's no limit on how many condiments you can buy so one day a whole pallet of ketchup might arrive."

"Smart money is buying the condiments and bartering those. Trade that ketchup for something you can use. I guess that they are taking and sending whatever they can get whenever it becomes available. Better to have something in stock than nothing."

"I love cinnamon rolls."

"Then I know where we're eating." She looked over at me and smiled. Flourish & Flavors was a nice small-town diner a block off Main Street and one of her favorite places. It wasn't as busy as I expected, perhaps because it was afternoon now. The girls were indeed at the end of their sleep cycle and woke up easily enough with the promise of pancakes. We had pancakes at home but everyone knows pancakes that are made out-of-sight taste better, plus for kids the restaurant made them in dinosaur shapes. "What were you doing at the candy shop?" I asked when we parked.

Raelene looked up from unbuckling Remy. "It was open and I thought I'd treat the girls."

"Mommy said we had to wait until we got home to eat our candy," Reya said crossly.

I tousled her hair. "Self-discipline is a good thing." At nearly eight, she did not agree.

"They pitched a fit," Raelene said. She looked good with our baby balanced on her hip and I told her so.

"Thanks." She smiled. It wasn't her makeup or her outfit, cleaned up as nicely as possible with a sponge bath in case she were to meet Doug, that I was complimenting. Yes, she looked more beautiful than she had in days, but she knew the flattering remark was more than just superficial.

Getting a seat inside the restaurant was easy after the lunch rush had passed. "Cash only, is that okay?" the waitress said.

"Not a problem." I noticed the dining room was chilly inside but they had plenty of Diet Coke. "That has aspartame in it, you know," Raelene said with an ironic grin. I picked up my glass and sipped it while staring her directly in the eye. She was screwing with me and I knew it.

The waitress came over and asked if we were ready to order. Without breaking my stare I asked, "Can you bring my wife a glass of Coke, the real kind?" Raelene started laughing. I knew her weaknesses.

Once the waitress came back for the order, she might as well have already scribbled down dinosaur pancakes for the girls. Reya was getting old enough to order adult meals but the fun shapes and colors were still more irresistible than an omelet. "Just so you folks know," the waitress said, "we only have scrambled egg dishes right now. No fried eggs."

"Powdered?" Raelene asked.

"No, liquid whole. Usually we crack and scramble our own, but that's all we can get at the moment." We could live without organic, regionally sourced brown eggs but not being able to get such a simple staple surely was another sign that things were drastically wrong. I had to modify my usual order.

Raelene collected the menus, just sheets of paper like during COVID, and handed them back to the waitress. They weren't for hygienic reasons but because the rapid price fluctuations made it impossible to keep changing the prices on the "good" menus. The kids' menu was $17.99 and our adult plates were $25.99. We'd hit a hundred bucks before the tip. How could these other people afford it? I looked around and from the cars outside to the people's general appearance, they didn't stand out as folks who could afford a hundred dollars a meal.

We had it really good with great jobs whose rates of pay kept up with inflation. Nursing had a labor crisis and my sector of IT was exploding. How were the people with retail jobs or mid-level clerical careers managing to keep it together? Credit cards?

"It's really good to see you order something different for once," Raelene said with a smirk.

"Oh yeah?"

"'Huevos rancheros, please,'" she said in a deep voice. "French toast this time, huh?"

"How are you supposed to have huevos rancheros with scrambled eggs?" The dish was made with lightly fried eggs so the yolk would run over the beans, tortillas, and salsa. "And why are you making fun of me for what I like here?"

"Because you take like five minutes to study the menu, sigh, and order the same thing all the time." She laughed. "If it wasn't for me, you'd still be eating TV dinners every night sitting in front of the TV watching *Star Trek* reruns. And yeah, I know you feed those to Reya when I work nights."

"How do you know I don't eat them?" I reached out and started to tickle her as a distraction.

She began giggling uncontrollably. "Oh yea? You eat Kid Cuisine?"

"Do you look through the trash when you get home?"

Raelene was still laughing. "No. Should I? You know Reya can't keep a secret."

I smiled at the carefree look on my wife's face. Heavens to Betsy, she was beautiful and all the more so when she found something funny. It could have been one of those moments to tuck away in the mind to cherish a joyous memory on a rainy day, but there was no chance to savor it. A shrill, loud voice rose over the general din of the diners from the host stand. "Whaddyou mean I can't use my card here? TV said we can use our cards at restaurants now."

I looked over to see a woman obviously from the city haranguing the young hostess. I could see the green card in her hand but already knew from the context the woman was talking about EBT. For years now, the cards could be used at any *participating* restaurant. This was implemented to supposedly ease the food desert problems in urban areas so residents without easy access to a grocery store could eat without having to travel too far. In reality this meant patronizing many fast food joints and the Internet rumor was that the program expansion was intended as a government bailout to the drive-thru industry. The state of emergency expanded this to any restaurant that could charge to the correct credit card merchant category code.

The woman was about my age, fat, and had four kids under high school age with her. Two older men and a woman, maybe in their twenties, stood outside the door. "We drove an hour down here and y'all ain't got no open stores and this is the only restaurant with no line. Ain't this some shit."

An older waitress, the sister of the owner I think, walked over. "Ma'am, I'm sorry, but our Internet is out and we are taking cash only. We can't process cards."

"That's bull. I saw on the TV that you supposed to be taking this shit." She slashed the card through the air like a knife.

The two men who had been waiting outside behind their party pushed through the kids and into the lobby. "Hey, what are you hasslin' my lady for?"

The older woman calmly explained. The adults in the group all made some dissatisfied noises and swore. They desultorily walked out, complaining loudly, and disappeared from view around the block. With the excitement over, the diners' eyes returned to their plates. The ordinary din of conversation and clinking of cutlery filled the air.

"Mommy, why was the woman so mad?" Reya asked with a puzzled look on her face.

"Nevermind her," Raelene said. "Some people get upset about anything."

Reya turned back to her coloring. I looked at my wife and made a sour face. How dare that woman cause a commotion and disturb my child? As they got older it was getting exponentially more difficult to shield them from the darker side of existence.

I zoned out for a moment watching my daughter intricately color in the shapes on the paper. She was turning out to be quite the little artist. If she had the skills to draw and if I could teach her to master some artistic software, she might have some winning career skills. A friend of mine had a daughter who designed on-screen graphics for multiple TV channels and made good money from it.

While I was lost planning my kid's future, Raelene struck up a conversation with a couple at a nearby table. "I tried that. I made an online order for pickup later this afternoon, but after I put in my address—who knows why it needed that—I got all sorts of error messages."

"That's because they aren't serving non-locals," the woman said. "If they accepted online orders from people outside the immediate area then all the city people would flock to the rural stores and clean them out."

"Not like they have much anyway," the husband said. "Our son is a truck driver. He's working but he refuses to go into any of the cities." The truckers were on an unofficial strike, mainly by declining to go into major cities with a lot of unrest due to the danger of hijacking. "You really think the free food distribution was just charity? No, it was a desperate attempt by the governor to forestall just this kind of thing. For the last three days he's been commandeering deliveries to rural areas to put the food centers together."

"Really?"

"Something's got to give," the husband said. "Supposedly rural folks are better prepared to weather something like this because of longer drives to get food. If it takes you half-an-hour each way to get groceries, you're more likely to shop more infrequently by buying in bulk. Every two weeks instead of every weekend. So, if it's let the rural people deal with shortages or have the cities turn into the Donner Party meets *The Purge*, it's a lot less risky to stick it to the provincials." The man shrugged.

The cold calculus made sense, but I wasn't seeing it doing much good. Whatever relief the government was sending to the cities was like peeing on a forest fire. I thought to ask the man what his experience was, to get a fuller picture of what was going on in the region, but we had an interruption.

Piercing, rapid-fire hollering caught my attention. Outside the front windows, a woman in her twenties careened up the sidewalk, her fury palpable, practically screaming profanities. Reya and Raelene turned to catch a glimpse, their heads swiveling in unison. The screamer wasn't alone; she was joined by two men and the younger woman from the original group with the EBT card issue. These disheveled figures, deprived of showers and clean clothes for days, banged through the door.

"How come you say my auntie can't eat here?" The hostess, caught off guard, mumbled a few words in total surprise and took a step back from her small stand. A black man sitting next to us rolled his eyes at the commotion, reaching for the Tabasco sauce.

"You gonna answer her or what, bitch?" one of the men bellowed, swinging at the mint tray, sending a spray of peppermints across the lobby across the room.

Barely eighteen, the hostess gasped, her surprise giving way to tears as she retreated into the back. "What's your problem, you racist bitch?" the screamer taunted, relishing in her distress.

Moments later, the older waitress from earlier emerged from the back, accompanied by a male cook wielding a spatula. "Excuse me, what's going on here?" she demanded, ready to confront the chaos.

"Raelene, we have to leave," I urged, sensing the impending danger.

"But the kids haven't finished eating, and we haven't paid the bill," Raelene protested.

Reya was turned around in her seat watching the confrontation with a mixture of childish curiosity and fear. The male intruder snarled, gripping a stool from the counter and hurling it into the pie display. "That's what's up!" he roared above the tinkle of broken glass, his anger escalating. The proprietress stood her ground, determined. "If this is how it's going to be, I'm calling the cops," she declared.

"The cops ain't gonna do shit," the screamer sneered, inching closer to the waitress.

I glanced at Raelene, no stranger to such turbulent scenes, having witnessed similar behavior during her time in Oakland and back east. It was much less common then. It was a much gentler time back then and such outbursts like this were aberrances. In today's fractured and polarized world, this sort of explosive turmoil had become the norm. The other diners, taken aback by the sudden chaos, exchanged worried glances. "Okay," she said. "We're going to the car." Already facing the door, I stood up and moved to the other side of the table, placing myself between the danger and my family. "Let's go girls."

Remy was too young, bless her heart, to care about anything except the strawberries she was trying to eat. The baby made a heart-wrenching wail as she was unceremoniously snatched away from her coveted treat. A swell of fury ignited within me; an indignant fire aimed at those callously ruining our lunch. Reya understood that something bad was happening without understanding what it was. She got out of her chair without looking away from the scene.

The group took a few steps across the lobby towards the waitress and cook. The cook took a stepped forward himself. Undeterred, he brandished his spatula. "So that's how it's gonna be, huh?" the male interloper growled. Uncertain of what to do, some diners whispered among themselves.

"Let's go," my wife whispered urgently to Reya, tugging

her towards the side door.

"Reya, follow your mother—now." She obeyed without protest.

One of the men noticed me standing my ground, his gaze meeting mine with hostility. "Why are you staring, fat ass?" he snarled across the room, moving toward a nearby table, anger radiating from him like a storm. Seizing a plate of food from someone's blue-haired *abuela*, he flung it against the wall, shattering porcelain and scattering vegetables across the room.

The screamer spat at the waitress. "That's it!" the cook declared, lunging toward the young woman. Instantly, she went berserk, her arms flailing in spasmodic arcs trying to clock both the cook and the waitress.

"Check please!" someone behind me called out.

A swift and powerful punch from the cook who had probably three hundred pounds on him knocked the screamer down, but not out. Two of the males instantly set on him, punching and kicking away. Up until now, my fellow patrons were watching in shocked disbelief, but with the violent assault underway, they began to yell and scream. The old Mexican ladies who had their meal interrupted now jumped up from the table. In doing so, one of them hit the third male who violently shoved the elderly woman down.

"Hey!" another man shouted. He was even less fit than I was and older too, but he was sick of this crap. The man's wife got up and scrambled behind the counter. This left the table undefended and between the third male and the man. Number three overturned the table, sending glasses and silverware flying in all directions. The cacophony of breaking glass and frightened screams filled the room. Everyone was standing up now.

Time to go, screw the bill, I thought. I turned around and saw Raelene already made it outside. Just before I slipped out myself, I saw one of the waitresses. "Hell of a day, huh?" I said with uncharacteristic humor. I slipped two fifties into her hands and went out the door. As I got outside, a siren was wailing in the distance. There were more out-of-towners running down the sidewalk towards the restaurant like hyenas to a fresh kill. "Car, now!" I ordered, scooping the crying Remy into my arms.

Thankfully the car wasn't far away, just a few spaces down the street. As we reached it, I heard two gunshots. "Reya, get in, fast as you can!" Raelene yelled. I handed Remy off to her and ran to my side. A short fusillade of return fire echoed.

I hit the start button, threw it into reverse, and backed straight down the street to the middle of the block. Now people were both running to and away from the disturbance. I knew the streets behind us dead-ended and we'd have to come past the restaurant, but there was an alley, so I took that. "What the hell?" Raelene asked.

"I don't know babe, I don't know."

"It's like *The Twilight Zone*. Has the whole country lost its mind?"

"That's about the size of it," I said as a police car, followed by another, flew down the street. I crossed the intersection and rolled through the stop sign back on to Main Street, ignoring the yell of a clueless pedestrian who must have not heard the shooting. The Japanese engine roared as I accelerated down the main drag for the bridge, ignoring some guy in a pickup who did the 'slow down' wave at me.

Two shootouts in one day! What in actual hell?

A minute later we were back across the river. "Mommy," Reya pleaded from the back seat. Raelene turned to see what the matter was.

"Ross, pull over. Reya's stuck." I did as asked. Reya, when I hit the gas, wasn't buckled in and slipped, getting wedged between the back seat and the back of the front passenger seat.

I took the crying, sticky Remy to try and comfort her while Raelene moved her seat forward to let Reya out. I bounced the baby on my knee and felt total and utter rage. Our first nice meal in days was interrupted by a bunch of no-class urban thugs who wanted to act rachet because they couldn't use their welfare credit card to eat with civilized human beings. So far we kept the girls from being directly exposed to the degeneracy and turmoil but it had become unavoidable. Was there no place safe anymore?

Two hours later, thanks to traffic being diverted due to all the flooding, we made it home the long way via the freeway. The kids got over the havoc, in a way. Remy cried herself to sleep and Reya put on headphones to watch her movies. Despite my anxious worries, nothing noticeably changed about the city or the river since we left.

The National Guard was still out. I'd been past their checkpoint so many times they probably knew my vehicle by sight. Back home, a new neighborhood watch stood guard at the entrance to our tract. Our "phase" of the development was separated by the other parts by a feeder road that hosted the schools and the park in the center of the tract.

The street we normally used was now guarded by three armed men. A pickup surrounded by cones lifted from a nearby construction site blocked off one half of the roadway. On the parking strip were two ten or twelve foot sections of pipe with metal spikes welded on it. A portable set of caltrops, I assumed.

"Daddy, are these bad guys?" Reya asked.

Great, now she's paying attention. "No sweetie, these are good guys, from our neighborhood."

"Like soldiers?"

"That's right. In our country, in bad times every man can be a soldier to protect us." I rolled down the window and stopped next to the man who seemed to be in charge. No one ordered us to stop or stood in the way, but they sure were staring at us rather intently. "Hi, I'm Ross. We live over on Canal Court."

"Where the shooting was?" the man asked rhetorically.

"Yes," I said without elaborating.

"Well then you know why we're here," he said. "We've formed a neighborhood watch group to keep a watch on our streets to keep looters and robbers from getting in. It isn't perfect, but its better than nothing." He explained they were having trouble getting volunteers. "We've called a meeting for the whole phase tomorrow morning at nine in the community association rec building. I hope you can join us."

"I'll try to be there." He thanked me and I drove through. "You wouldn't mind me joining, would you honey."

"No," Raelene said. "Just call Doug first before you volunteer for anything." She and I switched places when we got home so I could lift open the garage as she drove in. "Get those gas cans out of here and air the car out real good. I already have a headache. I hope the girls didn't lose any IQ points huffing that stuff."

"No, but if Remy grows up wanting to be a mechanic we'll know what caused it."

"Daddy?" Reya asked. "Are you going to be a solider?"

I never thought about that before. Legally speaking I was part of the militia, but that's not what she or I meant. Would I, and could I, throw on a plate carrier (if I had one) and stand on the front lines of suburban warfare if it came down to it?

D a y   5

Empty Pantry, Hollow Hope

This morning did not bring the expected positive change in temperatures, so I shivered in the garage as I took an inventory of our food. The tinnitus from discharging a shotgun multiple times in a confined space made it difficult to concentrate. 50 hours later and eeeeee seemed like it would be with me forever. Raelene and the Internet said it would fade after a week or two. The days would be interminable. Attempting to do math in my head was not easy and the calculations were kinda critical.

There's more misplaced peace-of-mind in these buckets than calories, I thought gloomily as I stared at what remained of our freeze dried food. At approximately 250 calories per serving and 25 servings per bucket that rounded to 6,000 calories, or three 2,000 FDA recommended average adult daily caloric requirements. If Raelene and I ate 2,000 calories each, between the girls they would consume the remaining 2,000.

That was one bucket per day un-supplemented by our pantry. With the "real" food we did have and me especially eating less than 2,000 calories, we were averaging a bucket and a half per-day. We were on our sixth bucket, out of twelve.

We had four more days left of food. Just visualizing what that meant froze me in the middle of the kitchen. Four days after today and we would not have any food. I failed my family. That is a thought that lands on you like a falling piano. A heavy, silencing weight descended upon me. It was not the burden of navigating the spot we found ourselves in I carried for the last few days; that I could bear. This was a crushing, wrenching despondency.

I could forgive myself if I was totally clueless and caught unprepared like the hundreds of thousands around me. Survivalism and prepping were always fringe ideas. Normal people didn't consider that the system of grocery stores and just-in-time deliveries that our civilization relies upon could stop. It hadn't since its inception over a century ago in most of the countries. The Great Depression was forgotten or unknown in most households.

But I, as St. Paul would have said, am without excuse. At my trial as a father, the empty buckets would be Exhibit A that I knew better. My brother had warned me, I had seen the signs, and I even took steps to have some level of resiliency and yet it was not enough. It was with emergency preparedness that my luck ran out and my penchant for doing the bare minimum necessary bit me in the ass. My exact attitude had been *Everything seems fine right now, why spend the money on something as kooky and far out as an implausible collapse?*

After COVID, I figured things could fall apart faster than I anticipated so I invested in the bare minimum and promptly assumed my bases were covered. From my academic career to my job, I had successfully half-assed everything I did and succeeded by luck. They say that intelligent but lazy people find the most efficient way to do things. My boss loved it when I did, except I was the one doing the work necessary on the backend to avoid a total shitstorm when the cut corner was the one that failed. Not having enough food and guns in a total disaster was not like some bodged software failing. I'd done that before and kept my job, the only consequence being 80 hour weeks and a small bonus that year.

Confronted with the monstrosity of what I had done, there was no longer anything to hide from myself. Whereas people like Grant saw prepping and carrying a gun as a way of exerting control over an uncertain world, I saw it as an admission of my fears. Intuitively I knew the economy wasn't strong, the nation fracturing, and the future dimming. No one wants to admit that their best years are gone and the ones ahead will be worse; definitely not a father with young kids.

Following my brother's example would be admitting my inmost fears were correct. I had plans. I'd retire early by fifty, sell this place and buy a big house with land on the poshest of country clubs. I'd buy new a Rolex instead of Casio. The girls would go to the best private schools and colleges. Raelene and I would travel the world in style. All of that was chaff before the wind now and perhaps their lives too. If the United States had widespread disasters like this one simultaneously as we fell into an economic depression while a literal communist revolution was starting, maybe the preppers were right about World War III or Mad Max.

"Daddy, I don't want to eat anymore oatmeal, I want my pancakes from yesterday," Reya said with disgust. She jabbed her spoon into the bowl, crossed her arms, and frowned defiantly.

"There is no pancake mix in this tub. Maybe tomorrow."

"No, today!"

Remy imitated her sister and echoed in toddler-speak "Today!"

"Reya, eat your oatmeal and behave. You are setting an example for your sister," I said through my teeth.

"No." She pushed her bowl away and looked off to the side, nose up in the air, like some twenty-year old Instagram princess sending back her dinner. Where did she learn that?

It was Remy's attempt at doing likewise that set me off. "Fine." I seized Reya's bowl. "Then you get NO OATMEAL!" I roared before throwing it across the room. It was made of plastic so the bowl bounced off in a flying mess, leaving a patch porridge that clung and oozed down the dining room wall. Reya stared in silence initially while Remy burst into tears, then they both began howling.

"Ross! What did you do?" Raelene called out. Her feet pounded on the stair treads.

"They wouldn't eat their oatmeal! Well guess what, maybe there won't be any goddamn oatmeal!"

Screw this. I stormed out the front door, slamming it behind me so hard the wall rattled. *Let her real father feed her, how about that? If Raelene wants to get pissed off at me she can consider how she'd be doing on her own as a single mom and no food in the pantry.* My grandfather told us stories about how German women would do anything for a box of rations or a package of cigarettes. In my senior year history class I learned what he meant by "anything" and the term "food prostitution."

Raelene would do it too if necessary; of that I had no doubt. She was so poor in college that she resorted to stealing food, dating men just for a free meal, and she met some sketchy photographers who bought her groceries. For what in exchange you can imagine. But two grand per shoot to a broke college girl living in Berkeley in the early 2000s was a lot of money.

After the initial shock and horror wore off, I learned to

forgive her brief experience with porn. That it was fetish porn—lesbian enemas to be specific—took a few weeks to get over. How would a 21 year old woman know that she would end up marrying a major geek who had access to military-grade facial recognition software that could comb the 'net? Turns out she was broke as shit so that's some consolation but I still think I might kill, or at least assault, the bastard producer if I ever met him.

A woman could always sell herself if she could do nothing else. Men, on the other hand, had no intrinsic value except as slaves or cannon fodder. Ladies might sacrifice their dignity and purity to survive, but men would kill. What could I do—what would I do—for us to survive? Others were answering that question all over the metro area.

I sat down against the garage door, which was freezing. I didn't care. The cold concrete and aluminum were my penance for being such a crappy husband and father. We were in this mess because I wanted to live a normal upper-middle class life, the one I'd strived for over twenty years. Cheap apartments, excruciatingly long hours, treading lightly among the rainbow colored diversity hires in Silicon Valley. We escaped, or so I thought, to a free state and a sane employer. The fruits of my labors, a big house, nice cars, a pool, and expensive vacations were finally at hand.

Doing the prepper thing would have been an admission that the United States we grew up in was on its deathbed. Despite the obvious signs of impending systemic failure and war, I knew I failed to do anything about it because if I did, I'd be admitting my precious lifestyle was on borrowed time. My dreams about watching the girls' grow up, threatening their boyfriends with a shotgun, and enjoying the good life with my wife felt like they'd crumble if I started stacking the place with crates of ammo and MREs. Instead I did the bare minimum to chase off the most tenacious feelings of doom that threatened to penetrate my fantasy.

Now here I was, losing my temper and wondering if I could or would kill to feed my family. If I got desperate enough, I'm sure I'd try and die in the process. Flabby men who sat in front of monitors all day didn't go on to become successful robbers. Hell, there might be some measure of masculine dignity in that versus pawning a twice-used Rolex on the street for a tenth of what it was worth.

Was this how it felt when someone in horrible circumstances knew they were condemned to die? I was angry at the world, bitterly disappointed in myself, and frustrated that, I as frantically, as I thought, I couldn't figure a way out. There was no peace, just a stinging sense of misfortune. It was the feeling that rose up like a ghost every time I considered making serious preparations for a catastrophe like this, only now I was seeing the whole iceberg. No peaceful resignation, just painful resentfulness, which since both involved a great deal of inaction, would result in the same fate.

Nevada

"Don't ever be afraid, son. Cautious, apprehensive, even wary; those are okay. But never afraid. I didn't raise you to be fearful." These words my dad told me on another cold, autumn day came back to me unbidden.

Before I even went into middle school I was convinced I was going to die. Well, worse than that: trapped in a wilderness purgatory. No one knew where we were. Dad and I had diverted off the beaten path on our drive to visit Grandma and Grandpa so I could shoot some jackrabbits before the first snowfall. The day had been a total washout for seeing any jacks so Dad let me take a few shots with my .22 at a Coke can.

Despite the wasted day and no mound of dead bunnies to pose next to with my trusty rifle from Kmart, it had been a good day. What boy wouldn't like to spend the day in the ruins of the Western frontier with his father? I was thinking about the nice warm dinner we'd have at the diner and wondering if they would still have any of the pie I saw at breakfast left over. Dad was listening to a tape of Buck Owens when it happened.

A jagged tooth of steel stuck up from a cattleguard and dug itself into the tire. It immediately deflated, but Dad proclaimed it safe to drive on until we got back to the highway. Dinner would be after dark, though. He would have to slow down to a crawl to keep the tire on the rim.

Not even halfway to the road the flat tire split completely and departed the wheel in the worst place possible. Even in the 2020s that place had zero cell reception, let alone in the 1980s. Overconfidently, I recalled the one time a few months earlier I changed a tire in the garage under close supervision (and lifting assistance) and thought this would be no problem. Had it not been late autumn, it probably wouldn't have been.

Half an hour later my dad tossed the pieces of a broken jack and inadequate tool box back into the truck. "That didn't work." He said with frustration and disappointment.

My unease had grown as I watched my father struggle and fail. When he threw the tools aside, that disquietude mutated into a kernel of panic. "Are we going to die?" I was probably white-faced and wide-eyed.

Dad laughed. "Not today Ross." He gave me a one-armed hug. "Work the problem. We need to find ourselves a piece of wood, like a plank. Even something with one flat side, like a split log, will do."

"How about a rock?"

"See any?"

I looked around as if I was going to find something on the side of the road. We were an hour outside Austin, Nevada, on Highway 50, America's Loneliest Road, and far off the pavement. What remained of daylight underneath the low, overcast sky was fading fast. Snow flurries were falling on the distant peaks. Not a single tree was in sight. The only vegetation was low cheatgrass and sagebrush, not the kind of stuff you could use to support a jack.

To my juvenile mind all we had to do was drive to where the road was more solid. Soft mud or not, the back wheels were mired and we needed the shredded tire replaced to crawl free. There wasn't any wood around. Earlier in the day I marveled at all the godforsaken wilderness that

Nevada had to offer and how its sparse flora gave the steppe a mystique the Mojave Desert didn't have. Near sunset, it was like being trapped in a nightmare.

I used to have these night terrors as a kid. They were different but all had a similar theme. I was confronted by a problem of such magnitude that I was helpless to even understand the scope. My arms couldn't wrap around a cylinder the size of a municipal water tank, the million gallon size, or I had to dribble a basketball the size of the Moon. If I didn't, I would die. Or like now, in one of the dreams I was trapped in a vast, empty space with no hope of ever getting out.

At nine years old I didn't have the perspective to know that there was always some kind of solution. Even laying down and dying was a solution but not a satisfactory one to my dad. So like in my dreams, I wandered around aimlessly. I listened to the harsh scratch of sagebrush limbs on my parka. A hopeless crushing feeling wrapped itself around my chest. Was I dreaming? Except for the details it sure seemed like it.

As I got older and computers went from something my mom used at work for typing to an interesting toy, the game *Hover* that came with early versions of Windows reminded me of the desert that afternoon. Distant, cold mountains and a dark, foreboding sky. Wandering around aimlessly on some sort of quest through a maze that looked the same at every turn. Funny how one unrelated thing can trigger your mind like that.

All I could think to do was wander. That's what I did in the dreams when I was trapped in that awful place of beige walls and silence. Rocks. I stopped and stared at this child's knee high mound of 50lb rocks. They were too heavy for me to carry but if I got my dad and brought him back here...

It clicked in my brain. Rocks stacked like that were done by a human. Peering around a sagebrush, I saw that the rocks made up the foundation for a headframe above a mine shaft. Dad's stories about the mining history of Nevada on the drive all came rushing back to me. In the grass lay the timbers of the headframe itself. They were far too stout to be useful without a chainsaw, but enough debris lay scattered around.

Someone had torn open the cover of the shaft to go inside. There were parts of a rickety ladder, shoring, and more lying in the grass. The wood was still strong after all this time too! I gathered up the biggest armload I could and drug it through the brush.

I appeared on the road a few yards south of the Bronco, huffing and puffing, with long green streaks on my jacket. Dad walked over from where he was searching for suitable rocks in a washout gully and looked me over. "Your grandma is going to just love scrubbing that out."

I just gestured at the wood. "Will this work?"

Half an hour later the spare tire was on and we were a mile down the road where the gravel resumed. "I was kinda scared back there," I confessed. It was an understatement. Coyotes had been howling in my mind. Mom and Grandma would never have known what happened to us if we hadn't figured it out. I thought we were so far away from civilization that someone like us in thirty years would find the rusted out Bronco. My dad had to know what I had been thinking.

Dad was a fighter pilot, tough as nails. He flew two tours in Vietnam and spent his whole adult career in the air. He'd look at me with a sad, disappointed look in his eye and wonder aloud why I was sitting in silence afraid. "Fear is God's way of warning, boy," he said. "You get up on a roof and look down to see that the ground is spinning. You got a few choices right then. Stop and figure out how to do whatever it is you're doing safely. Two, square your head away and get it done." He bent over to look under his Ford Bronco.

"That's only a couple."

"What?"

"You said 'a few.' You only said two. A couple is two."

He smiled. "That's right. The third is that perhaps you never belonged up there on the roof in the first place." A pause. "Don't ever be afraid, son. Cautious, apprehensive, even wary; those are okay. But never afraid. I didn't raise you to be fearful."

I must have fallen asleep on the ride back. The rest of the day is a blur. A brief snatch of being told to shower quickly so we could eat before the diner closed. Even the quick visit with my grandparents is lost now. That piece of advice is where the vivid memory ended.

Wipe your Ass and Work the Problem

This situation couldn't last forever. The rain would stop, the river would drop, and the temperatures rise. Even in the worst disaster in the country's history enough aid got in that people didn't outright starve. It would be uncomfortable and I'd feel like a jackass, but we would make it. The lesson would be expensive though, as I was down to the last few hundred dollars in my wallet.

So that was it. Wipe my ass, so to speak, get fueled up, and get the hell out of here. I would take us four and a half hours over the state line to where there was no disruption. We'd get a hotel room, some hot food, and I'd pull out a whopping amount of cash from the ATM. Between the accounts (if the machines had the money) I could probably get us $3,000; more if I took a cash advance on the credit card. Money wasn't the best preparation one could have but it sure beat having nothing.

The front door banged open. Raelene ran out, her Ugg boots slapping hard on the ground. "Ross!" she screamed, standing on the sidewalk and looking down the cul-de-sac. "Ross! Where are you?" she said with a crack in her voice. She scanned the houses to see if I was at a neighbor's door. I wasn't. She uttered a cry that wasn't quite words before turning around to see me.

Tears streaked down her cheeks. Her lips quivered holding back sobs. She inched towards me across the driveway like someone cautiously approaching a scared dog that might bite them. A lesser man, the one I was just moments ago, would have gotten defensive. Instead I rightly felt like shit. I got to my feet and kept my head down. *Your feet don't have any answers.* For a moment she stood a few feet away, uncertain if she should come any closer, until I raised my eyes and extended my hands to her.

She fell into my arms and the floodgates poured open. Raelene sobbed with abandon. "I thought you left us," she wept. In my anger I had forgotten that her father, in the early stages of mental illness, stormed out the door one day after fighting with her mother and never came back. The guilt was so heavy I felt I couldn't bear it. My wife, who had been abandoned by every man she had ever loved, thought I had done so too. I cried as well. I didn't care if someone saw us from their window.

"I'll never leave you," I sniveled. "I could never do better than you." She even may have laughed. She pulled away and we stared into each other's eyes. No love had been lost. She believed me because I hadn't walked away. Indeed I hadn't. I sat down with my back to the house, facing away towards any dangers. What's more she didn't let me go away either but came running out after me.

The words came tumbling out. I told her how I hated myself for being so willingly delusional about the future and about how rather than prepare to exert control over our destiny, I played the ostrich. I wasn't upset with Reya being a child, but instead terrified that soon we wouldn't be able to feed her.

"You have to tell me these things," Raelene said. "If we don't communicate the roots of our feelings, all we are left with are the surface level emotions and reactions. We can't respond to the problem if we are only dealing with the symptoms."

It sounded like hippy BS, and I'm sure she read it in

some Marin-county psychologist's book, but it was true. I wasn't angry, I was afraid, and men expressed their negative emotions most often through anger. "It's like Yoda said 'Fear is the path to the dark side. Fear leads to anger, anger leads to hate, hate leads to suffering.'"

Raelene sniffled and wiped her nose. "Did you just quote *Star Wars* to me?"

Dammit. I really have a problem with saying things I'm thinking aloud. "George Lucas was right though."

"I married a nerd," she said playfully. The spell was broken. All might not be right with the world, but all was right with our marriage.

Does Money Make You Stupid?

Raelene was not happy I was leaving, even to run errands. Precipitating my absence with a major fight and triggering her fear of male abandonment was a primary factor. We had a logical discussion about how any danger was slight, I let the neighbors know I was gone, and Hugo promised to check in every two hours until I was back. I even lent her the Glock, which made me feel more comfortable than it did her.

My wife calmly agreed that all would be well however I knew I failed to convince her on an emotional level. Under more ordinary circumstances, I wouldn't have left like that or I would have taken her and the girls along, if only to soothe her nerves. Couldn't have Mommy getting so nervous that she pops the cork on a bottle of wine before noon.

Driving away didn't feel good. The worst morning commute after a long vacation to my worst job ever paled with how much I didn't want to drive off. It felt like Groundhog Day getting off the island and over the river. Someone had ironically spray painted "Eat the Rich!" on the background of a RAISE Freedom Fund billboard, I noticed.

The one thing about living on the island was that the strategy of keeping a major terrain feature like a river between us and the city dramatically cut down on the rabble the that could infiltrate. One of the areas we looked at moving into was Forest Heights, the old-money section of River City that sat to the east of downtown. Being its own city didn't count for a thing. The predators who lived in the barrios and ghettos that separated the skyscrapers from the stately manors wouldn't be stopped by an invisible border. The arterials and residential streets all bled into one another.

That was the problem with urban sprawl, as I was learning. You could move away from the poor areas into an economic island, but nothing prevented the trouble from following you. The quality of the neighborhoods would decline as the city enlarged and the houses grew older. Suburbia was a constant process of those who had the financial mobility getting away from the problematic lower classes.

A half-hour south of the city, in minimal traffic, I should note, was where the agricultural areas began again. My destination was the small Indian reservation that was a few square miles of farmland and an Indian casino. They were blasting the airwaves about how they had fuel. Predictably the place was packed. The lines to the gas pumps wrapped through the parking lot like a snake doubled back on itself.

Cones and cops were everywhere. The tribal police agency probably only had half-a-dozen officers but it seemed like the entire tribe was a cop now. Each car had one of them sticking their heads in the window. One signaled me to stop at the parking lot entrance. "The wait is one to three hours to reach the pump. Your car will not make it waiting in line if the 'low fuel' light is on. I need to verify your gas gauge." Without asking, the man in the reflective vest leaned in. "Half a tank, you're good to go."

"What if I didn't have enough gas?" I asked out of curiosity.

"Then you can park and take a number for your turn. You still can if you don't want to burn the gas."

"Which is faster?"

"To be honest, probably waiting in line." A new car

arrived behind me. "Gotta go." I nodded and he moved on. The lines were coned off professionally and signs pointed out the exit for cars that quit the queue before reaching the pumps. *That's impressive.* We advanced at about one car length a minute, meaning the turnover was pretty good.

Security was tight. Armed men in reflective vests seemed to be everywhere. As I got closer to the pumps, I saw that there was a mixture of private guards on contract and tribal officers. The security guard quality varied from armed mall cops to military contractor grade guys. I swore I saw the flash of binoculars on the roof of the casino, implying they had armed overwatch. *Don't a few of the Vegas casinos have their own internal SWAT teams?*

Yet only a few of the tribal officers seemed to have any decent gear. In fact, many of them were old or out of shape, wearing cheap belts with little more on them than a holster and extra magazines. Their yellow vests looked like someone ordered a reflective traffic vest in bulk from Wish.com and ironed on a badge template.

At the hour mark I was finally close enough to see the light at the end of the tunnel. A gas tanker was making its delivery. Several more tankers were parked, under armed guard, at the far end of the parking lot. *I wonder if those are empty?* I decided to ask the bored kid who was standing guard over this section of the line. Since he was carrying a huge revolver jammed into a holster for a semi-automatic I assumed he had only been hastily deputized. No way this was a real cop, not even on the res.

"Excuse me, are those trucks empty?" I asked.

The kid looked around, confused, and saw where I was looking. "Oh, yeah. I think so."

"Getting a lot of gas delivered?"

"Yeah, but just today."

"What do you mean?" I probed.

"They said all the truck were coming at once, like in a convoy or something. I think they had the Army bring them here."

"Are they doing it again tomorrow?"

"I don't think so. They said we were just doing this today because it's when they could, uh, make it all, you know, happen."

"Gotcha. Thanks."

That was interesting. So the tankers were being escorted by the National Guard in a convoy. Arranging an escort for a single tanker, high-value target or not, would be a waste of resources so it made sense to have all the trucks come on one day. Bring them in together, transfer the gas when one underground tank goes dry, and then everyone returns to the terminal together. What kind of juice with the governor does that take? Or maybe none at all if the emergency managers decided this was to be a central distribution point. Today the casino gets the fuel, tomorrow the truck stop, and so on.

Probably the only thing keeping the customers from losing their minds was the constant movement. This was some pretty ingenious queue management taken straight out of Disney's playbook. In front of me, two teenagers were flirting back and forth from their parents' cars. Getting out and talking would have been entirely possible at this pace but I suppose they were having more fun. Some couples meet online, others through friends. These two met in an epic gas station line.

At 88 minutes, it was finally my turn to pull into one of the twelve pumps. Attendants were like hawks, hustling people out of their cars and straight to it. Pump and pay. No squeegees were present just to make sure not a minute was wasted by someone scraping the bugs off their windshield. Above the credit card terminal was a sign that read "10 Gallon Maximum." *Oh great.*

"Hey, what if I have gas cans?" I asked the attendant as I punched in my zip code.

"Gotta go to the back of the line, sorry."

Crap. I stuck the nozzle in the tank. The tank was just below half a tank, so if it held 24 gallons, adding ten would not get us all the way to where I wanted to go, but it would be far enough to reach somewhere else with fuel. I could live with that. It took about a minute for the pump to dispense almost ten gallons and then slow down to trickle out the last few ounces. *Click.* It stopped right at 9.99 gallons. Did I really want the extra hundredth of an ounce?

I looked again. No, I had the order wrong. It was ten gallons but $99.99. *Holy crow!* I looked at the little display above the octane selection button and the price was $9.99 per gallon. Prior to the Big Freeze, the national average was $4.85 a gallon. I was paying seven-odd dollars at the other stations, if they were open. "There's something wrong with the price," I said to the attendant.

"No," she said without even turning to face me, "that price is the only reason you're able to buy gas here today. The security doesn't pay for itself and before you start in on 'price gouging' the governor's emergency orders don't apply on the reservation."

She had a point and I was a free-market kinda guy, so I

didn't argue. I watched a confrontation while in line and the Indian cops, the real ones, didn't mess around. The wheel-lift tow truck siting on standby would probably just drag away the car from anyone who didn't cooperate.

The important thing is we could make it out of town now. *I worked the problem, Dad.* My nose tingled, my face rumpled up like a bulldog who ate a lemon, and my eyes went misty. Dad might be gone but his lessons would always be with me. I wasn't alone; I was my father's son and everything would be okay.

I shot Raelene a text. *Not dead. Home in about an hour.*

Her reply was nearly instant. *Don't put "dead" in a text. It's the first word I see & it scares me. I don't appreciate that kind of flippancy.*

Sry. I replied. *Home soon. Lvu.* Maybe guys appreciated more lightheaded dark humor than the ladies?

Being on this side of the river without a gun was suboptimal. I'd buy any pistol at any price. Only catch was I'd have to put it on the credit card until I could raid an ATM so a private sale was not possible. I dialed up the gun store that sold me the buckshot and gave me the tip on the Remington that saved our lives. I'd take their three-thousand dollar German .45. *Beep, beep, BEEP,* "We're sorry, the number you dialed did not go through. Please try your call again later."

No gun for you. If the phone lines were not working, neither would their Internet, which meant no credit card payments. No one in their right minds in the 2020s would write the charge up for later. What else could I do? I searched social media for recent mentions of open gun stores and there were either no mentions or the overzealous moderators deleted the posts. What caught my eye was a minutes-old post about an open gas station with no limits that claimed to be taking credit card payments via Starlink. "No limits! Hurry while supplies last!" the post urged.

Topping off the Lexus' tank and filling up all the cans was very tempting. We could run the generator all night. The location was in mid-town, which made it ghetto-adjacent, but not the proverbial other side of the tracks. I'd chance it. Better to have the gas than not and it was statistically highly improbable that anything bad would happen. I had to admit that my biases had more to do with my fears than any objective factors.

Aside from a few speeders treating the freeway like a German autobahn, there were no issues getting uptown. The area was in the process of gentrifying as the people who couldn't afford the residential areas downtown fanned out. A re-modeled 1920s bungalow inhabited by a pink-haired woman and her "partner" with a vasectomy could be raising their fur babies next to a dilapidated Section 8 rental house. The mix also brought in new small businesses without the reputation or customer base that would make more conventional shopping centers more affordable.

One strip mall hosted a porno store, a smoke shop, and a Chinese buffet. Traffic was thin. I didn't have any of the usual trouble in busier areas at the dark intersections where some cars inevitably had no idea whose turn it was while others ran right through. Looted and burned businesses made for little need for people to spend time here. Only the marijuana dispensary remained unmolested but it was fortified in a windowless, concrete building surrounded by two high fences. Someone spray painted on the plywood covering the door "No weed, no money." I was sure in time some tweaker would find a way in just to be sure.

Not many cars were at the gas station. I assumed there would be more, but perhaps I was just one of the first people to have seen the post and got here early. Security was poor. The owner must have rounded up kids from the neighborhood because it was all young people and teens. None of them seemed to have any warm clothes, though in the sunlight a hoodie might just be enough. One of them lazily waved me up to a pump.

I got out and stretched; my butt had been planted in the seat for going on two and a half hours. "Hey, the pump isn't working," a woman said on the other side of the island. Sure enough, the terminal screen was dark. There was no sound from a generator either. Mains power was out here, so why was there someone in that older car pumping gas? Something wasn't right. "Excuse me, sir?" the woman said as she walked towards a guy standing in front of the convenience store.

My new street-smarts tingled. *I'm getting out of here.* The store was dark, the pumps were dark, and I would swear that one guy was pretending to pump gas.

"Yo, yo, yo!" One of the 'security' guards on the sidewalk started yelling. I got in the Lexus just as a big diesel pickup pulled up and blocked the driveway behind me. Two four-wheelers came around the corner of the strip mall wall dragging huge tree trunk that looked like it had been freshly cut down in a park. They were boxing us in. The woman who complained about the pump was retreating for her car now.

By now the other hapless victims had all looked up from fiddling with the pumps to see we were trapped.

Everyone but me was confused as to what was going on. So we *were* being robbed. All of this had been a sham to lure people in, and when enough cars arrived, they sprung the jaws closed. "Wallets, cash, and credit cards!" a young man yelled as he waved a pistol with a comically long magazine around horizontally. No one had taught him to keep his finger off the trigger.

The guy on the sidewalk pushed the woman away from her car door. "Where's yo purse?" This was just a robbery, not a murder. The observation wasn't a relaxing one. My hand fell to my pocket and it stopped. I had no gun. Even if I had the gun, there were close to ten of them in all, probably all with guns.

The old advice from the stupid employee safety video at my first job was to always comply with the robbers fully so they wouldn't feel the need to use force. My wallet had enough cash in it to keep them happy and feel like they scored. Nothing they bought on the cards would be charged against me. *How would that approach have worked for you the other night?* a voice deep inside me asked.

In my basic handgun course the instructor explained that attitude had to go out the window. He played a few minutes of clips of murders where the victim complied perfectly and still got killed for it. These thugs were violent, unstable, unpredictable, and on the ragged edge of days without proper food, heat, or entertainment. The slightest thing that went wrong might result in gunplay or they might just kill us for no reason at all.

"Ay, yo. Get that green car. The Lexus," the thug in charge yelled at the fake gas pumper.

Uh oh, that's me. So they'd be taking the car too? It

would be found in a week or two, banged up, the interior trashed, and partially stripped somewhere. Insurance would cover it. Just more stuff that could be replaced, right? *Not gonna happen*, that resolute inner voice said.

A stab of the finger was all it took to start the engine. All the robbers' heads turned towards the Lexus. What to do wasn't even a conscious thought at this point. I was going all on instinct. I turned the wheels sharply to the right, shifted to drive, and tapped the gas as the fake gas pumper's hand touched the door handle. He jumped back but still fell to the ground after the back end brushed him.

I aimed the SUV for the small gap the tree trunk barricade left between the planter. I knew from Raelene's past experience that the Lexus would drive over concrete parking stops so there had to be enough ground clearance to get over the planter curb which wasn't much higher. There was. The two right tires hopped up over it with no trouble. The all-wheel drive compensated for the loss of traction that the ground cover caused too.

The idiot on the ATV could have caused problems if he drove it forward to put tension on the drag chain, but things were happening too fast for him to realize that. Give him a week's time and he probably would never have thought of that. Instead, he thought I'd stop if he ran in front of the Lexus. Nope. Lucky for him all those suicides sprints during basketball practice helped kept him nimble and fast. All he got was the fender scraping his leg when he realized that I didn't care if I splattered him all over the hood or not. Wisely, after hearing Bert's story about being mobbed by people, days ago I disabled the pre-collision system that would probably have applied the brakes at exactly the wrong moment.

Without looking back, I floored the gas pedal and roared out of there. Not a single shot was fired. I started to wonder why until I checked my mirrors.

Two motorcycles were chasing me and gaining fast. No way was I going to be able to outrun or out-maneuver them. My only two options were to keep going until they gave up or if they got close enough, knock them down. But legally speaking, I couldn't crash into them without some use of deadly force against me first. I might be considered the aggressor otherwise. Actually, I wasn't sure and the moment was such I couldn't call Doug to ask for a lawyer's opinion.

Nuts! I swore. The turn I took was the wrong one; there was no freeway on ramp here. Instead, I went under it. The precious seconds I bought by being out of sight evaporated. I had a vague notion to go the wrong way up the ramp in the direction of home for an exit or two. Traffic was light and I should be okay if I stuck to the shoulder and if I ran into a state trooper, that would be perfect. Okay, I'd try it again at the next arterial street.

I zoomed past houses going way too fast. Houses flew by like the background in a cartoon. Fortuitously these older neighborhoods didn't have the streets heavily cambered like in the newer ones so at every intersection the Lexus didn't bounce up and down over every gutter prolongation. The bikes kept up with my detour and were now a block behind me. My attention snapped forward again to see a group of four guys on dirt bikes approaching in the other direction. They stopped hard as we closed.

I swerved to the right and went around them. One held a radio in his hand. I cringed as the tires and rims scraped the curb, but the Lexus kept going. They all tried to turn around, slowly and awkwardly in the "all feet" way people do when they are new to bikes. The guys on the real motorcycles had to slow down to avoid their companions.

That bought me a reprieve. I took a hasty right, then went left, and right again up an alleyway that went under the freeway. After the narrow underpass, the alley terminated at two stout wooden gates. I was boxed in if they found me.

The gravel the tires kicked up scarcely stopped skidding about when I noticed a man in his late fifties or sixties closing the lid of a trash can. "Where you goin' in such a hurry down a blind alley?" he asked.

"They're chasing me on motorcycles and ATVs. Carjackers," I said breathlessly. Out on the front street, a motorcycle went by just then, the rumble of the exhaust echoing off the back houses. "They lured a whole bunch of us into a gas station, and tried to rob us, but I drove over the curb. Can I get through that gate and keep going down the alley?"

"That gate only goes to my backyard."

The man's son or grandson came out now with an AK-47 type pistol down by his leg. "What's up pops?"

"This guy here is running from some carjackers. Suckered in at a gas station."

"Man, you fell for that?"

"I'm desperate. My house got burglarized the other night, I shot a couple of them, but one of them got away and is threatening my family. We need this car to get out of state." The old man was taken aback.

"Man, that was you?" the young man said. "I seen the dude with the face tattoos on the news. You iced four guys and you're all worried about those fools on their bikes tryna boost your ride?" He laughed and used his free hand to mime shooting at a passing target. Multiple small engines approached the block and slowed down. "Guess they figured you in here."

The old man tossed his head at his son/grandson. "Help me with the gate. He can hide back here for a few minutes."

The younger one looked skeptical but did as he was asked. Safely behind the gates, I got out and shook their hands. "So why didn't you cap them?" he asked me.

"A Lexus isn't bulletproof. Besides, I left my gun at home with my wife."

"You left your gun at home and you ain't with your wife when some dude wants to kill your family?" the old man asked rhetorically. He shook his head. We all froze as an ATV came down the alley and stopped outside the gate. "Ain't nobody gonna see your car unless they peek they head above the fence," he whispered. The fences in back were ten feet high. "You sit tight here a minute and they'll be gone." The rider idled there for a tense few moments before turning around and driving off.

For the first time, I looked around the yard. There was a scraggly patch of lawn that was mostly crab grass, but the other half was taken up by a home garden. A stump sat next to the garage on gravel driveway with an axe stuck in it. Firewood was neatly stacked by the backdoor. Some drifted out of the chimney.

"You actin' like you never seen a fireplace before."

"We only have a decorative one," I said pathetically. I told them the whole story about coming back from vacation to an empty refrigerator and how much bad luck we had.

"Man, what kind of a fuckup husband and father are

you out here looking for gas and food in *that* car? With all your smarts and your money you don't got a pantry the size of a grocery store at home lookin' like something the Kardashians post on Instagram? Holy shit, remind me not to get rich. Money makes you retarded," the young man said. He walked off towards the house.

"Ah, don't mind my son."

"He's got a point though. In my defense I will say the neighbors are looking out for us."

"More than you can say for this neighborhood," he lamented.

"You're looking after somebody. That counts."

The old man smiled, then tossed his head back and laughed. "Don't you be thinkin' I'm a bleeding heart or anything. I'm actin' in my own self interest. Can't have no carjacking and shooting out back. That's the kind of incident that hurts my property value."

A few minutes later, the sound of the motorcycles died out. The son reported that he hadn't see anyone prowling around, so it was safe for me to leave. After prodigious thanks, I cautiously backed out and drove rapidly to the next freeway ramp unmolested. My wife greeted me in the driveway. "What happened to the tires? And why are there plants jammed under the bumper?" she asked.

I sighed. "Well, the driveway was blocked and I couldn't wait so I thought I would jump the curb and squeeze by. I guess I eyeballed it wrong." It was not a lie.

Raelene sighed. "Try not to be so impatient," she said with a kiss before walking inside. And that is how I got away with being involved in an attempted mass robbery/carjacking and high speed chase without freaking my wife out.

BOLO

While the girls were fairly oblivious to what really had been happening around them, they did bear their share of psychological trauma. Though they didn't doubt their mother's hastily concocted story that I "scared away the bad guys" with my gun, mental scars had been left. It might be Thanksgiving before they slept in their own beds. They didn't want to be on their own. Remy would start crying if she was alone and Reya followed one of us everywhere to all but the bathroom. The aftermath had left the girls on edge, their senses honed like razor blade, constantly vigilant for any signs of trouble.

"Dad, there's a car out front," Reya declared, her voice tinged with concern.

I peeked through the blinds with a careful touch. I spotted Detective Kimbrough making his way up the walk towards our front door. Sweat trickled down my forehead, despite the cool indoor temperature. Why was he paying me another visit? The thought sent a shiver down my spine, but I knew better than to show it. "It's okay, I know him. You can relax," I assured the girls, masking the trepidation that gnawed my insides. *I wish someone could reassure me.*

As I went downstairs, my mind raced, conjuring up images of handcuffs clamping around my wrists, the cold metal biting into my flesh. It was an irrational fear, I knew that, but logic had no place in the turmoil of my mind. If they were coming for me, it wouldn't be a lone detective at my doorstep. No, they would send a small army to haul me away. My face flushed with the heat of anxiety, my pulse pounding like a drum in my ears.

"I don't think I should talk to you without my attorney present," I said, my voice laced with uncertainty, as I swung open the door to face the approaching detective.

Detective Kimbrough's lips curved into a smile, his eyes glimmering with a mixture of amusement and understanding. He let out a friendly chuckle, a sound that seemed strangely out of place amidst the heaviness of the moment.

"That's wise, Ross," he replied. "But rest assured, I'm not here about the shooting itself. I've come to give you a heads up on a potential threat."

My heart skipped a beat, one fear momentarily eclipsed by a surge of another. A potential threat? What could it be? "Threat?"

"Yes, not specific but you and your wife should be aware nonetheless."

Raelene walked up then and put her arm around me. "What's going on?"

"Detective Kimbrough wanted to bring something to our attention. Where are the girls?"

"Watching their show. Why?"

"Let's go to the kitchen," I said. "Come in, detective."

We each took a seat and he opened his notebook.

"Before I get into it, I need to get some important preliminaries out of the way, so please pardon the suspense." He took out a packet of some forms. "I'd like you to look over a photo lineup to see if you can identify someone." He began reading the instructions. "'In a moment you will be shown photos of persons who may or may have not been involved in a crime. This does not imply their guilt for the crime or any other crime. If you recognize a person as one who committed the crime please describe to me how confident you are and your reasons for this belief. If you don't recognize anyone, you do not need to choose a photo.'"

I signed a form that I understood and he handed over what he called a "six pack" or six driver license style photos of similar looking men. I knew generally that only one of them would be the right one with the others chosen at random from their DMV photos. I immediately placed my fingertip on photo number 5, which was obviously the bastard who haunted my memory. "That's him. The man in my garage. I'm certain because his face from the video footage is something I can't ever forget."

Kimbrough went over a few more obligations with me and noted some forms. "If I never saw him face-to-face up close, why was that important?" I asked.

"Mainly to have it on record that you can positively identify this man by face and that you agree with our analysis of your security video that this is the same person."

Kimbrough put the forms away and withdrew a wanted poster with bold letters and bright red stripes across the top and bottom. The real name of "Uncle P" was Peter Fuentes.

He was tall, his head shaved bald, and had prison tattoos all over his face and head. The "wants" of murder, attempted murder, burglary, and conspiracy caught my eyes. My heart skipped a beat, causing me to involuntarily cough. I could hear Raelene's breathing speed up. We intellectually knew what the charges would be but seeing them in black and white—well, white on red—along with the ringleader's face was unsettling.

"Sir, the reason I'm here is that his parole officer spoke with him on the phone. When the officer got around to the subject of the incident, Fuentes first attempted to deny then made some indirect threats."

"Like what kind of indirect threats?" I asked.

"Generic stuff about 'maybe someone will come back to finish the job.' I listened to the tape myself and it's the kind of bluff and bluster you hear out of these guys, but I'm erring on the side of caution. We have reason to believe he's still in the metro area but lying low. If anyone comes across him, his parole has been revoked and he has a no-bail warrant. Let me reassure you that he would be stupid to come back here, despite his threats."

"But his last known address is in the Bottoms," Raelene said. It was right there on the foot of the flyer. The Bottoms was the ungentrified housing area of West River City across the ship channel. Rising house prices moved most of the low-class troublemakers out long before we moved here, but it still had an unsavory reputation and a higher crime rate.

"Mr. Fuentes is a member of the West Rats gang, or the 'Floaters' as they are known across the river." The original River Rats gang across the river objected to the unaffiliated gang using a similar name and gave them the sobriquet of a turd that wouldn't flush, the detective explained.

"What was he in prison for?" I asked.

"Carjacking, grand theft auto, and assault with a deadly weapon. He did two stints upriver, the last one being five years involving a shooting during an attempted carjacking. He's been in and out of jail his whole life for various misdemeanors. Drugs, fights, weapon charges, and so on. Nominally works in an auto body shop when he's not behind bars but that's probably just a front for a chop shop." Nothing like rape and murder.

"Did the kid in the hospital talk any more?"

"He did. The motive was a straightforward home invasion robbery. The reasons they chose your home was apparently some sort of 'beef' with over the donuts and the impression you were wealthy."

My brow wrinkled in puzzlement. "That's it?"

"Sometimes it's that simple. We're talking about low-IQ individuals here who are easily offended and carry long grudges. It could have been any upper-middle class family on the island, but a small measure of revenge seems to be the answer to 'why you?'."

"I'm sorry, that just doesn't sound satisfactory to me," Raelene asked. "Were they after the generator, the car, money; what?"

Kimbrough shook his head. "Food, mainly, and whatever valuables they could pocket and get away with. They had not and they believed that you *had*. Criminal motives are often quite simple when you realize many criminals operate under their own childlike logic. The basest of instincts and assumptions that people like us would rationalize make sense when you understand the rules."

He told us an anecdote about a suspect he interrogated. The young man had affiliated with gangs as a teen but led a normal life in his early-twenties. One day, after work he had an argument with a co-worker in a bar. The co-worker badly disrespected the suspect, humiliating him actually, in front of the entire bar. Causing an entire bar's worth of people to laugh at the suspect's expense was a grave insult to honor in the urban culture the men grew up in. Yet, instead of just fighting, the intoxicated suspect drew a gun and shot his co-worker in the head.

A more intelligent, educated person brought up in a more genteel segment of society would never have done such a thing. They would have been embarrassed, even angry enough to fight, but knew it was not a killing matter. Killing was too extreme of a response and carried deeply ruinous consequences. To the vast majority of killers, there was no past, no future, only an eternal present where their anger burned white hot.

"So what do we do?" I asked.

"Just keep an eye out. He would be stupid to come back here, especially knowing that you're willing and able to defend yourself. We got a ping off a cell phone in River City, so he's likely holed-up there." He yawned as he stood up to go. "Excuse me. I had to work the back half of a patrol shift last night. We're down officers."

"Desertion, like during Hurricane Katrina?"

"No, not that. Some questionable sick-outs, but a lot of guys are getting hurt. Cops are getting hard to come by. If this was a few weeks ago we'd have a task force with the marshal's office and metro PD hunting this guy down. Now I have to beg my partner for help." I showed him out and returned to the kitchen.

Raelene and I sat at the table after the detective left. Her fingertips rested lightly on the mugshots of the suspects. The papers he left us and his business card sat there like some macabre but low-effort tableau. Having the cops come to your home to tell you that someone is *very* determined to kill you is a very weird feeling.

Jim's Dire Warning

Jim came over about an hour after Kimbrough did. I appreciated the company. "Did you catch the new press conference this morning?" Jim asked. Officials had announced they expected the river to crest the levees, but not badly.

"No, just yesterday's. Sounded like they were trying to cover something up."

"They were. The Pine Valley Dam is failing. That's why the river isn't going down." The Buenaventura River that gave River City its name came from headwaters above Pine Valley. Pine Valley Lake was the largest lake by surface area in the state. We'd had a great summer up there because for the first time in five years the huge lake was full, thanks to two El Niño winters and freakishly strong monsoon seasons.

"Like all at once?"

"No, the lake overflowed the emergency spillway and is beginning to erode the soil on the other side, eating deeper and deeper into the soft bedrock. As the erosion continues the lake will pour through the hole, making the hole bigger as it goes. It's going to keep going for another day or two until the concrete is undermined. When that happens, it's a free-for-all until the water cuts down to bedrock."

"How far down is that?"

"They didn't say. All of this depends on the rate of erosion and the resistance of the ground. Could go faster, could go slower."

"So it doesn't sound like a big deal. Okay, so we don't get any more flooding because the rain stopped but the lake keeps draining. The river doesn't go down." I didn't understand his sense of urgency.

"Ross, this is one of those slow-at-first, then all at once kind of deals. Barring some miracle like the earth being harder than they think or the concrete cofferdam not being undermined, half of the lake or more will be drained."

Hydrologists had been attempting to lower the record high water level in the days just before the storm hit. The unexpected volume of precipitation and already saturated soils from the wet summer complicated their efforts because what they dumped from the reservoir went into the already deluged river. As the storm passed and our more normal autumn weather resumed, the water should be beginning to recede. Instead, it continued to rise rather anomalously, as the mysterious dissenter tried to point out in the press conference yesterday.

I lifted my phone to my mouth. "Siri, tell me what the depth of water would be over the River City metro area if Pine Valley Reservoir at full pool flooded the city."

"Okay, just a moment." The little thinking animation played. "Pine Valley Reservoir has a maximum capacity of 4.5 million cubic feet. Spread over the River City metropolitan area as defined by the US Census Bureau, which has an area of approximately 350 square miles, the depth of the water would be 159.7 feet."

Jim scoffed. "That's no help. The water will flood the whole river valley to varying depths, not just stack up over the city."

"I was just trying to visualize it, but even if the inundated area is ten times as large, basic math says that's 16 feet deep all across the basin."

"Well the entire lake isn't going to empty out. It's over

capacity so maybe half that."

Only eight feet spread out over an area the size of Rhode Island wasn't any better. The Interstate we needed to travel on to leave the state ran right through the bottom of the river valley that was about to be flooded. If we left now...no, we couldn't. We hadn't packed or readied the house.

"Why are you just telling me?" I asked Jim.

"Because I can trust you not to immediately spill the beans on the NextDoor app or something."

Jim swore me to secrecy because the city fathers did expect something of a panic and the infrastructure for a full evacuation wasn't ready yet. The voluntary evacuation of the lowest-lying neighborhoods based on the on-going flooding was necessary based on the so-far "ordinary" flooding but was also being used a as way to set the expectations for the public.

"I need a nap. I'll talk you later," he said. I shook his hand and let him go grab some shut eye.

So a flood is coming, I mulled disconsolately.

An impression that a giant wall of water was going to come barreling down the river valley and erase all civilization like the wrath of God wasn't accurate. Not this scenario, but something like it, had been planned for, and the excess water would be diverted through the massive flood works. A large floodway ran from the bayous northwest of the city south past the metro area.

Cold comfort that was. The emergency managers expected all of West River City to flood as in the realistic worst-case scenario, which meant in our neighborhood water lapping at the doorstep was just the best case. Old Town on the waterfront and the lowest lying areas would be inundated to rooftop level. The levees were expected to hold as long as the expected volume of water that they calculated arrived, but no more, and possibly a miracle or two happened.

So we weren't getting out of here after all. The Interstate we needed to leave the state was going to be submerged. Even if we left now there was no guarantee that the roadway and bridges would be intact or open to the public. Wonderful options. Stay here and possibly be murdered or flooded out, stay with my brother in a city that was trying to be taken over by violent communists, or drive east until we reached my sister's place in Arkansas.

Suburban Defense

Once Raelene and I recovered from the shock of Detective Kimbrough's news, I took a photo of the poster and put it out on social media. Ten minutes later I got a notification that it had been taken down for some reason. When I tried re-posting only the local news story from the other day about his escape, I caught a three-day ban. "Inciting violence and hateful conduct" was the reason. I went on another app and posted "someone is trying to kill me" only to get the post branded with a warning about self-harm and the phone number to a suicide hotline.

That left the old fashioned way. I went around to all the neighbors, including the teens next door and the new family, plus the houses across the cross street, and showed off the poster. Some of the people cared, others wanted to pretend that everything was fine. You'd think I'd be a hero for killing burglars on our street in a disaster or at least a sympathetic figure for what I went through. No, three houses treated me as if I were a leper.

Around noon Jim woke up from his nap after his overnight shift volunteering at the Emergency Operations Center. I could tell because he started sending a barrage of links, photos, and videos to our neighborhood chat group that the rest of us jokingly called JNN Headline News. I'd say that I caught it all on Channel 8 this morning, but catching a TV broadcast was not possible for us. Those cable boxes that sent the signals all the way to our house depended on electricity too.

Some of the headlines were:

- "Retailers asked to provide security for their own stores as strained police can't provide officers."
- "Woman critically injured after being run over trying to recover her stolen groceries."
- "Daring daytime home invasion robbery crew targets the elderly for food and toilet paper."
- "Home Alone: 8-year old boy recounts hiding as thieves ransacked the kitchen while his mom was out."
- "'I heard the doorknob rattling in the night'; Ring video captures frightening image of masked man trying doors."

The context made it clear what was happening. Food was running out in the stores, causing people to turn to burglaries to feed themselves. Gangs might have been reselling it, too. Without stores to loot or trucks to hijack, the only places left that had supplies were people's homes. Over a week into the worst of this and we were coming to the suburban looting stage of a disaster.

It was making sense to me now why FEMA's emergency relief efforts focused so much on establishing relief within three days. That's about how much food people had on hand to survive by themselves. Reality was showing it took longer to get sufficient aid into a large, devastated region. Maybe that's why the popular advice changed to two weeks without government aid or normal supply channels. If we and everyone else were fully stocked for two weeks on our own, our biggest problems might be boredom rather than near-anarchy.

A TikTok video showed a montage of empty grocery stores and then armed guards escorting or guarding delivery trucks. Discordant electronic music played in the background to create a tense mood. Old photos and clips of celebrity pantries flashed by faster and faster as the video progressed. It ended with a long, un-stabilized video of a suburban neighborhood filmed through the passenger window of a car. It ended with the RadCom logo over a black background. There was no spoken or written message. The message was in the images; the suburbs have food.

Beneath the video Jim added: *Recognize the neighborhood? It's the houses across from the middle school. They were on the island. It's time to put that group we discussed into action.*

As distressing as the video was, I had to remind myself that this video could have come from anywhere; taken from something unrelated, some suburbanite's blue-haired kid, or just generically filmed here. It didn't make sense for anyone to come to the island when they could stay on the metro side of the river and plunder the suburbs there.

Jim wrapped it all up with a Snapchat photo of a thug not more than twenty standing on the east bank of the river with the skyline of West River City behind him. The kid was pointing the muzzle of his gun directly at the cell phone he snapped the photo with. The banded caption across the middle of the image read: "Finna go shopping on the island." Jim added context from the police briefing. Looters were coming over in groups of two to four cars using stolen registration and IDs to get past the National Guard who really didn't have any authority to turn cars around anyway.

Chatter is indicating that RadCom is actively encouraging looting in suburban areas. Something about reparations from the bourgeoise although I doubt if their audience even knows what they mean when they say "bougie." I replied back that given Grant's situation in Red Rock, they were already way ahead of down here. Bert and Hugo responded with memes and angry emojis. When Jim suggested we organize a self-defense plan for our street, the three of us jumped on it.

Certain peculiar, but probably unrelated, events unnerved me, so I was all for doing something. Granted, one of the symptoms of acute stress reactions was hypervigilance, but seeing a drone overfly the neighborhood this morning bothered me. Raelene saw one our first night back. Occam's Razor and all that, it was in all likelihood a neighbor conducting a patrol for security or flooding from his backyard rather than walking around like a chump. What kind of looters would be using a drone?

I wasn't really amped up about the abilities of this ersatz neighborhood watch on steroids though. When the guys on the gun forums say, "No one's coming, it's up to us," that means your friends, family, and neighbors. You take 'em as you find 'em, for better or worse. There were six other houses on our end of the street if you thought of each end of the cul-de-sac as a barbell. All were good neighbors (I didn't say they were good *people*) but poor comrades-in-arms.

The ones next door—the other next door who weren't Hugo—ditched their kids to go to Palm Springs. Okay, the kids were college-aged and both of them had their girlfriend and boyfriend plus another friend over. None of them could take out the trash consistently so relying on them was not worth even asking. The next house was empty because an old woman lived there and she skipped town to Florida the same time we did. She was probably never coming back the way this early winter turned into the apocalypse.

There was the dude who lived on the corner opposite Jim that seemed like a really trustworthy guy. Three kids, nice wife, and had a solid job. So solid, in fact, that throughout all of this he went to work everyday. I was embarrassed to admit I did not recall his name. They moved in a few months ago in July.

Hugo was also dependable and into guns, but for his devotion to all things tactical what he needed was an up-armored Rascal. He was getting up near retirement and his joints showed the ravages of working physically intense blue collar jobs for decades. Hugo would get worn out if he stood in front of the grill too long on holidays without taking an Aleve. Bert was the most like me: average shape, reliable, but a little older. I don't think he enjoyed his stint in jail but in my judgment he would throwdown if necessary.

And that left Jim, Mr. All American. Jim was a veteran, of which branch I don't recall, and worked for the local government. He volunteered for more things than I could imagine and had his fingers in many pies. He shot competitive matches, he hunted, he went backpacking, and he kept himself in great shape. Heck, this whole thing was his idea.

At the appointed hour, I went to join the guys. Everyone was in Bert's garage again, including Darin from around the corner, huddled and chatting. "How come you never hear about a psycho torturing a moose? It's always pet hamsters, cats, and dogs."

"Did I interrupt something?" I asked. The tinnitus affected my hearing but it sure sounded like they were talking about something...macabre.

"Nah, just talking about psychopaths."

In what context and why? I wondered. Men had some odd conversations. That's what made us interesting. The six of us huddled in Bert's garage next to his Mr. Buddy propane heater. Next week's forecast of highs in the sixties and lows in the forties couldn't come fast enough.

Jim stood up and explained his idea. "We need to have some sort of defensive group for mutual defense."

"The HOA guys have the entrances squared away. So what do we do?" Hugo asked. His attitude was there was always someone else to handle things.

"We'll see their dedication in action if they're still out there between midnight and dawn today," Jim replied. "We need to keep a lookout for suspicious activity ourselves so something like a car coming down the cul-de-sac at 3 AM would be noticed right away." He explained that if someone had seen my attackers arrive, there would have been at least a minute's warning and someone could have come to my aid. Even just knowing trouble was brewing was better than being totally clueless until they knocked down someone's door.

"What do we do if something happens?" Bert asked.

"We'll play that by ear. Chances are, if five or six of us come out any troublemakers will just leave and go somewhere else."

No one questioned Jim. *What if they don't run away?* a quiet voice asked. I'm sure I wasn't the only one with the same thought. Not even I wanted to imagine aloud what we might be facing and how we would confront it. Statistically speaking, nothing at all would happen or Jim's evaluation would turn out to be right.

"That's it, just walk out if looters come?" Darin asked skeptically.

"And we tell them to leave. Plus I'm assuming we'll all be armed. Remember, they want nice, easy, compliant targets, not one that is going to shoot back. It's just intimidation."

"I'm not so sure that intimidation will work," I said. "I killed several of them as you are aware."

"Well the survivors ran like hell when you did, right?" Jim asked.

"True," I admitted. Everybody laughed.

"If we blocked off the road, they couldn't get down here in the first place," said Bert.

"And how is, uh, what's his name, the new guy, gonna get home from work? What does he do anyway?"

"Kevin? He's a systems operator for Fremont Energy," Jim said.

"Oh, so that's why he's always working, rain or shine."

"We can't block off the road. Not physically anyhow. Nothing to do it with," Hugo said.

"We've got cars," Darin said.

"Do you want to put one of yours out there? How about your boat?"

"Not my boat," Darin objected. His bass boat was precious to him.

"I've got a bricked Tesla we could use," I humorously suggested.

"I don't think we need to block off the street," Jim said. "The other guys from Saltgrass Drive are covering the nearest entrance to the tract."

"There are three more ways in."

"What I'm saying is we're pretty far in. This is my plan; we all take turns staying up through the night on watch. Should something happen, that person rouses the rest of us and we all go out to investigate or do something about it."

"Sounds fine to me," said Hugo. It was better than

standing around in the cold looking like a discount, middle-aged version of the A-Team.

"Does everyone have any of those bubble pack FRS radios so we can communicate?"

"Sure," Bert said. We all nodded. Everyone had kids and either went camping or had team sports so there was a pair of the ubiquitous cheap radios in every garage.

"That's one thing taken care of. Basically we need to keep watch and be ready to alert everyone and challenge any strange vehicles that show up on the street."

Each of us would keep a two hour watch from the comfort of any room with a view of the street. I'd be in the living room. Hugo would go first, then Bert, Darin, followed by me, and then Jim. I was the youngest, so I got the worst shift; couldn't sleep through the whole night nor go to bed late. The benefit to Hugo going first would be that he wouldn't fall asleep, though patrolling might be a bit challenging for him. He could make it as far as the mailboxes four houses past Jim's, right?

There wasn't much to the plan, just be a visible presence. I figured that would be all we needed to do. West River City wasn't a war zone filled with commie revolutionaries and none of us were soldiers or cops.

Things Hank Hill Never Taught You About Propane

I was dismayed at the fact I had no long gun and looter gangs were on the prowl. I knew from recent, firsthand experience how useful a shotgun could be. Now I wanted a rifle. The devastation a shotgun could wreak was nice, but reloading was awkward. Unless I wanted to go on a unicorn hunt and pay obscene amounts of cash, I was stuck out of luck on the rifle front. So I had to come up with some alternatives.

Idea one was a slam-bang shotgun constructed from plumbing pipe. This was a section of pipe that was slammed backwards to drive the shell into a fixed firing pin, hence *slam>bang*. This went directly into the "do not discuss with wife" category. A trauma nurse is not the kind of person you want to have get buy-in from before you construct something that could rapidly convert into an ersatz pipe bomb.

A 12 gauge shotgun shell diameter is nominally 18mm or .678" at the case mouth and .757" at the rim on the one I had on hand according to my calipers. I'd need a ¾-inch Schedule 80 length of pipe, at least 18" inches long if the ATF had anything to say about it, for the barrel. The barrel had to be thicker and tougher than the "receiver" in order to help contain the pressure of the expanding gases. The barrel would fit into the receiver pipe, which was 1.049" inner diameter one-inch Schedule 40.

The ¾-inch barrel had an outer diameter of 1.050" so I would have to lap the rear of the barrel a bit to get it down the necessary one or two thousands of an inch. A standard steel pipe cap would be threaded on the end of the barrel and have a hole drilled through its center to receive a short nail or pointed bit to act as the firing pin.

That was the extent of the gun; no trigger as forcing the shell backwards on to the pin was the entirety of the action. It was crude as hell. There was no ejector, so to reload, the empty cartridge had to be shook or pried out of the barrel and another manually inserted. Maybe one shot every ten seconds was the highest theoretical rate of fire, although the aim was so poor that if the first shot didn't count, you might not have a chance for a second.

What I really needed was a welder so I could attach leftover lengths of pipe as grips. If Harbor Freight was open, I'd probably go buy a cheap welding rig and maybe even a table top drill press. For a brief moment I was glad that I somehow avoided the gun rabbit hole. High-tech inside the house and a golfing hobby was expensive enough that I didn't need to add firearms and firearms accessories into the mix, but I was still without a long-gun.

I began looking around the garage for something. The approach of fall and the colder temperatures reduced the need for yard care, so a lot of the stuff was put away and not readily accessible. In the back of a Rubbermaid shed along the side of the house I found what I did with the propane weed torch.

Gas, the element of nature, dissipates quickly except under extreme pressure. A propane weed torch will project flame about a foot. Without heavily compressing the gas it's not going to jet out fifty feet like the M1A1 model the Marines in WWII had. I fired the thing up and all I got was a sensation of heat at arm's length. The blue flame would be a lot more dangerous if jammed into a body but if someone was that close I might as well use the pitchfork we had for some reason. I had to make the flame shoot out farther.

Inverting the tank does some things that the manufacturer and retailer really don't approve of. The propane in the tank is in a compressed, liquid form. Flip the tank over and now instead of vaporizing into the gas that stoves, grills, and torches are engineered for it remains a highly flammable fluid. Liquids are much denser than gases (duh) so the pressure, and thus flow, is higher.

The liquid propane actually evaporates (boils) as the pressure changes during its release from the tank to travel to the burner. This causes it to expand and loses heat, or energy. When this occurs rapidly the temperature drops so fast that the tank also starts to ice up or "freeze over." This is the refrigeration cycle and is how everything from the big cold food boxes in our kitchens to air conditioning and heat pumps work.

When the pressure drops, the liquid turns to gas. As I said before, the temperature drops as well. Our refrigeration devices work because it is taking the heat energy out of the atmosphere or whatever. Great if you want something to get cold but not in the case of a barbecue bomb. If the gas/liquid conversion continues, it needs an external heat source to keep from freezing. Fridges and A/Cs have thermostats; a propane flamethrower doesn't.

With a propane tank, this can cause the lines to ice up and stop working, which is part of the reason storing and mounting the tank with the valve up is so important. Dangerous? No, except for some frostbite danger if I touched it. Raelene saw a few cases in the ER of that from kids experiencing the same phenomenon by spraying a can of liquid air upside down until the exterior temperature dropped well below zero.

Heavy usage would give me problems with freezing but without knowing how long the fuel would last and what the flow rate was, I couldn't tell if this was going to be an actual problem. Any situation where I needed to use a homemade flamethrower was probably going to be over before the setup had problems. If I jumped up and down to shake or stir the contents of the tank, this would increase the heat a bit because the cold liquid would come in contact with less cold parts of the tank. The effectiveness of the shaking is limited and works about as long enough as kicking a stubborn mule might move it a few feet, but it is something.

The tank valve is designed to limit how much propane can come out. A larger tank and inverting it can only do so much. Liquid propane will expand up to 270 times its gaseous volume when exposed to air. This sounds impressive but isn't in practice. Actual flamethrowers use a liquid fuel, like jellied gasoline, which doesn't expand and also sticks to stuff (napalm sticks to kids). The designs are also different as it's designed to shoot flame and not just cook steaks. Thanks for coming to my TED Talk, "Things Hank Hill Never Taught You About Propane."

So what I needed to make was an accumulation chamber. People with low water pressure problems often have booster tanks to help increase the flow. My accumulation chamber, which I would make out of an empty green one-pound propane bottle, would hold some of the propane between the tank and the muzzle. This would give me longer bursts that shot further.

Drilling the little tank's valve open was a little sketchy

but I didn't explode. Next I had to figure out how to build the actual gun. Having a garage full of miscellaneous accumulated crap was helpful here. Using a spare steel-wrapped flexible gas line and a bunch of adaptors and fittings, I attached a pressurized paint sprayer to act as the gun. An electric "plasma" lighter became the ignitor with a switch rigged up near the sprayer's trigger.

If I squeezed just the trigger, a blast of cold, white gas came out the end with a loud hiss. Tapping the ignitor button just after activating the trigger gave me a roaring flame. *I hope Raelene didn't hear that,* I thought. The two-by-two foot ball of flame slightly warmed up the garage.

I strapped the tank down to an old military surplus ALICE pack frame. I hadn't used this thing for backpacking since I was in high school, but I still kept it around and was glad I did. For good measure I took some flame retardant insulation I had from an old project and wrapped that around the tank. Cutting that into strips allowed me to wrap it around the fuel line in a helix, like a Damascus steel shotgun barrel. This would both protect me from cold burns and keep the fuel liquid.

Time for a real test outside. The least visible part of the house would be the side yard. If I did it out front, the neighbors would definitely see and I'd probably get hauled away to the nuthouse for being "the guy who shot four guys and now has a flamethrower." In the backyard, the other neighbors or the kids might see. A quick burn on the side of the house would be as discreet as I could get. If anyone saw the flash, I'd claim the grill didn't ignite right away.

Flame shot out of the muzzle about 10 feet illuminating the side yard like the Aggie's big annual bonfire. *It worked!* I turned off the gas. *There are many flamethrowers but this one is mine!* The celebration was short lived though.

"WHAT WAS THAT!" Raelene yelled from inside the house. The kitchen windows faced the side yard. I probably should have noted that before performing my experiment.

I rushed back into the garage, slipped the pack straps off my shoulders, and set the tank upright. "Nothing!"

The garage door popped open. She was I-want-a-divorce pissed off. "Ross Porter, that was not *nothing*." The only other time I could recall her yelling my full name is when we got separated in the airport on our anniversary trip. "Nothing doesn't look like the barbecue exploded. And why is your face red?"

My face was red? Uh oh, I needed to attach some sort of flash shield. "It's to keep us safe."

Every married man knows the look that Raelene had on her face. Every teenage boy knows the look on his mom's face too. "Keeping us safe starts without you *not* blowing yourself up *or starting the house on fire!*"

"Okay, okay," I said meekly and put my hands up.

"Put that down and come inside so I can look at your face."

The flamethrower was obediently put down. Raelene took me by the hand and led me upstairs. "See, the redness is already fading," I said as I caught a glimpse of myself in the mirror.

"Luckily these aren't burns. Maybe a singe. I can't tell in this light. The heat causes your blood vessels to dilate so the extra blood flow carries away excess heat. It's a cooling mechanism. Like when you got heatstroke on our honeymoon." She rubbed some lotion into my skin. "If you fired that thing any longer you would have a real burn. First degree."

"The beard would have protected me some." That earned me a dour stare. "I'll build a flash shield and I promise I won't use it unless I have to."

"I'd rather you not use it at all. Why did you build that thing?"

"Because I don't have a shotgun and we need more protection. I should have bought an AR or a paintball gun. You know Grant's neighbor has an orange shotgun like the cops have to shoot bean bags? His friend, the fed, got a whole bunch of expired pepper balls that the government was just going to throw away. If I had stuff like that, I wouldn't need a homemade flamethrower."

She tossed the lotion on the counter, which knocked a hairbrush to the floor. She grabbed the brush, opened a drawer, and threw it in, then slammed the drawer. "Whoa, why are you being so aggressive and testy? Are you that worried about me?"

Her upper lip trembled. "I am worried." She hugged me and buried her face in my shoulder. "I'm scared. I just want to be somewhere safe with you," Raelene said. "Somewhere warm and quiet, all alone. I want you to wrap your arms around me and hold me tight. All I want is to be with you, to have sex with you, and forget about everything."

Not being able to get out of state as we had believed we could this morning was breaking down her resolve. Hope deferred makes the heart sick. There was nothing but lies that I could offer her in comfort. "Soon baby, soon."

Say Hello to my Little Flamethrower

After dinner, we huddled under the blankets and put on *Frozen* for the seven hundredth time for the girls. Raelene read a book while I tried to understand the mechanics, magical or otherwise, that would allow for the existence of an anthropomorphic snowman. How did a snowman get a Russian name like Olaf when this was supposedly set in Scandinavia?

"Olaf is a Norwegian name," Raelene replied to me without looking up.

"Did I just say that out loud or did I think it?"

"Ross, honey, if I could read your mind do you think I would let you know?" She had a point. Of course not. A woman who might spill that secret would be burned at the stake by the others.

No matter how hard I tried, I couldn't lose myself in the movie. I probably couldn't lose myself in anything, even *Star Wars* if this was 1987 and I was seeing it for the first time again when my dad brought home our first VCR. I had a sickening feeling in my stomach that was fear mingled with inadequacy. How often had my brother preached at me to get prepared?

I learned the wrong lessons from COVID and the riots. Like everyone else, we panicked and stocked up in case it was the end of the world. We weathered the shortages in good shape. Then it wasn't the end of the world and we went on living life as if all of it had been a giant overaction instead of the wake-up call it should have been.

What a monumental screw-up. I looked over at my wife to make sure I didn't say that out loud. I didn't. Dying men must feel the same way I did. I knew it wasn't the case but I felt like this was the last time I'd see my family. The emotions were one hellish combination. I couldn't tell if the sense of loss, the inadequacy, or the fear were the most powerful. I needed a beer. Anything to escape the parade of intrusive thoughts.

You know who wouldn't have to build a flamethrower? Know who wouldn't be afraid? James Bond. He would have it all squared away, ready to do battle with the zombie hordes. A secret agent, hell, even Grant, would have it all planned out with fields of fire and barricades, maybe even a couple of his fed buddies over for mutual support as well.

Presumably at some point when I was busy being a bachelor slaving away for Big Tech my brother was killing people. In today's world anyone with the pocket change for a trainer could learn all those skills, but had I? It was excuse after excuse. A new job, I'll do it after they lift the mask mandate, I'm not that into guns, am I really going need to this? Now I was desperately thumbing through the end-of-the-world survival guides I bought.

Cops, Marines, and Green Berets had all made their material as accessible as they could for guys like me but they couldn't distill what they learned through experience. Training was something but learning what stuff you were made of in a trial-by-ordeal was another. Academies, boot camps, and deployments were all the kind of test that let a man know what he was made of and what he was, and wasn't, capable of. Ross wasn't even a cook or some rear-echelon guy that at a minimum made it through basic training.

Every guy, I think, has a deep-seated need to take a shot at some difficult or adventurous thing like that. A rite of passage. I never passed any of those tests. There was nothing like that in my past, not even a fraternity hazing. All the men in my family had something like that, save me.

I took a deep breath and slowly released it. *This old horse again.* I had to tell myself it was no use comparing me to someone else. We were all different people and for all intents and purposes the mythical *he* didn't exist. Raelene was with me, not James Bond. She was my responsibility now and even though I didn't have the resources, training, or the flair I'm sure I was capable of defending my wife and our children.

Letting go of the machoistic BS was hard to do. Lord knows I griped about it often enough. While Grant was in Afghanistan, I was in college. He kept telling me I missed nothing by not going to war. "The Army is basically a jobs program. You have brains and options. You never wanted to be in uniform, so why are you deprecating yourself for not having served?"

Millions of Americans never served in the military and had happy, productive, and respectful lives they could be proud of. The point of the volunteer system was that guys like me didn't have to disrupt the economy or our lives, or give our lives, as my brother told me. He said that life wasn't like the Boy Scouts and joining the military wasn't collecting a merit badge that certified me as a man. Easy enough to accept over beers.

Kipling wrote a poem, "If", for his son (who died on a battlefield in France twenty years after he penned the words) saying that manhood was based on one's behavior and attitude. Wisdom, discernment, perseverance, and honor; that was what mattered to him and what he wanted his boy to know. He himself had never been a soldier—traveled with them as a correspondent, put their lives and perspectives into immortal words, yes—but he never took the Queen's shilling. In the opinion of perhaps the perfect embodiment of Victorian stoic manliness, it wasn't achievements that made the measure of a man.

From my commiseration I was ripped when the squelch on the bubble pack radio broke. I snatched it from the covers in time to hear Bert exclaim "Hey, get out here guys! A truck just did a slow drive-by. There's like four guys in the bed and there is a car with them too." Without hesitation I got up and put on my shoes and coat.

"Babe, get the girls in one of the back bedrooms. I'm sure it'll be okay once we run them off."

"Be careful," she said as she scooped up Remy. "Reya, let's go."

"But Mom…"

"You've seen it a million times before and we can rewind." I rushed past them and down the stairs to the garage, slipping out the side gate.

Another voice, this one in my mind, said *Get inside and stay inside!* But if I didn't go, who would? I met the guys who were standing in a short line in front of the vehicles we parked as a barricade. "Did you call the cops?" I asked.

"No service," Darin said in a quavering voice.

Why these thieves chose us I will never know. Being an upper middle class neighborhood in a relatively unaffected area might have been enough justification. Sometimes lightning did strike twice in the same place and I was the unlucky sap with the umbrella.

An '80s era pickup stopped in the intersection and all

the guys in the back jumped out plus the passenger. Two of Darin's project cars sat side-by-side in the street, blocking off our cul-de-sac. I met Darin, who was already kneeling behind a car, and Hugo and Bert came out a moment later. Jim was nowhere to be seen. Hadn't he been out here a moment ago?

The raiders formed a lose protective perimeter as the truck tried to push one of the cars out of the way. Why walk further with loot than you have to? I couldn't believe what I was seeing. The old pickup backed up, rammed the rear end of the car, then did it again. Using an old truck was the way to go because, stolen or not, there were no airbags or impact sensors to activate when ramming. With the weight of the car upfront in the engine, it took three solid hits to move the car far enough out of the way for the truck to squeeze by.

The formation of men went around the car barricade and stopped next to the truck, about thirty feet away from us. "We want your food and any jewelry. Give us your guns, your ammo, and any cash you have too. We won't shoot you if you don't shoot at us," one ordered.

These were the nicest bandits I'd met all week. If I seemed stoic right now, I did not feel that way. Crapping my pants had very favorable odds.

The five men that confronted us were carrying a motely collection of handguns, shotguns, and rifles. Since I did my gun shopping a few days ago I recognized that none of them were high-end weapons. Each goon wore dark clothing and what appeared to be body armor. I couldn't tell if it was real or just airsoft make-believe. I didn't see extra ammo protruding from them though. The men were young, fit, and most probably in a gang. They stood apart from each other in the open in what I assumed was a military manner.

If a gunfight were to erupt, we were at a severe disadvantage and would lose. There were only seven houses on our cul-de-sac, not counting the extension or the ones on the cross street. We were overmatched. The absent Jim had an AR-15 and a full tactical vest, Hugo had a WWII rifle for some reason, and the other two of us only had pistols. My pistol was inside with Raelene. So far, no one had reached for a gun on either side.

"Put the guns down!" one said, raising his rifle to the ready. Another took a liquid filled bottle with a rag from the back of the pickup. They would burn us out if they had to, or so his actions implied.

"Okay, okay!" Hugo said. He knew he was in no shape to fight it out. With his hands raised he backed away from the car all four of us were hunkering down behind.

"What are you doing Hugo?" Bert Vargas hissed.

"Trying not to die, that's what!" Hugo laid his rifle on some grass and reached for his holster.

"No!" the ringleader yelled. "Take the holster off the belt. Same goes for all of you."

Bert looked at me and shook his head. Hugo unfastened his belt and struggled to remove his holster. It held on snugly but he had to use his other hand to keep his pants up. At last he succeeded and set it on the pavement.

All of us turned when we heard a front door bang open. "What's going on?" Hugo's wife asked loudly as she shuffled down the walkway in a robe and slippers. "I heard a car crash and yelling." She stopped when she saw the men with the guns and assumed a deer-in-the-headlights expression.

"Get back inside!" one of the gunmen yelled.

"What? Hugo, I don't understand," she replied.

Both Hugo and the gunman yelled in unison. "Get inside, now!" The gunman aimed at her and flashed a red laser over her breast and face. She screamed before turning around and rapidly shuffling back inside the house.

With the interruption over, the lead gunman turned his attention back to us. "Come on, the rest of you. Disarm and open your garages. We want non-perishable food, gas, and cash." He pointed at me. "You. We want your generator."

Dammit. The drone was up to no good after all. It was the only way they could have known about it. Did these guys also know Fuentes and his idiot nephew? Were they the River Turds or whatever Kimbrough called them?

"Screw that!" Bert yelled. He stood up and dropped his hand to his pistol. To his credit the robbers didn't immediately gun him down. They must have not been prepared for that degree of violence or didn't want the heat it would bring.

"No Bert!" I yelled. *Time to shine, Ross. This better work.* "Everybody be cool! I'll open my garage. I don't have any guns. Just let me walk down there." I pointed to the house.

I didn't wait for a response or for permission. I didn't want to turn and see the looks of disgusted betrayal on the guys' faces. I walked as fast as I could without breaking into a jog into the garage. Being shot in the back was not appealing.

What did we think we were going to do against these guys? Ask them politely to leave us alone? My brother didn't have this problem. He was a freakin' genius compared to us. His street had purloined K-rail and razor wire that only the most determined lowlifes would try to circumvent.

I glanced back anyway. Bert and Darin had given up along with Hugo. One of the raiders was putting zip ties on their hands and this occupied all but the one of them who was following me. Arriving at the side gate, I slipped another look and saw three more of the robbers headed this way. My walking off must have taken the raiders off guard and made them suspicious. I shut the side door behind me.

I only had a few seconds to make this work. The first thing I did was turn the regulator valve on the propane tank fully open. I flipped it and the pack over and opened the safety valves I installed on the hose line and the sprayer. As I shouldered the pack, a voice shouted out from the street. "Open it up!" A hand slapped the garage door.

"Just a sec, it's stuck!" I replied. Getting the tank prepped took longer than I thought it would and the backpack was awkward to put on. When I finally was ready, the tank banged against the doorframe as I went back outside since it changed my balance. I could hear the liquid propane inside sizzle and pop as it boiled. It was already starting to feel cool on my back. *Click, click,* went my contraption.

"What the hell is that?" the bandit in the driveway asked, totally confused, when I came out the gate.

In the dim illumination of headlights from a hundred feet away it was hard to see what I had. Obviously it wasn't a gun but the backpack and wand thing was strange. The dude with the Molotov cocktail ran closer and with my neighbors subdued, this left only the isolated bad guys as the one watching over the prisoners and the truck driver. The four were walking right into a trap.

The ignitor on the tip of my device crackled with a

purple arc. Everyone heard it. *Come on, spark!* I thought. One of the robbers brought up a gun. He was going to shoot me because he thought I had some sort of homemade Taser. I could hear the gas blowing out of the tip of the wand. It wouldn't take them much longer to figure out what this was and shoot me. One of them with a rifle from far away could take the shot without much risk to themselves.

I poised myself to hear another fruitless *click* when suddenly a dragon's breath of flame leapt from the muzzle. Instantly the street was illuminated in orange, flickering light. The night chill was banished for a brief moment.

The closest raider's arm caught on fire. He jumped back and stopped for a second —the four that came up to my house all did. He couldn't believe his arm was on fire! Then he did an impression of the Wilhelm scream and ran away, looking for a puddle. Stop, drop, and roll must not be taught in schools anymore.

I recovered from my surprise before the other three did. Leveling the sprayer wand, I triggered it again in a long burst of flame that must have covered better than twelve feet. I was able to play the fire over them for about three seconds before the pressure started to drop. Two dropped their guns and ran. Their clothes might have been smoking but didn't catch. One of them seemed to have burns to his face.

The third must have been wearing cotton or maybe he had been siphoning gas that seeped into his clothes because he turned into a human torch. *What a little bitch,* I thought as he screamed. No, I saw a pool of flame on the ground and broken glass in the center. Somehow his Molotov cocktail ignited and he dropped it. *Did I do that?*

The human torch ran for the puddle where the first guy

had gone prone to shove his arm into. Together the two managed to get the flames out and coat themselves in mud in the process. Meanwhile, I turned triumphantly to watch everyone flee. The guy who had been restraining Hugo, Darin, and Bert stopped to watch the show.

Bert took advantage of the distraction to kick the captor's legs out from under him. Darin, who had his hands cuffed behind his back, slammed his body weight on the raider while Bert snatched away the gun. The driver in the truck reversed his vehicle out of danger.

The trailing car that passed by with the truck returned just then and stopped in the intersection. Someone with a rifle was getting out. *So they were together.* Before I could even think about being shot, I heard gunfire. Muffled shots came from Jim's upstairs window. He was using his suppressed AR to shoot the passenger! I saw the muzzle of the bandit's rifle fall as the body collapsed back into the seat. The driver panicked and floored it with his passenger's legs dragging on the asphalt as the door held the (hopefully) corpse in place.

The remaining stooges got up out of the mud and started to run for the pickup, which had already finished backing up and was about to turn to leave. Bert let his captive go. Apparently having some sense of decency, the captive grabbed the smoldering human torch from the wet storm gutter and helped him along. All of them ran after the truck yelling for it to stop. It did, barely, and they all jumped in the back, leaving the rifle of the one Jim shot in the street.

Trembling, I put down my flamethrower and struggled to turn off the valves. I looked up and saw Raelene's worried face looking down from my office window. Reya was next to her and her mouth hung open in admiration. Terror had turned to awe. I gave them a fake smile and a thumbs up. Reya flashed it back before her mom pulled her away from the window. Forget St. George slaying the dragon, I was the dragon!

"So that's where you went," Hugo said, rubbing his wrists where Bert cut away the ties. "I guess you don't screw with a guy who has a flamethrower."

Jim met all four of us in the street. The dead man's rifle was slung over his shoulder. "Guess I'm not going to the EOC tonight," Jim said emptily.

"What do we do now? We can't even call the cops!" Bert said, distressed.

Jim held up his fire department radio. "I called it in. They said they'll have someone here as soon as they can." He didn't seem rattled, not as I was after my shooting, but he was white-faced and appeared somewhat detached.

Eventually the police did come. I gave my perfunctory statement to the cops—I acted in self-defense, I was in fear for our lives—and my attorney (Doug's) phone number. Not what they wanted to hear, but no one took me downtown. Jim said the same thing but they took him back to his house to await the arrival of their sergeant and a detective. Since he fired the shots, he would be the star of the show.

Hugo handed over his security camera footage which backed up our story but created a lot of unwanted curiosity about my contraption. The flashes of light were obviously from me but the only evidence of anti-personnel use was burning and burnt thieves running in the edges of the frame. The police asked me to demonstrate my flamethrower "for investigative purposes," begged me actually, but I couldn't. Once they finished with Jim, they left us on our own again in the cold and dark.

None of us had any energy to play guards again. The fire, the screaming, the gunshots, and the police woke up enough neighbors so that everyone was on alert. A pair of additional cops had to be called in to string up crime scene tape and make sure the three dozen spectators the commotion drew didn't enter the crimes scene. Guys from the neighboring houses who walked over to see what the ruckus was about said they'd have our backs in the remaining hours until dawn. I don't know how sincere they were. All I knew is I went inside where it was at least ten degrees warmer.

Day 6

Pack It Up

If you think I went to sleep last night, you're nuts. We spent the night packing. We were getting out here to anywhere, be it Red Rock or Arkansas. Was it tiring? Yes, but part of me rejoiced to be out of here wherever that was. Even sleeping on the couch of Raelene's insufferable siblings or mother would be an improvement over freezing without running water and people trying to kill us.

Despite it being a full-sized SUV, the Lexus was not a Suburban and would not fit as much as I'd have liked it to. Two suitcases each, one for each of the girls, plus one bag with toys. The baby got her large diaper bag too. Reya could take a backpack of whatever she liked. The girls' footwells would have to hold these bags.

We had to decide what else to take and what to leave. All the food was coming with us. The buckets of freeze-dried food would form the base of the cargo area with the suitcases and other miscellany on top. Despite fearing we didn't have enough food, it took up a lot of volume and I ended up wedging the last duffle bag in the cargo area. In the end we started slipping various items, like the wedding photos, into open spaces between the buckets, bags, and boxes. The rearview mirror was useless.

The rooftop cargo carrier would have to be mounted and loaded in the morning. No way that it could be lifted in place if filled on the floor first. I doubted even Grant and I could do it. The less important stuff that we could afford to lose if it fell off, like clothes and pillows, would go here. I had no choice but to strap the gas cans up there which was fine because they were empty anyhow.

A lot of stuff was getting left behind. More clothes, books, and our entire kitchen. Forget about the electronics. Only our laptops and the bare minimum of peripherals were going. There was no room. I had no trailer, no way to get a trailer, and not even a trailer hitch. Thankfully Raelene was a minimalist and didn't accumulate the amount of stuff I did. Should our house be looted, the electronics would need to be replaced but I didn't think anyone would be taking our clothing or general household items.

To avoid any water damage should the house flood, we carted a lot of things upstairs. Furniture stayed. None of it was antique or heirloom. The big TV was at least five feet high so it stayed bolted to the wall, but I disconnected all the cables and taped them to the back. I carried the TV from the downstairs children's den upstairs and put it in my study. Any thieves would have to find it and lug it down the stairs. Immediately before I left the generator would get wheeled over to Bert's.

Raelene packed up the kitchen while I worked on the garage. Since we got married, the kitchen was her domain. If she really splurged anywhere on material goods it was her cookware. Whereas I might have made do with a single large sauté pan and a blender, she wanted a real wok and a stand mixer. My bachelor habit of using the blender as a chopper horrified her now. No way the Cuisinart was going to be left to drown.

With the glass half-full, we were all alive and that was what counted, right? The joy of having survived those deadly moments was intense, like getting married. I kid, but it *was* like getting married. The ecstasy and followed by the terror of thinking what would happen next. In both cases, I was still happily married and the gangs hadn't returned. Our more organized neighbors were also so impressed with the flamethrower that they had our backs in appreciation for almost bloodlessly running that crew off.

Raelene had her own thoughts. "Ross, what if we loose our house?" she asked.

For the first time in two decades, this had been Raelene's longest place of residence since childhood. It was *her* home, where she could express herself with the decorating and in her garden. There was no landlord to say he wanted to make it into an Airbnb or a boyfriend who wanted her to move out over the weekend. "This our home. Our home, that we built together."

She didn't mean by hand but as a family. This house was better than our condo and a place we hoped we could live in for a long time, if not until we were old but it wasn't everything. A home is a physical representation of the intangible bonds of a family. Our memories were more than the photos on the walls and tchotchkes on the shelves but the pencil marks on the kitchen wall, the scuff on the first stair tread, and handprints in the concrete steps in our garden.

To her, these tangibles made the reality of her motherhood and marriage a reality. A home, mortgage or not, was a kind of certainty she lacked since girlhood. I could live anywhere. This house was nothing, it was the people in it that counted, but we were two separate people. Seeing it on the rocks threatened the one place of stability she'd found in life.

"We have each other. That's all that matters." I kissed

her.

"Mommy, is everything okay?" Reya asked, sleepily. The last time her parents woke her up Dad 'scared off some bad guys' with a warning shot. "You're noisy."

"Of course, sweetie. Daddy and I are just packing up everything for your uncle's tomorrow." Raelene sat on the side of the bed and stroked her daughter's blonde hair until Reya fell asleep. "I hope it doesn't flood. I like our furniture."

Raelene had an incredible strength to not constantly dredge up what was bothering her and talk it to death, unlike me. She had her one moment and then put it all away. Only if something new developed or she came to a new conclusion would she bring it up again. I really admired that about her. She didn't tow it around behind her like a dead horse.

"I can drag it all up here if you want me to."

"Nah. You think it's really going to flood?"

"Not here. If it were still raining I might be more concerned." None of what I said was true, but I didn't need to say it. Worrying aloud about hypotheticals you couldn't change if they came true was a sin, wasn't it?

Evacuation

Grant called back in the wee hours. I don't know what time it actually was. He had good news. The National Guard was finally arriving in strength to relieve the beleaguered police. The RadCom activists that were organizing things absconded while their financiers sent buses for the lesser radicals. Suddenly without agitators, money, or behind-the-scenes support, the anarchist scum who gave muscle to the embryonic revolution were much less aggressive. Even the out-of-towners were finally starting to leave.

"A frickin' flamethrower Ross? Seriously?" he said when it came to my turn to talk. "Let's hope the cops pin that all on that dropped Molotov cocktail because I don't know how you're going to explain that to the Grand Jury."

"Relax bro, nobody got it on video. The actual burnings, that is." Due to luck of the camera perspective, there was no direct evidence that the burns were sustained by contact with my flamethrower. Doug said there was also a strong, but unorthodox, self-defense claim.

Grant cleared us to come up. With the security situation dramatically improving so rapidly he did not have the same concerns for four more people's safety that he did a few days ago. He also had more space than our sister and he and I got a long much better than either of us did with her. The far shorter drive would be nicer too. "Get some sleep Ross." I told him to do the same thing, then sat down to think if we had forgotten anything.

I came to, finding myself sitting in the recliner in my office with Raelene shaking me. I hardly knew I fell asleep. It was light outside now. "Jim is yelling outside."

I got up and went to the window. Jim was standing in the driveway yelling up at us. "Wake up, it happened!"

Opening the windows in this house wasn't easy, but I managed. "Jim, what happened?" I called down.

"The levee broke. Big breach by Miller's Lane that's widening by the minute. Probably an hour or less before the roads flood." The main arterial streets to get off the island all passed through low areas that would flood first and become impossible. "Go now!"

"Okay thanks." The window took some wrestling to close. The builder expected everyone would just use their HVAC systems year round I supposed or these windows were cheap. "What do you think Rae? Should I try to confirm it?"

She shook her head passionately. "Let's go! I don't want to have a campout on the second floor waiting for some volunteer in a rowboat to pick us up."

In ten minutes the last of the packing was done. All we had to do was toss the few things we were still using in bags and stow them in the car. The girls had just finished eating and of course we couldn't leave dirty dishes, but I did the washing up while Raelene got the girls ready. I wanted to change clothes before we left but decided not to chance it.

Once the house was closed up and locked, I raised the garage door while Raelene backed the Lexus out. Our garage door had a locking T-handle on the front so once I secured that, we were free. I threw a wave at Hugo, who was also packing his car, as we pulled away. Bert had a spare key and could get the generator himself.

"Do you think the bridges are closed?" Raelene asked.

"I seriously doubt it," but I feared it. Fear didn't have to make sense. Bridges were the last thing they would close.

Anxiety attacked from several different directions. You can reassure your wife all you want but not your inner doubts. Could we make it to safety? And was Red Rock really safe now? I also suddenly felt sentimental. I was leaving the dream home I worked my butt off to buy. Our stuff we could replace but the house was still stuffed with the memories of our small family. Would we see it again?

Later I realized that in this moment a large component of my apprehension was worry about the future. In the past few days, everything I knew and understood about the world fell apart. This year was not just a tumultuous election cycle but a sign of worsening things to come. The world my wife and I grew up in no longer existed. I didn't have the benefit of years of adjustment to the doomer perspective of the world that men like my brother and his friends did.

There's a theory that when complex systems breakdown, the signs are obvious along the way, but typically only noticed in hindsight. Going forward, the observer thinks that everything's fine until a rapid collapse occurs. It's called sandpile theory or Seneca's cliff. *How did you go broke? Slowly at first, then all at once.* That was how I realized that Grant's theory about America being in decline wasn't paranoia built on the trauma of the Iraq War. I don't want to say that Alex Jones was right, but he was. Today was just another chapter in the life of a guy who just figured out what was going on. Hooray for me.

"Why is the ramp to the expressway closed?" Raelene asked.

A cop car sat perpendicular across the road. The yellow suited officer was setting orange cones out in the lanes. I stopped in the turn lane and rolled down the window a few inches to speak.

Maybe asking a police officer if the road was closed was a bad idea. He made a face like he was disgusted. "No, those are just submarine cars in the water, like in *The Spy Who Loved Me*," he said sarcastically. Beyond him the roofs of cars showed above muddy water in a low spot where the ramp curved. More than a few people hadn't heard the slogan Turn Around—Don't Drown. "What do you think?" He pointed to my right and shouted. "Go!"

I went. "Don't say it Raelene, don't say it." She didn't, but I saw her turn away to hide her I-told-you-so smirk and stifle a laugh at my expense.

Traffic was moving down Port Boulevard fairly efficiently. Aside from the light drizzle, there was nothing to tell you that the levees had failed. The police calmly waved traffic through the intersections, merging in the cars coming off of terminating arterial streets. There didn't seem to be any sense of panic. As we reached the Old Bridge, traffic backed up a little, but within five minutes it was our turn.

The two lanes had been reversed in a contraflow pattern using both lanes. Driving the wrong way didn't feel as odd as I expected. The white foam of the waves in the brown water occasionally lapped at the bridge sides. To the right water poured continuously over the top of the lock gates from the river. We were getting off the island just in time.

To get traffic back on the right side of the road, our lanes peeled off left down the south bank road. "I've got cell service," Raelene said, head down, studying her phone. "I think they're trying to take us around downtown to the West Main exit. Traffic is that dark red color all the way to the Interstate."

"What if I swing up through one of these residential streets, go through the Bottoms, and get on at Newlands?" Newlands was the last Interstate on-ramp in West River City.

"Mostly green."

We turned out of traffic and drove up a residential street. There wasn't much activity. A few people were packing up their cars. Others were placing sandbags along the garages and front doors. All the signal lights were out but traffic wasn't very heavy. As we passed under the Interstate, a lot of cars were headed in both directions. Unless an ark showed up, the water wouldn't get high enough to reach any portion of the freeway here. Imagine the irony of being a commuter who has to survive the flood by sitting in his car on an overpass for a day or two. Yuck.

On the other side we drove through the end of the retail district. The low-end shops and small businesses that catered primarily to the lower income people who lived in the Bottoms were gutted. Buildings had been burnt. Those that stood were boarded up or had their windows broken. All were graffitied. The "other side of the tracks" feeling was strong here.

Water was pooling in the streets as it back flowed from the storm drains, coughing out like a drowning victim vomits water. Down the streets to our right, or upriver, in the far distance towards the ends of the blocks, water had already submerged the yards. The near total absence of cars told us that the police had evacuated this part of town last night when the river topped its banks. Over the last few days I had already become accustomed to the ghostly deserted feeling of the city.

The inch or two of water that covered the streets grew

deeper, far beyond what even last year's powerful monsoon dumped on us. Now we were making waves and throwing up spray in places. It didn't seem to get better. "Turn behind that auto shop and go behind it. Take the alley to the service road," Raelene suggested. It would be a few feet higher than the avenue we were on.

It was higher and drier, but the pavement was terrible. I followed the service road for a half-mile behind mostly mechanics, body shops, and towing yards. As we went through one intersection, we saw about a dozen men loading vehicles onto flatbed trailers. *Evacuating the shop or stealing the cars?* The road curved and I saw the embankment of the cloverleaf above the buildings. Almost there.

The curve dead-ended at the embankment itself. Stupid me, I should have known but I was too sleep deprived to think I needed to get back out on the other road. There was no alley here so I executed a three-point turn and headed for the last intersection. We wandered into a trap and I was oblivious until the jaws began to swing shut.

Everything happened in a weird time warp like the shooting. Time seemed to move like normal except there was much more detail and thoughts than the seconds ordinarily allotted. A big Ford diesel pickup that was towing one of the trailers pulled out in front of us at an angle, blocking the road. I started to think they didn't see us right up until I saw the passenger doors open and men get out holding pistols. "Oh god, Ross what is this?" Raelene shrieked.

It was a carjacking, that's what it was. We just drove by car thieves in our $120k car. Several of the men who had been loading vehicles were walking over towards us now. The Lexus was creeping forward now. *Do I shoot? No, there's at least two guys with guns and you've got your family in the car. They'll shoot back if you shoot and there are the guys on your left flank. Flank? I'm thinking like my brother!* In a life-threatening situation it's amazing where your mind has time to go.

The me of a week ago probably would have stopped, not so much afraid of causing an accident but in doubt that I could squeeze through. Old me would have rolled down the window and tried to negotiate, only to lose the vehicle and leaving us huddling in a looted body shop waiting for cops to find us. Or a Coast Guard helicopter if the flooding kept up. Shooting burglars in your home and facing off in the street with a looting gang has a wonderful way of making you reconsider calculated risks.

One of the faces of the approaching men was familiar. I made the connection just as I saw his face change with recognition. He remembered our vehicle; he inspected it pretty closely as I saw in the garage security video. It was that Fuentes guy—his empty gaze and tattoos was seared into my mind. Of course he would be over in the Bottoms. His hands reached for his waistband and he picked up the pace, breaking into a jog.

There's gonna be shooting. "Everybody duck!" I shouted. Raelene instead unbuckled her seatbelt and tried to lean back towards the girls. I grabbed her neck with my right hand and shoved her down into my lap in a manner that would otherwise have looked most inappropriate. As long as she was below the line of sight I didn't care what it looked like.

I accelerated the Lexus and turned the wheel to squeeze through the narrow gap between the pickup and the curb. The two men on foot saw me hit the gas and ran out of the way instead of shooting. The slower guy got clipped by the mirror, the second bad guy this thing clocked this week. I couldn't avoid the open front truck door and hit it, bending it back against the front fender. My side mirror was knocked in against the window glass.

No one fired a shot at us as we sped away. Why they didn't shoot at us as we sped away, I'll never know. I guess life is not like action movies. We made it out on to the avenue again. Remy began crying because she didn't understand why the other car was so close to her window and what the bang was. "Mommy, what's going on?" Reya asked.

"Just a little fender-bender, honey," Raelene said as she leaned back to comfort Remy.

No one was following us, blessedly. *Thank you Toyota Motor Corporation for making this thing AWD all the time.* The water was up to the rocker panels now and I could really feel the drag that the water was putting on the car. If the water was moving it was deep enough to carry the car away. *Not much further now.* As long as there wasn't any surprise dip in the pavement we'd be fine.

Except there was a gutter in our path. The nose of the SUV dipped and the bow wave flattened out. If you've never been in a floating car it feels like when the boats on Pirates of the Caribbean start out. As the car lurched, Raelene, leaning back over the center console, knocked into me, then fell face forward into the rear footwell. I had barely enough time to register what happened, let alone feel any trepidation. The dip must have been for a storm drain because as soon as we started to sink, I felt a push upwards and we floated forward until the tires touched again.

I pressed the gas gently, but firmly as soon as I felt the weight settle on the tires again. The engine surged as huge clouds of steam rose up behind us. The tires spun but we moved forward. Then we were climbing out of the water up the cloverleaf. All of a sudden we were on wet, but "dry" asphalt.

In the rearview I saw Reya unbuckle and try to help her mom up. Raelene awkwardly fought her way into the front seat again, smacking and kicking me in the process. As this was happening we were going around the curving ramp up and away from danger. Who knew a soft white yuppie guy in a Lexus could drive like that?

"Daddy, a car is following us," Reya said. She had unbuckled herself and was kneeling to look over the pile of stuff in the back.

"Sit down and buckle up!" Raelene said. I looked in the mirror and sure enough the pickup truck, sans trailer, from the alley was coming after us. No way it was just coincidentally entering the freeway here at the exact same moment.

A noise and a flash in the sideview mirror caught my eye. For a bizarre moment, I thought the orange light was a strobe light. Hey, the pickup could have been used for construction, right? No, it was a muzzle flash.

"Everybody get down!"

"Why, are they shooting at us?" The crackle of gunshots answered her question.

I didn't have time to be afraid. I had to find a way out of this. So we were northbound on the Interstate now heading away from town in moderate traffic. The pickup was accelerating but his V10 engine or not, I doubted with that light rear end he could be as free with his maneuvers as I could. The Lexus had traction control and more weight over the rear axle, so in theory we'd be less prone to slipping and sliding.

I punched it. *Come on Japan, gimme whatcha got.* We leapt forward and began weaving in and out of the evacuees' vehicles. The truck imitated my acceleration but its wheels lost traction and the rear started fishtailing so the driver had to back off a bit. Even so, I couldn't drive through the rain on wet pavement at 90 MPH hoping the driver didn't figure out how to accelerate safely. *Think Ross, think.*

I needed a piece of wood. Not literally, but figuratively. In that same way that my dad had us search for planks he knew to be around when we got mired in Nevada there had to be another answer out there. We were on the causeway now with no exits or ramps for miles, so getting off the freeway wasn't an option for us. There were openings every mile in the median for the troopers to turn around on though. One was coming up fast.

The Lexus' traction control and ABS triggered when I hit the brakes then spun the wheel to the left. The SUV shuddered as the brakes pulsed and tires fought for a grip on the wet concrete. She kept stable as we made the U-turn through the gap. Raelene had taken off her belt for some reason and was bracing, wild eyed, against the dash.

"Daddy, drive normal. My stomach hurts," Reya said.

The pickup attempted to follow the maneuver and was now coming to a stop after entering a wicked serpentine back-and-forth skid at 80. I accelerated again, the Lexus no worse for the wear. I hoped the National Guard was still manning the checkpoint over the river.

We made it two miles before the truck driver figured

out how to safely go fast and began to catch up with us. The driver was still hanging out the window and shooting. I couldn't tell, but it seemed to be Fuentes. Where was the heavy traffic when you needed it? "Are they trying to kill us?" Raelene asked in a whisper, trying to keep the girls from hearing her. Reya was curious, not scared (yet) and all Remy knew was she was on a roller coaster ride.

"I think he's just trying to scare us into stopping so he can carjack us." A shot-up luxury SUV wasn't worth much in Mexico even if the bullet holes were patched. But yeah, he probably would kill us if we stopped and surrendered.

We were back in the city again and entering the approach to the big river bridge. I gunned it around the curve and felt the wheels starting to slip on the wet pavement. The cones began to narrow and then there it was: Humvees, orange traffic barrels, and flashing orange lights. A military checkpoint never looked so beautiful.

I braked, cut around the stopped cars through the delineators, turned on the hazards, and honked while flashing the brights. *Please don't shoot us*, I prayed. The Guardsmen suddenly spread out into a tactical position and took a knee, no doubt inspired by gunshots and my erratic driving. I slowed down to a crawl about a hundred yards out and crept forward.

A machine gunner got into his position on top of a Humvee and was training the big .50 caliber towards us. At twenty-five yards, I stopped, slowly opened the door, and got out with my hands in the air. "Someone is shooting at us I yelled." They didn't seem to understand me and were yelling their own commands. Drivers in the waiting cars attentively watched the show.

A ripple of gunfire made me jerk. The pickup was coming around the curve. Fuentes had his handgun out the window and fired another long burst. Pistol rounds bounced off the pavement all around me. *I think they call that a 'Glock switch,'* a part of my brain said. I ducked. Many heads in the queued cars dropped low as well.

The Guardsmen didn't seem to appreciate being shot at, although none of them were hit. An M16 opened fire. Even I knew it was a stretch for automatic fire from a 5.56 at that range, but the big .50 cal machine gun didn't have that problem. The staccato *da-da-da-da-da-da* was followed by a sharper, snapping sound as the bullets passed over my head. A white cloud of steam appeared where the radiator was punctured on our pursuer's Ford. Right away the truck began to slow down.

By the third burst of the machine gun that shot right over the Lexus, the red tracers shooting by like laser beams, the pickup veered off and crashed into the K-rail. The M16s were still firing as someone shouted, "Cease firing!" The shooting stopped then.

"My family is in the car. My wife and girls," I said to the sergeant who approached me. He could see I was trembling involuntarily. The muzzle of his gun moved away from my head. That felt a lot better.

"Are they hurt?"

"I don't think so, unless they got caught in the crossfire."

The sergeant stuck out his hand and helped me up. He turned to his men. "Put a Hummer or something behind that SUV. Then get second squad up and clear that enemy victor!" The platoon leapt into action.

With an up-armored Humvee acting as a shield, the guardsmen got my wife and kids out of the Lexus. Raelene got out of the car and embraced me in a wet hug. Over her shoulder I saw the girls bouncing up and down in the car seats waving at the soldiers, both of them totally at a loss for what was really going on. Their tear-stained faces were mixed with joy at seeing Daddy was all right and for the soldiers who had saved them. I'd miss this innocent age.

Contrary to my expectations, the state troopers showed up fairly quickly and got my statement in record time. Since I didn't do any shooting, Doug didn't need to be here. Like with the burglars, the whole interview seemed far more abbreviated that it should have been. If we had an accident, it probably would have taken the troopers longer to investigate than what was a Guard-involved shooting.

The real answer was that the freeway had to be opened for evacuations, so the on-scene investigative work would be the bare minimum. There was an argument with a trooper lieutenant who wanted to impound our vehicle for investigation, but the major incident sergeant prevailed with him to let us go. No tow trucks, too much time, and we were evacuating in the vehicle. His boss settled for detailed photographs.

Raelene and I were operating in a daze the whole time all of this was going on. Our kids complained about the drizzling rain but otherwise seemed to have recovered from the excitement and reveled in all the attention the soldiers, troopers, and firefighters gave them. The girls got junior badge stickers from the trooper and candy from the soldier's MREs. To them, it was *Paw Patrol* in real life. I just wanted a drink and a warm chair.

Maybe I didn't go to Afghanistan or Iraq or live some big adventure where I was supposed to have proven myself as a man. This week was that moment where I established my self-perception as a man in my own eyes. Ross had seen the elephant and everyone came through alright. Nobody could hurt me by calling me a pussy again. I could stand up there with James Bond.

"Daddy, drive normal now or I want Mommy to drive," Reya said. Raelene and I laughed, letting all the tension and fright fade away as the city disappeared behind us. It didn't work like that, but for a few minutes we were enraptured by the levity and exhilaration of being alive.

Denouement

"The Guy in the Glass" by Dale Wimbrow Sr. (1934)

When you get what you want in your struggle for self,
And the world makes you King for a day,
Then go to the mirror and look at yourself,
And see what that guy has to say.

For it isn't your Father, or Mother, or Wife,
Who judgement upon you must pass.
The feller whose verdict counts most in your life
Is the guy staring back from the glass.

He's the feller to please, never mind all the rest,
For he's with you clear up to the end,
And you've passed your most dangerous, difficult test
If the guy in the glass is your friend.

[...]

About the Author

Don Shift is a veteran of the Ventura County Sheriff's Office and an avid fan of post-apocalyptic literature and film. He is a student of disasters, history, current events, and holds several FEMA emergency management certifications. You can email him at donshift@protonmail.com or visit www.donshift.com.

Fiction works include the Ventura Sheriff EMP series, *Hard*

Favored Rage and *Blood Dimmed Tide*, where deputies must survive after a devastating electromagnetic pulse destroys the electric grid. *Late For Doomsday* and *Limited Exchange (1 & 2)* are novels of surviving and evacuating after a nuclear attack.

All works explore the realities of emergency planning and personal survival in the face of low probability, high impact events that highlight the shortcomings of a technology and infrastructure dependent nation. Non-fiction titles include *Nuclear Survival in the Suburbs* and the *Suburban Defense, Suburban Warfare,* and *Rural Home Defense* guides.

Made in the USA
Coppell, TX
27 June 2023

18585832R00157